CHARMS & CHOCOLATE – CONNECTED TO SOIL

JENNY SWAN

JENNY SWAN

V

THE WITCHES WORLD-FOLDS SAGA

- Volume 1: Awakened by Fire
- Volume 2: Carried by Wind
- Volume 3: Immortalized in Iron
- Volume 4: Protected by Water
- Volume 5: Connected to Soil

"You can also commit injustice by doing nothing."
(Marcus Aurelius)

PROLOGUE

She was in the house by the cliffs that often served as her retreat. Never for more than a few days so that nobody, not even those she belonged with, could track her down.

It hadn't been easy to return to them, but she had done it. For herself? For them? For him? She had no idea. Her heart had been pounding so hard that she'd almost changed her mind. But she had pulled herself together and taken refuge behind her mask of equanimity.

As expected, most had reacted to her return hesitantly, if not harshly. If there were such things as outcasts among her kind, she was definitely one of them. Even if, strictly speaking, she had chosen the path of solitude. Was it possible to cast yourself out?

The waves roared and crashed against the high rocks on top of which her hut was situated. She'd turned a log into an armchair and was sitting on the porch, staring at the endless sea. The sun had long since disappeared, but a pale bright glow that was clearly visible along the horizon would keep absolute darkness away for a few more minutes. Nobody knew about the place and that was a good thing. Not even her sisters would find her there. At least that was her hope. After all, they had found her in Norway. But she'd been in a public world fold there, whereas this one was her own. No one lived here except her and it would stay that way.

Her chest tightened as she recalled how she had met him. He had no idea who she was and he couldn't find out. Although she had stood by him, just as her sisters had asked, things that had not been part of the plan had taken place. Should she have returned sooner? Or should she not have gotten involved in the first place? It was a strange feeling to return to the field after having become accustomed to leaving the fate of the world to others, to standing on the sidelines as an idle spectator. Should she have stayed in the shadows? Whatever the case may have been, her sisters were unlikely to achieve their goal, so she was no longer necessary.

Her crow Leo cried out and perched on her shoulder. The delicate feel of his claws on her and his weight, light as a feather, comforted her. He was the only living being with access to her and in whose presence she felt comfortable.

He cried out again and brushed his little black head across her cheek. She had been crying without realizing it. An image formed in her mind. He wanted to share something with her, but she shook her head. She needed rest, to collect herself, and make a decision. Should she continue to remain in the shadows or assume an active role?

As the last bit of light disappeared over the horizon and an impenetrable darkness settled over the coast, she made her choice. She stood and squared her shoulders as her crow's screeching echoed through the darkness like an omen.

1

M ayla blinked several times, but her eyelids were leaden. Blackness surrounded her, her head hurt like hell, and her body ached. Everything about her was exhausted, sore, and shattered. A pair of green eyes flashed and a voice murmured something, then another. Or was it the same one? Mayla struggled to break free from the stupor and open her eyes again, but she couldn't. She drifted off.

She was startled by a scream. She blinked again. This time it was easier and she cautiously opened her eyes. Orange light blinded her. She lowered her lids until she grew accustomed to the brightness. As she lay on the bare ground, she heard murmuring nearby. Was it just an effect of her stupor? She felt weak, but she leaned on her hands and slowly sat up, little by little.

She was in a forest. How the heck had she gotten there? And who had screamed? Had it been part of a dream? Though she was seized with dizziness, she slowly turned her head. What had happened? She pulled in her legs in order to get up when she saw something large lying motionless on the ground. Wait, that wasn't just anything. It was Georg.

In a matter of seconds, her power of recall returned. They had jumped to the chateau, looked around, and then followed someone into the forest. As fragments of memory slowly came back, she leaned on her hands.

"Georg?"

He didn't react.

She struggled to her feet, swayed, and with all her force managed to remain upright. Paying no mind to her dusty blouse and dirty skirt, she staggered toward Georg. She collapsed on the ground next to him, barely even feeling it as her bare knees scraped against a stick.

"Georg?"

She shook him gently, causing him to groan.

"Mayla? What happened? What... Look at you!" He sat up too quickly and became dizzy. He put his hand to his head and collapsed on the ground, his face as white as chalk.

"Slowly, Georg."

He rubbed his hands over his eyes and then sat up again hesitantly. "What happened?" As he asked the question, his eyes cleared. He remembered. Then he looked her straight in the eyes, took her hand, and pressed his lips together. When he began to speak, his voice was deeper than usual. "Mayla, I saw who it was. The one who struck me..."

She frowned at him. Georg had seen the shadow they had followed? She was about to ask him about it when she suddenly remembered. The last part of the memory fell into place.

Tom.

Blurry images pushed into her consciousness and tears welled up in her eyes. She needed to be brave and strong, but she couldn't do it. Sobbing, she sank lower. Georg hugged her and she leaned her forehead against his shoulder.

It had been him. He had struck her — and Georg before that. Tom. She had clearly recognized him. There was no doubt about it, dammit. Her body shook as she sobbed. "Why did he do it?"

Instead of answering, Georg stroked her back and waited until the flood of tears subsided. Her head hurt and was throbbing terribly. But this was nothing compared to what was burning within Mayla: despair, disappointment, betrayal. She felt broken, as if when Tom had struck her, he had injured not just her body but her soul as well.

She looked down and saw that Georg was trembling. Beads of sweat glistened on his forehead. He was worse off. She had to...

There was a crack in the undergrowth. Mayla stifled her sobs and Georg pulled out his wand. The bushes in front of them shook and Karl came bounding out. He ran up to Mayla and jumped into her arms. Meowing piteously, he looked at her, licked her fingertips, and nuzzled his forehead against her hand. She felt deep love and hugged him gratefully.

There was orange glow making its way

through the dark treetops, and the morning sky was pierced by the hoot of an owl. Creola circled overhead. She descended gracefully and landed on Georg's shoulder. The barn owl hooted softly and brushed her head along his cheek, which was smeared with damp earth. The dark eyes in her heart-shaped face rested on him. A smile appeared on his bloodless lips and he gratefully patted her head, which she tilted as she looked at him. When Georg nodded, she blinked once, then spread her wings and flew away into the bright morning sky.

Georg stood up and held out his hand to Mayla. "We should leave. Who knows who is in the forest or who might be watching and listening to us."

Who do you think? Mayla wanted to scream, but Karl's presence calmed her. He nuzzled her tenderly and made her feel like everything was going to be okay. "All right, but I'm not going to Donnersberg Castle."

"Then let's jump to my place. We can freshen up, talk to Violett, and plan. She'll be worried sick."

Mayla nodded and held out her hand to Georg, who was struggling to maintain his balance. Did he even feel capable of casting a spell? Before he could use the last of his strength, Mayla wrapped her arms around him and thought,

Perduce nos in domum Violettae!

As Mayla was swept off her feet, she hugged Karl to her. She had never jumped with him before. Hopefully, nothing would happen to him. As long as the little guy stayed with her, it should work.

The light of the morning sun and the forest mixed into a muddle of orange and green. The next moment, they landed on a wooden floor, and Karl was snuggled in her arms, purring.

"Where have you been?" rang out Violett's shrill cry before Mayla could get her bearings. Violett jumped up from the wide couch, her blanket sliding to the floor. Obviously, she hadn't spent the night in her bed.

Holding Karl tightly, Mayla stood in her friends' colorfully decorated living room without saying anything, gazing at the abstract paintings, countless gnome figurines, vases with artificial flowers, and framed photos on the walls. She felt almost overwhelmed by how idyllic the home was.

"Oh my, look at you two." Violett threw her arms around Georg's neck and hugged him, who swayed under her enthusiasm.

"Careful, Vio!"

Shocked, she looked at him before urging him to sit on the sofa. Then, she rushed over to Mayla. She opened her mouth, but before she could say anything, she closed it again. Slowly tilting her head, she fished a dry leaf out of Mayla's hair and brushed the dirt from her shoulder.

"Come, first sit, and then tell me." Without looking, she pointed her wand in the direction of the kitchen where there was a gentle clattering sound. She pushed Mayla gently but firmly onto the couch next to Georg and a few moments later, a coffee pot, cups, and a basket of raisin rolls floated over and landed on the coffee table. Violett served herself enthusiastically, her eyes fixed on the two.

"We were both knocked unconscious," Georg began. Violett gasped loudly, bringing her hand to her mouth.

"I'm sorry, what? Knocked unconscious? You mean attacked with a spell?"

Georg shook his head. He did it remarkably slowly. "No, knocked down, as in with a club."

"What? Who'd resort to such a barbaric act? You were in a world fold, weren't you? Did you see who it was?"

Mayla didn't yet feel up to talking about the previous night. Luckily, Georg took over. She waved her hand and the pot poured coffee into the cups. She picked up her cup groggily, blew the coffee to a comfortable drinking temperature, and took a sip. The warmth and aroma immediately invigorated her limbs, if not her heart, which beat only as often as necessary to survive.

"I followed the shadow into the forest to a waterfall where I momentarily lost sight of it. Since there was water nearby, I was able to use a spell to resume the pursuit quickly. Before following the tracking spell, I noticed something small lying on the ground. When I bent down to pick it up, someone hit me from behind. As I fell, I turned my head and caught a glimpse of Tom before I passed out."

Georg had seen something on the ground? Wait, hadn't there been something in his hand when she had reached him? A bag with a hard object in it? Ah, yes, she had taken it from him. She recalled feeling the edges through the fabric.

Someone had taken the bag from her.

Tom...?

"It was Tom?" Violett turned to her, her gray eyes wide in disbelief. "Is that true?"

Mayla merely nodded, not sharing the memory that had just come back to her. As Karl purred on her lap, she sipped from the cup as if this were an ordinary coffee klatch. She sensed that the cat wanted to calm her down and she was grateful. She gently stroked his fur. Had one of the magic stones been in the bag?

"What does this mean?" Violett demanded, interrupting her thoughts.

Georg ran a hand through his copper-red beard. The gesture was slower than usual. "We have to find out. But first, I need a shower to clear my head. Or would you like to go first, Mayla?"

She shook her head.

Violett's voice cracked. "A shower? You need to go directly to the hospital. Look at you!"

Mayla barely heard their conversation. Suddenly, her mind was silent. No thoughts were flooding her mind. No chaos. There was absolutely nothing going on now that the last missing bit of memory of the stone was restored. Everything was clear and made sense, requiring no further consideration. She stroked Karl's head again, barely noticing that Georg had left the room. When she turned her head, she spotted Violett's pitying gaze on her.

Mayla took a deep breath, her voice barely a whisper. "Why did he do that?"

Violett reached for a second roll and picked a raisin out of the bread. "I've known Tom longer than you, but not as well. He always had his reasons."

Mayla sighed heavily. "I know. He does. But knocking down his fiancée and, before that, a friend...?"

Violett popped the raisin into her mouth and immediately started digging for another. "It's probably hard for you. It's the same for me, no question, but... well, he..." She shrugged.

"Yes?"

Suddenly, Violett jumped up and waved her slender arms in the air, sending a few crumbs flying across the room. "He's got to have a reason... even if it doesn't justify knocking you unconscious."

Mayla simply nodded. She knew Tom had his reasons. He just had to. Nevertheless, the betrayal weighed on her heavily, more so than the physical attack itself. She inhaled deeply, unable to answer her friend.

"Then he just ran away?!"

Mayla wanted to nod again, but an image popped into her mind. Had she merely imagined it or had she heard a voice and seen a pair of green eyes? Had he come back to take care of her? Her heart wanted to scream *yes*. Yes, yes, yes — he had returned, sorry for what he had done, regretting he'd had to do it because someone had forced him to. But no feeling stirred within her.

She raised her head. "I don't know. I was unconscious." Violett gestured wildly in the air. Her friend shouldn't get so upset. She was pregnant, after all. Mayla swallowed and tried to make her voice sound normal. "Come, sit down, and stop eating just raisins."

Violett rolled her eyes. "Georg always says that, but I never would have expected something like that from you." She waved her wand once and a flat box flew to them, landing with a flourish on the side table in front of Mayla. "I can rely on your discretion, can't I?"

Mayla grinned weakly. "My lips are sealed." She automatically pushed the lid aside and reached for a truffle. She stared at it for a while, her thoughts on Tom, before finally putting it in her mouth. Karl's purring and the taste of the treat she loved so well calmed her and she closed her eyes. Her head was still pounding, so she reached out and placed her hand on the back of her head. "Sana!" The pain subsided until only a slight ache remained — a throbbing that served as a persistent reminder of what Tom had done.

2

After healing her skinned knees with a spell, showering, and cleaning her clothes, Mayla hurried downstairs to the ground floor and into the living room where Georg and Violett were sitting on the couch. Karl had disappeared.

Georg looked pretty worse for wear even though he was clean and wearing fresh clothes. He and Violett were holding each other's hands, talking quietly and looking at each other like couples in love do. Violett was talking insistently to Georg. Mayla picked up words like hospital, doctor, and examine.

She stood in the doorway, hesitating. The picture was so idyllic, so cozy, and... intimate, she didn't want to intrude. In this home, she felt completely out of place. She would have preferred to go outside and finish what she had started. To stop the hunters so she could finally get her daughter back. Her mother's heart was crying out for her. They had never been separated for so long. She knew it was only reasonable that she hadn't heard from Emma and her grandma. Still, she wished they would send a Nuntia spell so she could see her daughter's kind face and hear her sweet voice.

"Mayla. There you are." Violett smiled at her.

"I don't mean to intrude. Thanks for the coffee and shower."

"You're not bothering us." Georg stood up, but the dizziness hit again. Violett steadied him and pushed him back onto the couch. He didn't resist. As soon as he regained control of himself, he turned to Mayla again. "I think we should go to Paris to see Julie Martin. Tom had a private conversation with her. Maybe she can give us a lead."

"You're not going anywhere, Georg! You can hardly walk a straight line. No, no, I'll take you to the hospital first."

"But, I..."

Violett looked at him sternly and he fell silent.

Mayla felt like grinning, but the corners of her mouth weren't about to play along. "Violett is right, Georg. You definitely need to be examined. I couldn't heal you with the Sana spell. Who knows if it was one of those ancient spells that hit you."

Georg grumbled and nodded in resignation.

Violett's face relaxed, though she still looked at Georg worriedly. "It's best if we go straight to the Marienstein City Hospital in Frankfurt, where Dr.

Merch practices. He's a friend of my father and a world-renowned doctor." She stroked his shoulder lovingly before turning to Mayla. "And you get checked out too. That hit you got must have been fairly strong for you to have been lying unconscious all night."

Mayla waved her hand. "That's not necessary, I..."

Georg looked at her sternly. "If it's necessary for me, it's necessary for you!"

"I wasn't hit that hard, and I healed myself long ago. See?" She demonstrated by walking a straight line across the floor without losing her balance. "I don't feel dizzy, nor do I have a headache." Okay, she did have a slight one, but she didn't need to tell them that.

Violett sighed. "Still, it would be advisable. I mean it's better than doing nothing, right?"

Mayla tucked a strand of hair behind her ear nonchalantly. "I won't be doing nothing. I'm jumping to Paris to confront Julie Martin."

"What?" Georg retorted, but Violett immediately shoved him back onto the couch. That she could do this effortlessly showed how truly weak he was.

Mayla shrugged. "I believe she'll tell me things she wouldn't admit to you, Georg. After all, you are a policeman and officially after Tom and the hunters. I'm certain she's on his side no matter what he's done in the last few days. I can probably achieve more on my own."

Georg shook his head. "No, Mayla, it's too

dangerous. You can't leave without backup, especially after what happened to us yesterday. I mean, Tom didn't just knock us out, he left us lying there helpless. It doesn't take much imagination to think what else could have happened to us."

No, he hadn't left her lying there completely helpless. Someone had come and checked on her, and maybe Georg, too. There was only one answer to why the person hadn't woken her up and taken her to safety, and it came in the form of the green eyes she had seen. Tom must have returned that night. Probably because he regretted it... Anger tried to fight its way up inside her. With anger, everything was so much easier to bear. But she didn't give in to the feeling.

Mayla waved her hand firmly. "I'll manage."

Georg sighed in resignation. It sounded weak and she wasn't used to that from him. "I think it's too dangerous for you to travel alone, but I won't be able to stop you today — unless my beautiful future wife does it for me."

Surprisingly, Violett shook her head. She peered thoughtfully at Mayla. "It is dangerous, but let's not forget she's a von Flammenstein. And she had the best protection spell teacher."

Mayla smiled. It was good that Violett believed in her. And it would be good to just be alone, to sort through her thoughts, to make decisions without anyone else's input, and, above all, to track down Tom. She was certain she would locate him. However, she didn't know if she would be happy with what he'd have to say to her.

"I'll be careful." She was about to turn when Georg called after her.

"You are aware of how it's going to look, right?"

Mayla paused. It would look like she was allying herself with Tom by going to see him. Mayla shook her head. She didn't care what the police or former outcasts thought. Now it was about much more than that. Once the hunters had all the pieces of the stones, they would try to abduct Emma again so she could bring together the magical stones for them. Mayla had to prevent this from happening at all costs.

"Whether I go alone or you tag along, they will suspect me anyway. They already do."

Violett bit her bottom lip. "Not all..."

Mayla smiled at her. "I know, and I am so grateful for that."

With tears in her eyes, Violett rushed toward her and they fell into each other's arms. She wasn't usually so sentimental.

"You are always welcome here. Please, never hesitate to come to us if you need anything. You can sleep in our guest room any night. We won't tell anyone."

"I appreciate that very much. Thank you." Mayla kissed her on the cheek and hugged her. When she turned, Georg was standing in front of her with his arms crossed. Even though it took a great deal of strength, he remained upright. He was pale, and his gray eyes flashed with concern.

"I don't like this, Mayla."

She smiled. "I know, but don't worry, I'm not completely alone." With a flick of her hand, the box of chocolates flew to her. "I'll take this with me. Wish me luck." Before she could change her mind or her friends could sow any seeds of doubt, she clutched the amulet key and thought, *Perduce me ad locum Pont Neuf!*

As Mayla's heels landed on the stones of Pont Neuf in the heart of Paris, she immediately created a protective shield around herself. "Tutare!" She remembered when they had been unexpectedly attacked all too well. Since she was on her own, she would play it safe. After all, it was possible a few hunters might run into her again.

With the bluish, shimmering protective shield now up, she looked around. Except for her, there was no one else in the tiny world fold. Numerous passersby strolled across the bridge, but none entered the magically sealed area. This mean that none of them were witches. It was funny to watch them disappear on one side and then the next moment reappear on the other, as if Mayla were in a bubble. But she didn't have time to continue making such observations. She would come here with Emma one day. It would be fun with her, along with a box of chocolates... The idea encouraged her and she cheerfully removed the protective shield.

She paid attention to the flow of people before she stepped naturally out of the fold and mingled with them so quickly that not a single one looked up in surprise. The conversations of passersby were muffled to her. As she marched purposefully north with a French tune in her head, she paid no attention to the voices or the mild wind that whistled across her nose and promised to have a pleasant cooling effect on that hot August day. However, the cheerful mood from last time failed to return; in fact, the melody faded as she stared at the spot where the ancestral home of the de Bourgogne family was supposed to be — there was nothing there.

She quickened her pace, her heels sounding out a constant clack, clack, clack against the stones, but she didn't notice it, nor the Frenchman who was shouting something and whistling at her. The world fold was not visible. How? Why? Was it... locked?

She left the bridge behind and crossed the street. She looked around cautiously. Where exactly did the world fold begin? There was nothing noticeable, no subtle sparkle or crack in the building facade. There was just one classical apartment building lined up wall-to-wall with the next. There was no sign anywhere that in between there was a hill full of lavender and a chateau.

Why had the world fold disappeared? It was strange that not even the faintest sparkle of magic could be seen. Did someone have something to hide? Had Julie Martin left town, or maybe she didn't want visitors? Was she perhaps hiding Tom and...

Mayla didn't hesitate for a second. She frowned and considered. Back in southern England with Artus von Donnersberg and the others, she had opened the von Eisenfels family's closed world fold. Even though this time she had no assistance, maybe she could still do it.

She stood with her legs apart, tilted her head left, right, and left again, and raised her hands. She imagined the world that lay hidden in the world fold in great detail and thought, *Te aperi, munde contracte!*

Nothing happened.

Shoot! Were her powers truly not enough? But she was a von Flammenstein and her strength had grown over the last few years. Maybe she was simply too exhausted. It was no wonder, since she had been lying unconscious in the forest all night and hadn't eaten a proper breakfast. Although... Smiling, she reached into her handbag where she'd stashed the box from Violett. She fished out the biggest chocolate and ate it with relish. Savoring the sweetness, she closed her eyes in bliss before opening them again, then raised her hands in determination and thought, *Te aperi, munde contracte!*

A delicate sparkle appeared, and the classical buildings moved aside gradually to reveal the purple hill with the de Bourgogne family's country estate. The scent of lavender immediately filled her nostrils. Mayla nodded happily. She had always known it — the power of chocolate was immeasurable!

More confident than before, she stepped onto the path that wound its way up the hill. Too bad she couldn't jump straight into the fold to the front of the door. She had no choice but to struggle up the hill.

She completed the journey without taking a single break. The uncertainty of what was going on with Tom and her longing for Emma fueled her strength as well as her impatience. She was breathless when she reached the top and panted until her racing pulse calmed down. She took in one deep, intentional breath, touched the necklace with the heart pendant that she had worn for years, and collected herself. Then she knocked firmly on the door.

She shifted from one foot to the other and slung her handbag from her right shoulder to her left. She peered in the windows but didn't see anybody moving behind them. The last time, Julie Martin hadn't kept them waiting long. The young man who helped her around the house could have opened the door for Mayla if Julie was unavailable. But maybe he wasn't there either. She knocked again, more forcefully and more insistently, but no one answered.

What should she do now? Return with nothing to show for the trip? Never! Extraordinary events required extraordinary measures — that was clear. Without further ado, she raised her hands and thought, *Dirumpe!* and the door burst into pieces. The pieces of wood rumbled to the ground. Mayla stepped over them and entered the courtyard. Without turning around, she raised her hand, pointed at the shattered door, and thought, *Refice!* and the fragments came together and the restored door landed on its hinges as if nothing had happened.

"Hello? Anybody home?" The banging noise might have scared everyone...

Nobody answered.

She suddenly felt uneasy. Should she continue even though no one seemed to be on the premises? Actually, she wasn't the type to commit crimes, but why else had she smashed the door? Well, she had broken in, so she might as well enter the house and snoop around, right? She had already broken the law anyway. Still, it felt odd. Without a moment's hesitation, she fished out another chocolate and put it between her lips. It was a vanilla truffle and her eyes lit up. She definitely felt better now. Now to see how Julie Martin lived — and if Mayla could discover what Julie might have secretly shown Tom yesterday.

She crept across the inner courtyard, making her way amidst the columns decorated with vines. Blue grapes, ready to be harvested soon, were hanging down, giving the property a picturesque atmosphere. Did Julie make wine? Well, that definitely didn't matter.

Mayla looked around. Where should she go? There was the door that Julie and Tom had disappeared through the day before. She hurried purposefully toward it. With a spell on her lips, she raised her hands but then stopped. Maybe it was unlocked. She grabbed the knob and turned it. The door swung open as if it had been waiting for her. It was dark inside, so she blew a flame onto her fingertip. Being a Fire Witch came in handy. Wind, water, or earth power would have been of little use right then.

She crept into the chateau and through the entrance area, which was comfortably furnished. The windows all had heavy curtains and had benches in front of them. In addition, there were wicker chairs with cushions as well as a few half-columns with busts on top of them — the only thing that made a stately impression. The large pictures on the walls showed regions that were unfamiliar to Mayla. Maybe they were other world folds? Her passion for travel had certainly been rekindled by current events. Together with Emma and Tom, she would...

Together with Emma and Tom? She wanted to believe in Tom and his good intentions, but based on what he'd done the night before...

With her shoulders sagging, she followed the corridor that branched off to the left and ended up in a spacious kitchen. Next to a fireplace, she discovered shelves with dishes. There was also a small dining nook with a rustic corner seat and matching table, and a windowsill with clay pots containing basil, rosemary, coriander, and thyme. Were the herbs watered with a spell or would Julie be returning soon? There wasn't anybody in the kitchen and there was nothing unusual in the inventory.

Mayla hurried back, passed through other

hallways, and encountered countless rooms, all of them welcoming and in no way ostentatious. There were numerous paintings on the walls. The depictions of flowers and natural landscapes exuded as much coziness as the numerous pillows that appeared to be hand-embroidered.

As she searched the floors, she discovered several bedrooms, bathrooms, a dining room, and a drawing room — this last seemed the most personal of them all. Inside was a grand piano, a narrow shelf full of books, and an easel with an unfinished oil painting. It depicted a flower arrangement in a basket with the handle sketched but not yet colored in. Pretty. Was this Julie's hand-iwork? Had she painted all the pictures in the house?

Mayla rummaged through the various items there, but a remaining spark of decency prevented her from going through the documents and cupboards too thoroughly. She sensed Julie wasn't hiding anything from her, except perhaps the knowledge she had shared with Tom but not her. She would hardly find this information in the cupboards and drawers.

Disappointed, she returned to the foyer. She hadn't even found anything unusual in the base-ment, let alone any trace of Tom. He wasn't there, and neither was the lady of the house. Strange that Julie had disappeared overnight even though she had told them the day before that she was a recluse. That couldn't be a coincidence.

Mayla's eyes burned, possibly because of the poor lighting, and the throbbing in the back of her head had intensified. It would be better if she took a break. But where? Violett and Georg were at the hospital. Even if they had already gone back home, Georg needed to rest. She wouldn't be going to Donnersberg Castle, that was certain. She was about to retreat to one of the cozy bedrooms in the chateau when she was struck by an idea. Not just any idea — no, it was the perfect idea. How she could take a little break and meet a loved one at the same time. With a smile, she clutched the amulet key and jumped.

4

She landed on cobblestones that had no trace of lavender or French flair, but it smelled of apple cider and good old city air. Mayla greedily inhaled the familiar scent. How long had it been since she had visited Frankfurt? The big city still felt most like home even though she hadn't been here in years and had technically grown up in the suburbs. She had gone to high school in Frankfurt, studied there, and lived in Bornheim for several years. If there was one place she could call home, it was Frankfurt.

With a smile on her lips, she strolled past the main police station. Her steps felt lighter as she exited the world fold and tottered across the street. She passed St. Catherine's Church and strolled through Katharinenpforte until she reached the small shop. The dream catchers in the large store window were swaying back and forth when Mayla spotted the hand rearranging them — the hand she used to hold in hers so often, that would reach into her box of chocolates, and that would clap joyfully when Mayla said something.

A broad smile spread across her face as she entered the esoteric shop. A wind chime accompanied her arrival and she heard the familiar voice calling out, "I'll be right there." The smell of incense filled her nostrils, bringing another smile to her face. For the first time since the incident, she felt comfortable. She turned happily and looked at the woman standing on a stepladder who was hanging wind chimes and dream catchers.

"No problem, I have time."

Heike widened her eyes and turned abruptly. Her foot missed the step. "Mayla?" She flailed her arms wildly and fell.

In a matter of seconds, Mayla scanned the store, found no one there but them, and thought *Vola!* so as to gently float her friend to her feet. Heike didn't even notice, but immediately rushed toward her, her arms outstretched.

"Mayla? Is it really you? How nice. How wonderful. I've missed you so much."

The two were already throwing their arms around each other. The familiarity of her long-time friend filled Mayla with a sense of warmth and she hugged her back gratefully. "I've missed you too, Heike."

Heike took the glasses off her nose and wiped them clean with a cloth. "What are you doing here? I thought you weren't coming until next week after Emma had settled in. I can't believe I haven't met your little girl or Tom yet. At least you're back. Tell me! How is your new home? It's a shame I can't see it."

Mayla laughed halfheartedly. She wanted to hide it — her anger, her worry, and her disappointment. And her fear. But when she shrugged and began to speak, her voice didn't sound as untroubled as she'd hoped. "It couldn't have gone more wrong."

Heike furrowed her eyebrows, put her hands on her hips, and peered closely at her. "What happened?"

She was briefly overcome with grief and she started to sob. Heike wrapped her arm around her. "Come on, Mayla, let's sit down and then you can tell me in peace." She led Mayla to a seating area and maneuvered her onto a divan-like upholstered piece of furniture covered in pink and orange cushions. She quickly rushed to the shop door, locked it, and hung up the "Be back soon" sign. Then she scurried into the back and returned with a pot of tea and two cups, which she placed on the small side table. After pouring the steaming liquid, she reached into a drawer and pulled out a box of chocolates, which she held under Mayla's nose. "What happened?"

"There's a pot of tea and chocolates — were you expecting me?" Mayla made an attempt at a crooked smile but didn't succeed.

Heike chuckled. "Let's put it this way. This morning I felt like making a whole pot of tea instead of only half, as if my subconscious knew you were coming." This sounded particularly spiritual for Heike and Mayla grinned.

Her friend winked mischievously. "I always have chocolates here anyway. I learned a lot from you at the agency — in particular, that you should have stockpiles in various places so that you never have to do without when you truly need them."

With a smile, Mayla recalled the years they had spent together at the advertising agency. It had been a nice time, especially since she had been able to see her friend every day. Five years had passed since they had last spoken face-to-face. The time had passed quickly. At first, they had written letters to each other and later, Mayla occasionally left the world fold on Lesbos to call her friend from a payphone. But such exchanges could by no means replace personal interactions. At least they had kept in touch and Mayla knew Heike had quit the advertising agency two years ago and became co-owner of Nora's esoteric shop. Now, they ran it together and Heike was happy.

"So what happened, Mayla?"

Mayla took a chocolate and smelled it. Cinnamon and bitter cream. Yummy. How was she supposed to explain to her friend the monstrous thing that had happened?

"There was a kidnapping attempt, which is why Emma is living in hiding with my grandma. Then, last night, Tom knocked me unconscious and hasn't been seen since."

"What?" Heike's mouth dropped open. She stared at her in disbelief. Over the chocolates and tea, Mayla told her the long version, even describing the little bag that Tom had snatched out of her hand and that she suspected contained the magic stone. She knew that if there was anyone she could trust, it was her friend Heike. Plus, she lived outside the world folds.

Nora had taught Heike a lot about the world of witches, but she still looked up in surprise when Mayla spoke about the magic stones. She even confided in Heike that Emma carried the ancient magic within her and the consequences that might be in store for her little one. It felt good to get everything off her chest and Heike was a good listener. And her optimism was unbeatable.

"You have to look at this in a positive light, Mayla. If Emma was born with it, there's a reason for it. She is destined for great things." Heike enthusiastically bit into a crunchy truffle and pondered, happy to be involved in solving the problem. "What's gotten into Tom? I can't believe he knocked you out and took that bag from you. Why would he do that? Do you believe one of those stones was in it?"

Mayla shrugged. She didn't know whether to be outraged because Heike wasn't more upset about her being betrayed or relieved because her friend thought the same thing she did. Tom was still on her side.

Meanwhile, Heike continued to consider. "He told you that no matter what happens, he was doing it for your daughter. Do you think he wanted to prevent the hunters from getting the stones and that's why he stole them?"

Mayla unexpectedly raised her arms but

stopped herself at the last moment before shattering all the angel figurines on the shelf across from her. "I assume so. But he could have told me. Together we are stronger. And it doesn't explain why he knocked me out. If there was one of the stones in the bag, it was safe with me — as was the Fire Circle Stone."

Heike sipped her herbal tea. "If I remember correctly, he was never particularly communicative, was he?"

Mayla grumbled and reached for another chocolate. The smell hinted at a cognac filling, which was exactly what she needed.

"You need to find out why Tom did what he did. I bet he was the one who came back that night and made sure you were okay. He didn't want to hurt you, he was forced to, don't you agree?"

Mayla grumbled again. "I hope so, for his sake. Otherwise, God help him."

Heike sat on the edge of the seat and leaned forward. She seemed content, as if she were solving a puzzle like Miss Marple and all this wasn't bitter reality for Mayla. "So here's what you do now. Search for clues as to what Tom has been up to lately. Where was he? What did he find out? What texts did he study? Who did he meet?"

Mayla furrowed her brows. "I would love to know who the woman he spoke to in our bedroom was. If she's a hunter who fought the man who tried to kidnap Emma — what was his name? Richard von Pommern — or if it was a power struggle at the von Eisenfels family's ancestral home?"

"Quite a power struggle if she killed that von Pommern guy, don't you think? Even though he deserved it. My goodness, poor Emma. No, I think this woman has something to do with Tom's disappearance. She's his ally."

The words stung Mayla. He preferred for the stranger to be his ally instead of her!

"You have to look for her, too."

Mayla raised her hands helplessly. "How am I supposed to do that? We've been searching for something to lead us to her and the hunters for days. We've found nothing except crumbs of earth that led us to Mont Saint Michel."

Heike chuckled happily, which seemed to Mayla just as inappropriate as the joy she seemed to take in the whole conversation. But she couldn't be mad at her friend. She even noticed a little how Heike's cheerful nature rubbed off on her.

"You found that locket in the Mont Saint Michel cemetery? Where is it now?"

Mayla reflected. "I think at Donnersberg Castle. Violett and Angelika examined it more closely."

"I would get it back if I were you." Heike took another sip of tea. "Yes, you have to get the necklace and then jump to the south of England, to that country estate belonging to Tom's family. There, search the room again where this stranger fought the hunter, and especially make sure to search that secret library. I bet that's where Tom left a message for you."

"What?" Mayla laughed unhappily. "Why would he leave a message there?"

Heike winked at her. "Because he took you to the secret library, a place where few people can enter. Where else would a message for you be safe?"

Mayla expelled a breath loudly. That sounded logical enough. Maybe Heike wasn't entirely wrong. She tilted her head and looked at her friend. "Okay, thanks. That was quite the investigative interview."

Heike chuckled. "Yeah, right? Fantastic. I learned that from the crime novels I've read."

Mayla also chuckled. "Since when do you read crime novels? You've only ever devoured esoteric books."

Heike made a dismissive gesture. "Since I started working here, Nora has been teaching me a great deal, so I needed something else in my free time. I ran across an Edgar Wallace film by chance and since then, I have been fascinated by crime thrillers. Last week, I even took part in a murder mystery dinner — you must join me one day. It was so much fun. In any case, I definitely have special knowledge that I can use to help you." When Mayla laughed again, Heike raised her hands defensively. "I know, I know, these are all just made-up cases. Still, I learned a lot about how investigators work. That's why I'm convinced Tom left you a message somewhere."

Mayla smelled the chocolate candy she was holding in her hands. Heike was probably right. She was equally convinced that Tom had meant her no harm and certainly hadn't sided with the hunters. But all the same, her wounded pride still grumbled at how quickly her friend had taken his side.

"All right, then I'll be on my way."

"Fantastic." Heike clapped her hands. Her eyes lit up as if she were on a mission of discovery herself. "Oh, how I would love to come with you. Too bad I can't enter any world folds. If you think of any spell that can provide normal people with magical abilities or allow them to enter world folds, you'd tell me, right? I'm counting on you, Mayla! Are you going to come back later? I can help you with the other things as well."

Mayla smiled. How she had missed Heike. "Thanks, that is nice of you. How late are you working?"

She waved her hand dismissively. "Don't worry about that. Any time you need me, Nora can handle the store without me for a while. So? When are we meeting?"

"I can't promise anything. Who knows what clues I'll come across, but I'll be back as soon as I can." She winked mischievously at Heike, who nodded happily.

"Take care of yourself, Mayla. When all of this is over, come visit me with your little one... and bring Tom. Okay? I would like to finally meet them. And I promise you, I'll have a serious talk with Tom. He's not going to get away scot-free for hurting my best friend!"

Mayla smiled and her heart warmed. Heike was a great friend. Even though they hadn't seen each other in five years, they had simply picked up where they had left off. That was real friendship.

She said goodbye, promising Heike she would return. The wind chime tinkled behind her as she left the store, sounding a bit like the starting bell signaling that the search for the truth, Tom, and the stranger had begun.

5

Mayla decided not to look for the locket first. She wanted to postpone a confrontation at Donnersberg Castle and perhaps even avoid it altogether by asking Violett about the necklace. Maybe her friend could get it.

Tom hadn't told her the spell to access his family's secret library, but since the room's primary protection rested on the fact that no one could enter the place unless accompanied by a family member, she hoped she could cobble together a spell. She thought for a moment, imagined the dark cluttered room, and thought, *Perduce me in bibliothecam occultam familiae Eisenfels!*

The buildings of the main police station swirled around her and the sunlight disappeared along with the blue sky, giving way to a gloom that Mayla welcomed like never before. She quickly blew a flame onto her fingertip. Had the spell worked? The flickering glow pushed back the darkness and revealed the table where she had stood with Tom, spreading out countless scrolls. In the background, barely visible, were the many plain shelves.

She had done it. That was a good sign! She did a little mental dance before she blew on a three-armed candelabra and looked around the deserted room. The interior appeared to be the same as last time, with countless scrolls and old books stacked on the simple shelves, with nothing to give the impression that anyone had spent any length of time there over the past few weeks. Had Tom been there, as Heike suspected? Had he left her a message?

Could anyone other than her and Tom enter this library? The last time they had been there, someone had overheard them. So, at least one person other than the two of them knew about the hidden room and how to get inside. That meant it wasn't completely safe to leave a secret message there. Had Tom done it anyway?

She walked to the end of the room. To make sure that no one would surprise her and that she truly was alone in the library, she peeked around the last row of shelves. No one was around, but she was still troubled by a sense of uneasiness.

She quietly hurried to the shelf she and Tom had pulled out many scrolls from the previous time and carefully searched for a piece of paper among the books and rolled-up texts. She wanted to believe Heike's theory, to hold on to the belief that he had a plan and would let her in on it, but she discovered nothing. No piece of paper, no sealed envelope, nothing that hadn't been there before. She also hunted for items that weren't part of the inventory. Tom may have left her a Nuntia charm. But there was nothing to be found.

Where else could she look? Should she scour the shelves? But he would never have thought she would do that. No, he knew her too well. If he had been expecting her to come there and had left her a message, then he would have chosen a location or object with a significance that only she would notice.

Had something happened the last time, or had they talked about anything he would use? Mayla frowned, lifted the candlestick higher so that its light reached into the far corners, and considered. She walked slowly through the aisles. Her eyes slid over the metal shelves, darted over the scrolls and the picture frame and — wait! The picture frame?!

The last time they had been there and were overheard, the eavesdropper had left behind nothing but a picture frame with broken glass. Tom had said he couldn't remember ever seeing one in this library. Was that his clue? The one she was searching for?

She stumbled over to the shelf where the frame was and picked it up. She looked around warily so that no one would take her by surprise again, but there was no one to be seen or heard. Wait. The last time, the person had remained inconspicuous. She closed her eyes and felt the magic in the room. She couldn't sense any source of energy other than her own. There wasn't anybody there.

She placed the candlestick on the floor. She didn't have the time — or the patience! — to go back to the table and examine the picture frame there. Instead, she peeled back the supporting cardboard in the aisle and looked behind it. There was nothing there. Was it hidden by a spell? Mayla tucked a loose strand of hair behind her ears.

Aperi! she thought, trying to make the cipher visible. But nothing changed. Strange. Wait, was the whole frame possibly a Nuntia spell? She raised it to her lips, concentrated on a message, and whispered, "Te aperi!" But even then, nothing happened.

But the frame had to hold a clue! Tom hadn't charmed it back into one piece and placed it back on the shelf last time — no, he had taken it with him... right? Shoot, she hadn't been paying attention.

Disappointed, she reassembled it and turned the frame so she could look at the picture. Wait! There hadn't been a picture last time. Now it held a photo of an unfamiliar landscape. A simple cabin in the middle of a forest. Who took snapshots of something like that and then framed it? It was unremarkable. Wait, maybe the picture itself was the clue.

Deep in thought, Mayla slid to the floor and fished for a truffle. Oh dear. Her supplies were running low. Hopefully, they would last until everything was cleared up. All the same, she didn't deny herself the comforting treat. Slowly and with all of her attention, she placed the confection in her mouth, let the chocolate slowly melt on her tongue, and enjoyed it to the fullest before studying the photo again.

A cabin in the forest. Had Tom ever said anything about it? No, as far as she knew, he only owned the cabin in the Pyrenees. Did he possibly want to lead her there? The frame was a bit dirty. She ran her finger over the place where the wood and glass met. Something stuck to her fingertip. It wasn't dust. Frowning, she sniffed the finger and her eyes widened. It smelled like... earth. It was the clue she was searching for! Tom's tip wasn't the broken picture frame but the new spell she had learned when Georg and Tom had discovered the dirt in their home. The earth would lead to the house. Or at least to where Tom thought Mayla should go.

Hooray for Heike — she had known.

Mayla jumped to her feet and thought about it. What was the spell Georg had used to trace the dirt in their house back to Mont Saint Michel? When she remembered, she clapped her hands happily. She concentrated on the earth and whispered, "Ostende, unde venias!"

The fine bits of earth came off her finger and rose into the air. They stopped at eye level and turned faster and faster until they slowly sank to the ground. An image appeared in the air and Mayla's breath caught when she recognized it.

It was the Eiffel Tower.

The Eiffel Tower? Tom was summoning her to the Eiffel Tower? Why in the world couldn't he have done this as part of a romantic getaway sometime over the past two years?

She inhaled deeply and massaged her temples. She had to think. Obviously, she would jump to Paris. There wasn't any doubt about that. But what was there? She clenched her hands. There was only one way she would find out.

Determined, she rose and brushed the dust off her skirt. Was there a world fold at the Eiffel Tower? Probably, given that witches had appeared at every tourist attraction Mayla had visited. Without further ado, she grasped the amulet key and considered the translation before imagining the landmark that was the very symbol of Paris. Luckily, Tom had taught her that trick so she could avoid translating every single word she didn't know in Latin for the Perduce spell.

"Perduce me ad locum Eiffel Tower!"

With a wave of her hand, the candles went out and darkness surrounded her, only to give way in the next moment to a bright blue sky. The sun was blinding so Mayla held her hand in front of her eyes.

Sure enough, she had done it. She now found herself standing before the symbol of Paris, near the stairs leading upward. With a smile, she tilted her head back and her gaze followed the metal framework to the top, which reached for the sky. Madness. It had been ages since she had been there, most recently on a graduation trip with her school class. If someone had told her back then that next to the entrance to the Eiffel Tower was a world fold that only witches could enter, she would have laughed. Who knew if she had been one of the tourists who disappeared before the witches' gaze, like now, on one side of the fold to then reappear in the blink of an eye on the other?

She looked around warily. The world fold was larger than the one on Pont Neuf, but was barely ten square meters There were a few witches inside, joining groups of tourists chatting happily as they crossed the magical threshold and mingled among the normal tourists to make their way up the stairs. Apparently, there was no separate entrance for witches, but at least she didn't have to join the long line at the ticket booth.

Her gaze went up the staircase, searching the higher levels. Was Tom waiting for her up there? Or was he hiding among the groups of tourists standing at the ticket office paying for tickets? No, his height would have attracted attention. She shielded her eyes again with her hand and surveyed the area, but she didn't see him in the park, by the nearby trees, or across the street. An old-fashioned carousel that children scampered around caught her eye, but she didn't see him there either.

Well, the clue had pointed to the Eiffel Tower and not to the surrounding area or Paris itself. Without further ado, she scurried out of the world fold and mingled with a group of Italians who were chatting loudly as they headed up the stairs. Within a short time, Mayla fell behind. Countless tour groups passed her until she finally reached the first level. Phew. What had Tom been think-ing, sending her there? It just kept getting worse.

If he was hinting that she should get in better shape, he would get an ear full. Panting, she leaned on the railing and put one hand on her hip. She was tormented by stitches in her side. Shoot, she should have brought something to drink.

While catching her breath, she gazed out over Paris. The city was beautiful. She would have loved to sit down in the little cafe by the park, drink a café au lait, and snack on a petit four. Perhaps two or three. Maybe she could do that once she'd searched the Eiffel Tower. After all, nothing helped to think as effectively as a beautifully decorated confection and a cup of coffee. Mayla's mood immediately lifted.

Her pulse had steadied and she strolled along the platform. She looked thoughtfully at the stairs that led up to the second level, then shook her head decisively. Tom would never have asked her to go higher and he certainly wouldn't have expected her to look there for a clue. This meant that the next clue had to be somewhere on this level. She walked along the balustrade and explored the bars above it, inspected every telescope that had been set up for visitors, and examined the bar tables and every corner. She found nothing. There was nothing. No trace of Tom or his whereabouts. It was a dead end, darn it!

She wanted to try a spell, but unfortunately, it would be too conspicuous. Everyone would notice the glitter trail left by the search spell. Darn. Now what? She glanced briefly at the staircase that led to the next level. No. Like in the library, he had chosen a hiding place that only the two of them would recognize. Insider knowledge. But what?

Sighing, she turned her head — and her eyes landed on the cafe. Of course, Tom would have known she'd be wanting a coffee straight away. He had hidden the clue there. It just had to be there. Wonderful. Now she could kill two birds with one stone. Happily, she entered the stylishly furnished establishment and sat down at one of the last free tables. Hopefully, it wasn't important for her to sit in one specific seat. Given the crowds, it would have taken forever to search every table.

Excited by the prospect of a second and much more substantial breakfast with a breathtaking view, she reached for the menu and her eyes lit up. Petit fours. At least now it was clear. All the angels in heaven were on her side. Or magical beings, supernatural energies, or esoteric structures. Oh, whatever. It didn't matter. Mayla crossed one leg over the other and waved to the waiter.

"Un café au lait, s'il vous plaît, et trois petit fours. Merci beaucoup."

A smile crossed the waiter's lips as he wrote down the order and bowed. "Avec plaisir, Madame."

It didn't take long before Mayla received her order. Fantastic. She enjoyed every single bite. Sure, the situation was serious and time was short, but this break gave her strength. Thrilled, she hardly left a single crumb on her plate and sipped the last of her coffee. Now she felt prepared to consider what to do next. As she waved to the waiter so she could pay, he approached with a grin.

"Did you enjoy it?"

Why was he speaking English to her? There were probably so many tourists that he picked up bits and pieces from them. "Yes, thank you. It was delicious. I would like to pay."

"Your man already did that and he gave me this letter to give to you. You're welcome, Madame." He bowed and held out a small silver tray to her. There was a sealed envelope on it. The seal was a combination of a flame and two hammers. It was from Tom. Unbelievable.

Mayla stared at the waiter wide-eyed. "When did he give this to you? Where is he? In the kitchen?"

The waiter shook his head. "No, Madame. I'm to tell you to read the letter. It's all in there."

"What?" Stunned, she looked from the waiter to the letter and then at the swinging door that led into the kitchen. Okay. Tom was hiding there, watching.

The waiter took the envelope and handed it to her. "Please, take the envelope, I have to get back to work. Au revoir, Madame." He bowed discreetly again and turned his attention to an older gentleman waving him over.

Mayla stared at the envelope lying on the clean white tablecloth in disbelief, as if it were innocence itself. She reached for it nervously, unable to wait a second longer, and broke the seal. There was a short note inside, and she unfolded it.

Tears welled up in her eyes when she recognized the familiar handwriting.

Dear Mayla,

I'm sorry for what happened. You know I am always on your side and would do anything for Emma and you. Trust me and step aside. I'll take care of everything. Hide at Donnersberg Castle and wait. In a few days, everything will be taken care of and you and Emma will be safe.

I love you.

Yours, Tom

Mayla stared at the words. Wait, what? She should hide? This was the secret message for which she had struggled up those horrid steps? No hint as to how she could help him. Where was he? Had he wanted to buy time and keep her busy, actually distract her by sending her on a scavenger hunt like a child? Was this supposed to be a joke?

Mayla read the lines again and again, scanning them in the hope that she had missed something, but there was nothing there but trivial words.

Dammit, Tom...

She waved to the waiter, who approached with an tray overflowing with dirty dishes.

"Please, can you tell me where the man went after he gave you the envelope?"

"No, sorry." He bowed and hurried into the kitchen.

Shoot. She wouldn't be getting anything more out of the waiter. Now what? What did Tom actually think of her? That she would listen to such nonsense? She had never sat patiently in an armchair to just wait around for him. Well, that wasn't true... She had been doing that for the last two years. But things certainly were different now. She definitely wouldn't be dissuaded. Besides, what did he mean by writing that she and Emma would be safe? What was wrong with him? Why hadn't he included himself too? Something wasn't right.

She stood up resolutely, stuffed the note and envelope into her handbag, and began the descent. She didn't pay attention to the phenomenal view but kept her eyes glued to the steps so she could get back into the fold as quickly as possible. She would locate Tom. She would learn about all these schemes. To do that, she would follow the trail they had been pursuing together over the last few days. Mayla was convinced that answers were waiting for her somewhere along there.

6

H ome was her first destination. She hadn't been there since she'd searched it with Tom and Georg. Since no one could enter the property without her permission — except apparently the hunters, darn it — she believed she was safe from the police and the people at Donnersberg Castle.

As soon as she landed in the hallway, she put up a shield and looked around carefully to make sure the hunters weren't waiting for her. Luckily, she didn't see or hear anything. She let the shield fizzle out and roamed the living room and kitchen. Everything had changed since the hunters had ravaged her home. For a moment, her fingers itched to clean everything up with a simple spell and restore the sense of a cozy atmosphere, but she refrained from doing so, and instead hurried upstairs.

Tom had spoken to the stranger in her bedroom. Had the two met there or had he caught her by surprise? Did they know each other from before? Had Tom recognized the woman when they had watched the fight between her and Emma's kidnapper at the ancestral home in southern England? Dang it. These endless questions weren't getting her anywhere. She had been spinning in circles for far too long.

She entered the bedroom purposefully. The large double bed was made, the blanket neatly folded, and the novels Mayla had last read were lying on the nightstand. What books were on Tom's bedside table? She quickly moved to his side of the bed and sat down. On the nightstand was a small lamp and a photo of Emma, Tom, and her. It was a picture of them at the beach. Emma had built a large sandcastle and was grinning at the camera between her parents. Her grandmother had taken the picture. Mayla sighed, picked up the picture, and hugged it to her chest.

Oh, please, let this all end well!

She placed the picture in her purse and opened Tom's bedside table drawer. It didn't feel right going through his private things, but that's what he deserved. She rummaged through the few belongings with her fingertips. A watch, a few coins, and tissues. There was nothing else. Mayla closed the drawer and opened the compartment underneath. At first glance, it appeared empty, but as she leaned forward, she spotted a small box nestled in the back. She slowly pulled it out. What was inside? If it had been extremely important, Tom would have taken it with him — or the hunters would have absconded with it when they ransacked their house. If it didn't have at least some meaning to him, he wouldn't have hidden it.

As she carefully opened the lid, her heart beat faster and faster. She didn't know whether it was because she was excited or because she was ashamed of going through his things. But that wasn't what mattered right then, for goodness' sake.

The lid flipped back to reveal layers of red velvet. Frowning, Mayla pushed the fabric aside. Underneath was a white gold necklace with matching earrings inlaid with tourmaline. The bluish-black stone shimmered. Why was Tom keeping this box and jewelry?

She carefully stroked the surface of the earrings. The jewelry didn't look new, as if he had bought it recently to give to her. No — in fact, it looked as if it were hundreds of years old. She stroked the chain reverently, traced the ridges of the molding the jewelry was in so it wouldn't slide haphazardly around in the box, and felt another hollowed area. Wait, was something missing? And as she moved over the empty place in the box, her eyes fell on the ring on her finger. The one Tom had presented her with when he'd asked for her hand in marriage. She paused, stared at the ring, then at the necklace and earrings, and back again. The ring was part of it; it was an ensemble.

Mayla's heart beat faster. Why had he only given her the ring and not the other pieces? Did he want to give them to her at their wedding? Or had he consciously withheld it? Where did it come from? An antique shop or maybe... his ancestors?

When he'd given her the ring, it hadn't occurred to her that it might be a family heirloom. Had old Bertha also worn this ring? And the jewelry? Mayla shuddered. A strange thought. The necklace and earrings in the box had a slight yellowish discoloration, as white gold tended to acquire over the years. Her ring appeared newer and more polished, but he'd probably had it restored so it would match her other shiny jewelry and make a suitable engagement ring.

Mayla lowered the box into her lap and stared off into space. She knew about Tom's background, who his father and grandmother had been, and what they and some other ancestors had done. The family had a bad reputation. Mayla had repeatedly insisted that not all members of the von Eisenfels family were evil. Nevertheless, the ring on her finger suddenly felt heavy, as heavy as hundreds of years of dark history, brutal power games, and ruthless intrigue.

She looked at it, played with it, and slid it up and down her finger. If she had known it was an heirloom, she would have been just as happy about the piece and the proposal! At least that is what she told herself. In reality, it was different. The truth was that it weighed heavily on her. Anything else was a lie.

Why hadn't Tom told her where the jewelry had come from? If he had explained it to her, told her it was important to him to preserve the heirlooms, she certainly wouldn't have objected. But finding out by accident... Mayla shook her head.

She breathed in deeply, put the box in her

purse, and stood up. She wouldn't put it back in its hiding spot. The jewelry was probably of little use to her in her search, but she still couldn't leave it behind. It meant something. Besides, she planned to ask Tom about it.

Disappointed, she plodded around the bed. The trip hadn't provided her with any clues... but wait a minute. Her face brightened a bit. She could at least stock up on chocolate. She walked to her side of the bed, reached into the nightstand, and retrieved her emergency nightly stash from the bottom shelf. The handbag was slowly filling up, but it didn't matter. The box had to go in, especially given that Violett's was almost empty.

She glanced around the room one last time and left with a bitter taste on her tongue. As she passed the nursery, her heart felt leaden and her steps grew heavier as she approached the narrow bed. Her eyes scanned the pink and green bedspread and the flower mobile that dangled from the ceiling. Slowly, she sat down on the mattress and stroked the pillow as if her daughter were lying there. Emma, however, wasn't there. Would she ever sleep in this bed again? Would she ever open her dark eyes, look at her mom with a smile, and ask what great things would they would be doing today?

The memory of Emma and the knowledge of the blood flowing through her daughter's veins helped. Her daughter was also a von Eisenfels and she was a wonderful girl. From now on, whenever she looked at the ring, she wanted to think of Emma and how her daughter was part of the family from which the jewelry originated. She stroked the pillow one last time before picking it up and pressing it to her face, breathing in the beloved baby scent that clung to it faintly before putting it back and leaving the room.

Her shoes clacked on the stairs as she hurried downstairs. Every step attested to the seconds — to that valuable time — that passed while she was in this house without finding any significant clues. In the house Tom had chosen for them and where they had planned to live a safe and good life. Protected and happy. Mayla stared at the ring on her finger and balled her hands into fists. Like hell was she going to let the hunters win. She wanted her happiness back. Her life, her family. And she swore to herself that she'd get it, whether in this house or another.

MAYLA'S next stop was southern England. She was planning to calmly search the von Eisenfels ancestral home, especially the room where the stranger and that cursed kidnapper, Richard von Pommern, had fought. At least there she would find a useful lead. She swore on her supply of chocolates — no, better not. Like hell would she give up. Tom had yet to see the type of woman he was intending to marry.

She clutched the amulet key and imagined the impressive estate where Tom had grown up. "Perduce me in villam familiae Eisenfels!" In the time that it took her to take another breath, she found herself in the entrance hall, warily scanning the area. It was quiet, not noticeably quiet, more like... deserted. Again, Mayla assessed the area as best she could, but other than her magic, she did not detect any pulsating energy coming from a living being. Still, she kept her head down as she set off.

She didn't want to search the office that belonged to Tom's father. Tom wouldn't have hidden anything there, not in a million years. She was certain of that. In any case, it was unlikely Tom would have left a clue anywhere. For too many years, he had lived as a shadow, hiding his past and origins, and leading such a withdrawn life that no one had even imagined that the mysterious hermit could have been the son of Vincent von Eisenfels. No, she wouldn't find anything left by Tom unless he wanted her to, but maybe she'd find something from the mysterious woman.

The situation was so desperate that her only choice was to remain optimistic. She hurried up the stairs to the first floor and crossed the dark hallway. Although it was light outside — and rainy, typical for a late morning in England — the pictures on the walls were in shadows. Only the oil portrait of one individual caught her eye. It depicted a tall, slim woman, her chin raised, her long black hair slickly styled. She looked breathtakingly beautiful, not likable, but with a symmetrical face, large eyes, and elegantly curved eyebrows. She could have posed for a glossy magazine and become famous.

Her pride radiated from the picture, and Mayla almost wanted to hang her head. But she didn't and instead approached the portrait. No name was on or under the painting. Yet the brown eyes — dark as night — and strong chin seemed so familiar to Mayla that this woman could only be one person. Valentina Victoria von Eisenfels, aka old Bertha, when she'd been younger, probably around forty.

This imperious woman was a great con artist, considering she'd run a hotel for so many years undetected right under the eyes of the police officers whose station was not three hundred meters away. How could she have remained calm as Mayla, a naive new witch, sat before her asking questions? With just a slight wave of her hand, she could have killed Mayla back then. Did she truly not know who Mayla was?

In the painting, Bertha was clutching a stick. No, it wasn't a stick but something like a scepter, and there was a signet ring on her finger. Mayla narrowed her eyes. It wasn't the one with the mountains that Mayla had admired at the hotel. This signet ring depicted two hammers, the insignia of the von Eisenfels family, and their metal circle.

Mayla shuddered. She turned from the portrait and walked down the hallway, passing other paintings, including Vincent's, but she didn't spot Tom in any. Frankly, there was not one single family portrait or children to be seen. Tom was probably not among them because he had left the ancestral home and renounced his lineage long before he had become an adult.

She passed one strong chin after another, all

with dark eyes and black hair above them. She found herself comparing the people portrayed to Emma, but even if certain external characteristics were the same, her daughter lacked the arrogance and imperious character exuded by all of those who were represented.

She looked away from her child's ancestors and fixed her gaze on the door leading to the room where the fight between the stranger and hunter had taken place. It was halfway open. To be on the safe side, she checked the property again to see if anyone had arrived in the meantime, but apart from her energy, that of the tall trees on the extensive grounds, and the magic that pulsated in the world fold, she didn't detect anything.

With her hand on the knob, she pushed the door open. The room was still trashed but continued to exude a certain comfort. There were shelves containing not only books, but also small figurines of elves, fairies, and knights. There was a globe off to the side with the countries and oceans depicted in bright colors — apparently revealing a few world folds because the outlines of Europe and Asia were definitely irregular. The upholstered furniture in the room was not covered in black or white leather but common fabric with plush cushions.

Mayla glanced around in disbelief. Because of the chaos created by the fallen shelves, chairs, and table, she had completely overlooked the fact that this room didn't fit with the rest of the property. It was different, so much more personal and... warmer. It wasn't a child's room — otherwise, she would have immediately guessed it had belonged to Tom. Moreover, there wasn't a rocking horse, cuddly stuffed animals, or any other toys. Even the small figurines appeared merely decorative.

The choice of furnishings suggested the room belonged to a woman rather than a boy, and certainly not a man. Who had decorated this room? Had a von Eisenfels defied the reigning style and claimed this space as her oasis? But Vincent would have surely redecorated the room in accordance with his sense of style when he had been living alone with Tom on the property.

Or else someone had lived here in recent years. Someone who had made the room their retreat by simply claiming the space since the property was no longer used by the hunters. The country estate had frequently been searched by the police, but the officers had long since confiscated everything they considered important and removed the barriers from the property. So, who had designed this refuge? The stranger?

Mayla slowly entered the room, careful not to touch or change anything. She didn't want to inadvertently ruin a clue by trampling it or accidentally kicking it under the sofa.

The mood of the room differed from the rest of the property. It wasn't as cold and gloomy, but rather welcoming and uplifting. Had the stranger lived in the room? She had made such a cold and hostile impression — she couldn't possibly be the interior designer of this room. Mayla shook her head. No, it was too hard to imagine.

Up ahead, the two had fought each other.

Having suffered a fatal blow, the hunter had fallen when the unknown woman had snatched a bag from him. Had it contained a magical stone? Did that mean she was one of their opponents after all?

There had to be something in this room!

As Mayla crouched down and examined the floor, she suddenly felt a magical presence. She immediately raised her hands, ready to cast an attack spell when something glittered in front of her and a woman unexpectedly appeared.

It was Anna Nowak.

7

"Anna? What are you doing here?" Mayla looked incredulously at the Polish Earth Witch, whom she had met at Donnersberg Castle and to whom she had never really warmed up. At first, Anna had felt an inexplicable dislike for Mayla. Even though they had grown closer during Melinda's liberation and worked together while fighting Vincent and Bertha, they had never become friends. It wasn't necessarily Mayla's fault, but the feeling that Anna had nothing but contempt for her had never gone away, which was why she hadn't made any effort to improve the relationship.

Anna raised one of her perfectly plucked eyebrows and stood confidently in front of Mayla as if she were the mistress of the house and Mayla the trespasser. She was taller and more athletic than her — which wasn't surprising. She also had practical knowledge of a variety of complex spells and had expertise that few possessed. She was certainly Mayla's equal even though Anna didn't belong to a founding family. "I'm here to help you."

Mayla's eyes widened. She wasn't here to attack her because of Tom's... betrayal? But Mayla didn't have to ask. If anyone at Donnersberg Castle swore loyalty to Tom every time without being asked, it was Anna Nowak. Even when it leaked out that Tom was Vincent's son and the others believed he was an informant.

"That's... nice of you, I..." Mayla hesitated. She didn't know if she could trust Anna, if the witch would truly stand by her when things got rough. But given her almost unwavering loyalty to Tom, she would hardly lead Mayla to her ruin, would she? She would have refused anyone else from Donnersberg Castle, but Anna's knowledge and experience with the most extraordinary magic could come in handy while searching for Tom. "How did you know I was here?"

Anna waved her hand. "I wanted to search the places you, Tom, and Georg talked about. I found the fight and the dead hunter peculiar, which is why I came to the property first. Do you know where Tom is now?"

Mayla looked at her thoughtfully. Anna's knowledge must have been limited to Tom promising to come to Donnersberg Castle that evening and not showing up. She had also heard how the others had suspected Tom of stealing some of the magic stones. Did she know what Tom... did after that? Probably not. How would she react?

"Tom is... not with me. He..."

Anna shrugged her muscular shoulders. "That does not surprise me. Tom has always been a lone fighter." She raised a skeptical eyebrow. "So, you haven't found any trace of him yet?"

Should she tell Anna? Mayla inhaled deeply and made her decision. If she didn't trust anyone, she would become as much of a lone warrior as Tom, which she didn't want. Mayla was convinced they were stronger together. Knowing Anna was on her side made her want to tell her the unvarnished truth of what had happened that evening.

"He knocked me and Georg out in France. Georg probably found one of the magic stones Tom took from us. We were lying unconscious in the forest all night. Georg even had to go to the hospital, so I went on without him."

Anna merely nodded and kept her inquisitive eyes on Mayla. She knew there was more, so Mayla abruptly decided to tell her the whole story so that someone would help her. "I received a message from him earlier. He said he would take care of everything and that I should trust him. He's doing it for Emma and me."

Anna laughed, sounding loud and brash but not unpleasant. Mayla had rarely seen anyone so confident. "Typical." She turned to the upended shelves and scanned the book titles and delicate figurines. "You saw the strange woman and the hunter fighting in this room, right? Did you notice anything about her?"

Mayla crouched and continued her search, stroking the floor. Perhaps the strange woman had left behind a few bits of earth. "She was wearing a long dark cloak and hood. Only because her long black hair was peeking out and her silhouette was visible under the cloak, did I know it was a woman. Her face remained completely in the shadows even though she didn't notice us at the beginning. I didn't hear her say anything either."

"Did she have a wand in her hands?"

Mayla stopped. She tried to recall the duel in detail. "I don't know. I only saw them fighting from behind. When the hunter was dead on the floor, she turned toward us."

"Your story suggests she is a powerful witch. A powerful witch knows how to cover her tracks." Anna bent down for something that Mayla couldn't see from a distance. When she raised her thumb and forefinger, Mayla marveled at what her new ally had found. A long black hair.

Mayla walked over to her. "So... how does this help us? Is there a spell, like for dirt, that helps us find the owner of the hair?" She was expecting Anna to make fun of her because she didn't know as many spells as she did — and she probably knew only half as many as most other witches her age. Although she had learned a lot and coped wonderfully, situations like these brought to light just how much she was missing because her magical abilities had only awakened in her early thirties.

Anna shook her head. There was no mockery in her expression or voice. "Unfortunately, there isn't one, but the hair is still a valuable clue. We can use this to find out the person's age and origin as well as their state of health and where they spend most of their time."

Huh? Like the crime series on Thursdays? "Are you sending it to a forensic lab or is there a spell?

Anna rose, pulled a small paper bag out of her jeans, and placed the hair in it. "Neither. We need a kettle and water to make a brew."

"We're preparing a magic potion?" Mayla shook her head in disbelief. There were so many new things for her to discover.

"It's not a real potion. I'll show you." She was already clutching her amulet key when Mayla pointed to the remaining mess.

"Don't you think we might find more clues?"

Anna shook her head. "She covered her tracks thoroughly. It's pure luck that we found a hair of hers."

Mayla pushed a loose strand of hair behind her ear thoughtfully. "Or intentionally. Maybe it's a trap. She may have quickly pulled out a hair or shaken it from her cloak, or it may not be hers at all but someone else's to lead us astray."

Anna pulled the hair out of the bag and held one end under Mayla's eyes. "No, look. The marks show it clearly. The hunter must have thrown a burning attack malediction at her, which she managed to dodge, but this hair was separated from her head and fell to the ground. She definitely didn't plant it."

Mayla peered at the tip of the hair. There was no root or traces of skin to be seen and Mayla couldn't see what Anna saw. Still, she wanted to believe the experienced witch. "All right then, let's brew the potion."

"Good. Let's go, there's no time to waste." She took her hand and Mayla felt powerful energy emanating from her. She was an extremely powerful witch. Perhaps Anna would one day take Phylis's place as Head Witch of the Earth Circle since the de Rochat founding family had been completely wiped out and head witches were chosen based on their powers. Either way, it was reassuring to have Anna on her side.

"Let's jump into the forest, where we won't be disturbed."

Mayla nodded and the next moment, the ravaged room swirled around her, with the disorder seeming even more violent to her, until it was replaced by a soft green that was peppered with shades of brown. She heard the rustling of a mouse scurrying away through the leaves.

Mayla's heels landed on dry leaves. Every step she took crackled. "Where are we?"

"In Germany. If you walk that way, you'll end up in Poland." She pointed east. "Rarely is anyone here. The forest is quiet and deserted. Over the last few years, I seldom have met a witch, so we can safely build a fire."

Mayla scanned the area and all she saw amidst the beech trees, moss, and a few slippery jack mushrooms was a large pile of stones, so she relaxed. Anna, with her wand outstretched, flew in twigs for the fire, piling them up much neater than Mayla could have managed. Mayla reached for an acorn, imagined an iron cauldron, and whispered,

"Converte!" She'd had to cast this spell for her daughter so many times that she could easily convert objects even into other materials. "Is there a river nearby?"

Anna nodded. "There is a spring behind the stones. It's small, but it'll suffice."

Mayla listened but didn't hear any splashing. She trudged after the Earth Witch with the cauldron. As they made their way through the previous year's dry leaves, every step was accompanied by a rustling, and it was a while before they heard a faint trickle. They reached a hill and with it the spring, which was a delicate, weak spurt that seeped out of the earth and flowed into a small stream.

Anna took the kettle from Mayla and held it under the flow. Having a water wizard along would obviously have been beneficial.

"It's a shame Georg isn't here. He could have strengthened the stream." Worry settled over Mayla as she thought about her best friend. "Hopefully, he's okay. Tom hit him rather hard. Not even my Sana spell could help him."

"Oh," Anna waved her hand, "you're overthinking it. Tom would never have seriously injured him and Georg is tough."

The blow had been so hard that Georg had needed to go to the hospital, but Mayla didn't want to start an argument. Once the cauldron was sufficiently full, they hurried back.

Anna flew the vessel onto the stacked branches and placed her hands on the ground. With this, a vibration so slight it was barely perceptible traveled through the earth. Curious, Mayla watched.

"What did you do?"

"I reinforced the ground so that the flames stay on the branches and we don't start a forest fire."

Mayla watched Anna carefully. She had never observed an Earth Witch perform spells before. Although she had lived in Phylis's house for a while, the Earth Witch had rarely stayed with them and Mayla had been far too preoccupied by Tom's health and her pregnancy to notice anything.

Mayla bent down and blew on the branches, igniting flames that licked up the dry wood. To brew a magical potion, the water couldn't just be charmed until it warmed. The interaction of the elements was important in order to ensure efficacy.

"Are you adding any herbs to it, or what do you do with the hair?"

As if on cue, Anna pulled the bag out of the back jeans pocket and fished out the discovery. "We whisper a spell and throw the hair in. We will read the answers on the surface of the water."

It was unbelievable what tricks Anna had up her sleeve. Mayla couldn't suppress an impressive whistle. "Wow, I definitely missed a lot."

Anna shrugged. "Few people know the spell. Not even police officers and detectives."

"Where did you learn it?"

"I read a lot. That was not always so. My child-hood was sheltered and I was naive until everything got out of hand. Since then, I have lived by the principle that knowledge is power."

Mayla couldn't help but shiver. What had Anna experienced that made her become this strong woman? Regardless, Mayla thanked her lucky stars that the Earth Witch was on her side. Without thinking, she took Anna's hand and smiled at her. "Thanks for coming."

A warm glow that Mayla had never seen in her before appeared in Anna's dark eyes. She squeezed Mayla's hand briefly, but only for a moment, then pulled away and held the hair over the now bubbling cauldron. "Listen, you wait until the water reaches its boiling point, then concentrate on the hair, and say, Quis es? and add the hair." Anna released her thumb and index finger and the long black hair slid into the water.

Curious, Mayla leaned closer. It was taking its time and she was about to ask if something had gone wrong when the bubbles finally subsided and the water immediately stopped boiling. It was as calm as a mountain lake with no one swimming in it. The hair was no longer visible.

Gradually, it took on a greenish-bluish tint and cloud-like configurations began to appear that mixed together until... Mayla widened her eyes... a Roman numeral appeared on the water.

LIX. Fifty-nine.

Mayla was about to give Anna a questioning look when the cloud-like number started moving, so she kept her eyes fixed on the cauldron. The shape balled up before changing to something that resembled an outline of a country or something similar. Was that England? The shape changed so quickly that Mayla wasn't certain. Next, it changed into another form, which seemed so confusing that Mayla didn't know what to make of it. A blink of an eye later, as if someone had snapped their finger and dissolved the spell, the fire went out, the colors disappeared, and nothing remained but the calm water reflecting the trees and sky.

Perplexed, Mayla straightened up. "Wow, that was... impressive. Did I see that correctly? Did it say fifty-nine?"

"Right, that was the age. What else did you see?"

"England?"

Anna nodded. "Good. The greenish-bluish color told us the state of health. She lives a healthy lifestyle, spends a lot of time outside, and eats little, but in a balanced way. But her soul is unhappy. I've never seen such a sad soul."

There was pity in Anna's voice, and it affected Mayla. Who was this woman? What had she experienced? How much practice did it take before you could read a cauldron as well as Anna? Mayla looked at her, impressed. "Were you able to read anything else from the cauldron? Her whereabouts? Didn't you say we could find that out too?"

Anna rocked her head back and forth. "Normally, yes, but this woman is a nomad. All I can say is that she lives in seclusion. She is not someone who jumps from conference to conference to talk to various witches in the world as some do. No, this woman lives in secret. She has gone into hiding and no longer takes part in society. This would also go with the dark blue soul. Something must have happened."

"Amazing. How could you see that?"

"It is hard to explain. After England, the pattern could not decide on any country, touching on one only before immediately changing again. It showed that this woman moves on before people remember her and connect with her."

Mayla nodded thoughtfully. "Exciting. Where did you gain the knowledge for this spell?"

Anna shrugged. "Let's say I once helped someone and in return was granted access to an extraordinary library. That's where I came across the spell and noted the various possible interpretations. The more you use it, the more practice you get and interpretation becomes easier. But enough about magic. Now we finally have some information about the unknown woman. Late fifties and from England. Interesting. I wonder if Tom knows her."

A memory that Mayla hadn't shared with Anna yet flashed through her mind. "He knows her. I've seen the two of them together."

Anna immediately furrowed her fine eyebrows. "What? You didn't tell me that! Where did you observe her?"

Mayla ignored the accusation. "In our house on the Rhine. After the hunters' attack, I went back there with Tom and Georg to search for clues. Tom was upstairs and as I headed up, I heard him talking in our bedroom to the woman. They didn't see me." Mayla put a hand on Anna's forearm. "You're going to keep this to yourself, aren't you? I don't want to create any more trouble for Tom."

Anna laughed. "Don't worry, he is doing that all by himself." She stared off into the distance. "He knows her, I knew it. What did they talk about?"

Mayla focused intently until she remembered. "The woman asked if anyone suspected anything and he replied that they trusted him. He probably meant us. Then they said goodbye and she jumped away."

"So, she knows more and might be able to tell us what Tom is up to. I'm just afraid she's as good at covering her tracks as he is, so it'll be next to impossible to find her if she doesn't want to be found. But maybe we haven't tried everything yet."

"Do you have an idea?"

Anna pursed her lips, put her hands in her pockets, and looked out. "Perhaps. I would like to check something. Come on." She held out her hand.

Mayla paused, skeptical. "Where do you want to go?"

"Donnersberg Castle. Angelika's library is extensive."

Mayla hesitated. "No, I'm not going there. Last time, they let me go, this time they might stop me. I don't want to risk defending myself against them — and I don't want to give Andrew or John a chance to follow me."

Anna frowned suspiciously until she gave in. "I'm afraid you're right. The two of them are angry and are claiming that you and Tom planned to steal the stones from the beginning. But they don't know I'm on your side."

Mayla was about to get upset about John and Andrew's accusations when she thought of something. Heike had given her another idea. "Do you think you could try bringing back the locket we found in the Mont Saint Michel cemetery? The necklace with the image of Charlotte de Bourgogne?"

Anna put her hands on her hips. It was amazing how quickly the mistrust returned to her eyes. "What do you need it for?"

Mayla shrugged and looked her straight in the eyes. She didn't want the Earth Witch to think she was being devious. "I don't know if I need it, but Marianna was looking for it. I prefer to have it so I can use it as leverage — or use it ourselves. After all, it's me who found it, not Angelika or John. Don't you think it might be useful?"

Anna nodded. "I'll see if it's possible to get it without appearing suspicious. Where will we meet when I'm done? Here?"

Mayla laughed. She would never wait in a forest, twiddling her thumbs. No, that was out of the question. "Send me a Nuntia spell as soon as you're ready. We will meet in the room on the von Eisenfels property. I'll try to find out something too."

"Okay. Good luck." Anna grabbed the amulet key and disappeared without another word. Mayla stayed behind in the silence and looked around the forest, perplexed. What could she do in the meantime?

8

Mayla pointed to a broken branch lying among the leaves on the forest floor. "Converte!" It turned into a comfortable wicker chair, and she immediately sank into it. She grabbed the chocolates and leaned back, staring off into the forest. Yet she saw neither the trees nor the midday light that filtered through the treetops and bathed the surroundings in a warm glow.

The stranger came from England and was fifty-nine years old. Therefore, she and Tom could not have played together as children. It was more likely that Tom had only met her recently.

He could hide things from Mayla, no question about it — but unlike him, it was possible to read her like an open book. Tom knew how to mask his emotions and thoughts, but being by his side for the past few years, she had learned to recognize subtle signals. When he didn't want to continue talking about a topic and tried to distract her, he'd ask her about something he knew was on her mind. When he claimed he had plans to do something so he wouldn't have to accompany her, he would scratch his chin for a second, and when he had plans to do something he didn't want her to know about, he would avoid eye contact. They were tiny things, but they were signs he wasn't being completely honest with her.

As they had watched the duel between the strange woman and the hunter, she hadn't noticed any of those tiny gestures. Even afterward, when they had talked about the stranger, he hadn't avoided the topic. So, he did not know the woman at the time of the duel. Had they met in their bedroom? Goodness, how that sounded. Tired, Mayla grinned and placed a truffle on her tongue. The tart taste of the dark chocolate coated her taste buds. She closed her eyes and relaxed.

Had Tom caught the woman by surprise in their bedroom, and then they'd started talking? Or had they met prior to that? No, Tom had been with her the entire time from when the duel had taken place and the conversation she'd overheard. First in her house on the Rhine and then at Donnersberg Castle. So... had the nameless one been waiting for Tom?

He'd gone straight up while Mayla and Georg had searched the garden and the ground floor. Was it purely coincidence, or had they arranged to meet? Perhaps the stranger had sent him a Nuntia charm to introduce herself and tell him the meeting place. Why had she only approached him, excluding Mayla? If the woman knew Tom or had been watching him, she had to know that Mayla was loyal to Tom.

Something was wrong. She had missed something. But what?

She reached for another chocolate and held it under her nose. She deeply breathed in the soothing scent of vanilla and closed her eyes in bliss.

Tom, what are you hiding from me? What have I missed?

She heard a meow and as she opened her eyes, Karl landed on her lap. Smiling, she stroked his little black head.

"Hello, little one. How are you? Do you have a message for me from Anna?"

He meowed and nuzzled her knuckles. Then he began to purr, kneaded her lap, and curled up.

Mayla laughed. "You want to keep me company. That's kind of you, darling." She gratefully buried her fingers in his soft fur. His presence was comforting. She turned her gaze back to the forest. Now she was waiting in the forest after all, twiddling her thumbs while Anna was out and about. However, jumping to random spots wouldn't do much good either. She resigned herself to her ruminations again. Perhaps Karl's constant purring would help her organize her thoughts.

She glanced at the had she was stroking Karl's head with and her eyes fell on the ring Tom had given her as an engagement gift. The blue-black stone shimmered. She turned it back and forth. Did it have any meaning for Tom?

"You're still wearing the ring," a female voice said.

Startled, Mayla's heart almost stopped.

The strange woman stood in front of her.

She was tall and the wide cloak didn't reveal anything else except for her feminine silhouette and the long black hair that fell to her chest. The hood cast shadows across her face, so Mayla couldn't make out any facial features even though the two of them were less than a meter apart. She had her hands hidden in her cloak and it didn't appear as if she wanted to attack Mayla.

Mayla jumped to her feet, causing Karl to hop off her lap. "Who are you?"

"That does not matter. We need you."

Ready to attack, Mayla watched her, uncertain of what to make of the stranger's arrival. "I'm sorry, what? What do you mean by we? Is Tom with you?"

"The others will explain that to you. Come on." Before Mayla could object, let alone make her own decision, the woman grabbed her arm, causing the forest and her comfortable wicker chair to spin in a circle. Mayla lost her footing and abruptly landed on stone. She glanced up. They had landed in a sacred complex. Large stone pillars rose to form the frames of individual temples, some of which were large, others small, and reminiscent of ancient ruins — except these temples were completely preserved. In the middle stood a tiny stone house that was closed off by a heavy lattice door that had wreaths of flowers and lavender bouquets in front of it.

"Where are we? Why did you bring me here?"

"Come."

She was as taciturn as Tom. The strange woman was already heading toward one of the temples in long strides. Mayla quickly decided to follow. Considering Tom had talked to her and allied with her, she probably wasn't an enemy. If necessary, Mayla could grab her amulet key and jump within milliseconds.

As she hurried after the stranger, she looked around. The sun was warm, but no hotter than in Germany. That meant they were probably not on any ancient temple grounds in the south. The buildings were mighty and impressive, but the area still seemed deserted — as if the site had once been important but had lost its purpose over the years. Only the flowers placed in front of the tiny temple house showed that someone remembered the site and its significance.

A feeling of ancient power surrounded the complex. It was magic, no question about it, but in a form Mayla had never encountered anywhere else.

Her mind was teeming with thousands of questions, but she held back, suspecting that the strange woman would not answer her. Where was she taking her? Who were the others she had spoken of, these individuals who were supposed to explain everything to Mayla? Tom was one of them, Mayla assumed. Why else would the stranger have come for her?

"When will I see Tom?" she inquired, unable to help herself.

The woman didn't reply, but instead pointed to a round temple hidden behind one of the larger religious buildings. It was a simple construction consisting of columns arranged in a circle that supported a stone roof. This building also reminded Mayla of the round temples of the ancient Greeks and Romans.

In the shadow of the small temple were four people in dark cloaks and hoods just like the stranger. She allowed Mayla to go first, and as she hurried toward the cloaked figures, she realized Tom was not among them.

She glanced uncomfortably from the strange woman to the others. She didn't feel threatened or in danger, but she did get an odd feeling knowing the stranger was behind her. Now what? She had expected to be taken to Tom. She needed answers. She had to help him and thus her daughter, but perhaps these people in cloaks would support her.

Her fingers gripped her purse straps as she approached the round temple. The clicking of her heels echoed through the facility like drums announcing something important. She used the time to examine the people in the shadows of the temple as much as possible. Female silhouettes could be discerned under their cloaks. Apparently they were women, five total, along with the one who had brought Mayla there.

One stepped toward her and pulled the hood off. Surprised, Mayla slowed her pace. She hadn't expected the others to be more open than the stranger behind her. But this was probably their workplace, so they felt safe despite Mayla's presence.

When the woman had pulled the hood off her head and Mayla could see her face, she stopped abruptly. She knew this woman. She had met her yesterday. And she had broken into her house in Paris that very morning.

It was Julie Martin.

Her snow-white hair was pinned up, though her glasses weren't resting on top. But Mayla recognized the round face with the wide nose and blue-green eyes immediately.

"Julie?"

Smiling, she clasped her hands together in front of her body. "That's not my real name, but more on that later. Welcome, Mayla von Flammenstein . I'm glad you found us." She took Mayla's hands and smiled warmly at her.

"What are you doing here? Who are you?"

Julie smiled and pointed to the veiled women. "These are Ignatia, Agatha, and Aura. Madeleine brought you to us and my name is Teresa. We are the last descendants of the high priestesses. We brought you here because you have to help us unite the magic stones."

Mayla looked from one to the next in awe, but apart from Julie — rather, Teresa — no one had removed their hoods. She turned to the side to check out the strange woman who had brought her there, although she too hadn't removed her hood. Madeleine. She was also a descendant of the high priestesses? Mayla had never expected this. And Tom worked with them. If he trusted them, she could too, right?

"You are descendants of the women who protected the magic stone when it was whole?"

"I see you've done a little research on us." Teresa smiled, her face widening . She seemed so friendly that Mayla wanted to trust her even though she'd initially introduced herself with a false name. If Teresa was a descendant of the high priestesses, she probably had to exercise caution and conceal her true identity, just like the other women.

Curious, Mayla glanced from one to the next. "That's right, I did some research, but I didn't find much. I didn't even know the high priestesses still existed."

The women let out a discontented murmur that died away when Teresa gave them a warning look. What was going on here?

"Why should I help you? I lost the stone and do not possess the ancient magic to piece together the fragments even if you have them." Were they hoping for Emma? To be on the safe side, Mayla wouldn't mention her daughter. Perhaps they hadn't yet learned that Emma was born with the old magic, although it suddenly seemed unlikely to her.

"We work with Tom. He wanted to help us collect the fragments. Originally, we possessed three except for the Earth Circle one that the hunters stole, and the one from the Metal Circle. Vincent or Bertha hid it well. They didn't even tell Tom where it was hidden when he was younger. But it won't work without him."

"So... did the hunters steal the first stone?"

Teresa nodded. "We had to make sure the others didn't fall into their hands, which is why we asked Tom to get them for us."

"I see. Where is Tom?" Mayla's eyes immediately scanned the area. She didn't see him anywhere, or anyone else for that matter. Behind the temples there stretched an unknown and mountainous landscape. Was he hiding in those woods? It wouldn't be the first time he'd lived in a secluded hut on a mountain...

Teresa shook her head. "He's not here. We only allow women to enter this world fold and the grounds, and usually only those descended from the first high priestesses. However, the situation is serious, which is why we are making an exception for you."

Mayla looked around hesitantly. "Do you know where he is?"

Teresa peered at her earnestly. The dimples in her cheeks disappeared. "He's with the hunters."

"Certainly not voluntarily! I'm sure he's not one of them. Tom would never..."

"We know that," Teresa interjected. "He went to them to find out if they knew where the Metal Circle Stone was. They also have the Earth Circle Stone, which we also need."

Marianna Lauber and her people had stolen

the first stone and had thus started this mess. "So, where are the other fragments now?"

"We kept the other three safe in our facility, but now they're gone. Tom had to take them with him to prove to the hunters that he wanted to reunite the magical stone with them. He offered to perform the spell."

"What? Why would he do that?"

Teresa clasped her hands in front of her stomach. "He needed to gain their trust so they would tell him the location of the Metal Circle Stone. He also wanted to return the Earth Circle Stone to us."

"And that's why he..." She looked questioningly from Teresa to Madeleine, who was standing at a safe distance from the other high priestesses. Why did she remain in the background?

Teresa nodded. "Yes, that's why he knocked you and Georg out. He had no choice. He is under their control. As long as he stays with them and agrees to cast the spell, they will leave Emma in peace."

Mayla's heart sank deeper. So, they knew about Emma and her abilities. Her mouth went dry as she looked at each of the high priestesses. "Emma is much too small. She's useless to you and to... "

Teresa put a hand on her arm. "Emma is neither small nor useless. She is a powerful witch and there is so much more to her that you cannot even begin to imagine. But at the moment, that's not the point. We have seen that you stuck by Tom even though he did everything he could to keep you away. That's why we decided to trust you even though you come from one of the founding families."

Even though she came from one of the founding families? She looked from Madeleine to Teresa in disbelief. "People usually trust me because of my heritage. What do you have against my family?"

Once again, a murmur went through the women in the background. This time, Teresa didn't shoot them a warning look to try to quiet them down, but instead peered at Mayla, the expression in her eyes not as friendly as before. "I don't know what you know about the time when the ancient magic was divided, but the founding families and the high priestesses were not on the same side. It is your family and those of the other circles that are to blame for the fact that we cannot fulfill our important task and that the power of magic has diminished. But that was a long time ago and in times of need, we should forget old grievances and instead, move forward together."

She paused as if to give Mayla a moment to digest what she was saying before continuing. "We all agree that the hunters should not be allowed to reunite the magical stone — and certainly should not control this powerful object. That's why we are hoping for your help. However, I would like to make it clear that our goal is to unite the fragments. We want to take up our task again and protect the stone and with it the world of the witches. So, we won't return the Fire Stone to you. Will you help us anyway?"

Mayla had a sinking feeling in her stomach.

She didn't understand enough about the situation. How important were the stones to the circles? But in the past few days she'd been able to see that the members didn't lose their powers when the head of the circle didn't have it in their possession. Still, she hesitated. Mayla would have preferred for her grandma to make such an important decision. But perhaps the high priestesses had chosen her precisely because she was more impartial than others who had been told the tale from the perspective of the founding families over and over again during their school years and beyond.

She looked from Teresa to Madeleine, then to Agatha, Aura, and Ignatia. Would these women bring the needed balance to the world of witches? Would the reunification of the stone possibly bring peace? Would she be involved in the collaboration? How would her grandma react? And what about Phylis, Gabrielle, and Andrew? Tom, at least, had apparently decided to support the high priestesses in their cause. If Mayla trusted anyone, it was Tom, even though it would have been helpful if he had shared his reasons with her.

"I am ready to work with you. If Tom was on your side, I want to trust you — especially since I can understand your motives. You have been robbed of your task. But what happens to the world of witches when the stone is reunited? What effect does it have on the magic of those who belong to one of the covens? Will the circles be eliminated?"

Teresa clasped her hands in front of her body again. The friendly dimples had returned to her cheeks. "Everyone retains the magic they were born with and the covens will persist if the head witches want them to continue. We don't know how it will affect the hunters and Tom. However, there is a possibility they will be able to cast the old magic without powerful spells being fatal to them."

Alarmed, Mayla listened intently. "Isn't that dangerous? Wouldn't that make the hunters overly powerful?"

Teresa shrugged. "That remains to be seen, but we must take the risk. You should especially think about your daughter. As soon as word gets out about her abilities, people will ostracize her. However, if others in our world possess the ancient magic, perhaps even people your daughter can protect others from, then she will be accepted. In the eyes of the witches she will be a gift, not a threat."

Mayla's mouth dropped open. "Emma should fight the hunters? Never. She's only four years old."

"She won't stay that way forever. We've been watching her. Her powers are strong and it would be wrong to teach her to suppress them."

Mayla began indignantly, "I didn't teach her to suppress them, only that she should hide them when others are present."

Teresa smiled slightly. "What's the difference?"

Mayla stared at the women, stunned. She still couldn't see anyone's face except Teresa's, which was perplexing. Why were these women watching Emma? Why did she hear concern and kindness in Teresa's voice when she spoke of Emma? Could it be that this high priestess had taken Emma into her heart? Why?

Before Mayla's thoughts began to run amok, Teresa spoke again. "Right now, this shouldn't be about Emma. So, what do you say? Will you help us get the stones back?"

Mayla hesitated and glanced over the temple grounds, then back at the women. "I will, but I want to see your faces. If you want my trust, I deserve yours too."

The women hesitated, mumbling something, when Teresa turned to them with a smile. "I understand her wish. Now it's up to you, Ignatia, Aura, Agatha, and Madeleine. Are you willing to trust a von Flammenstein descendant as you would like her to trust you?"

Mayla eagerly watched the high priestesses, who seemed unsure. They whispered amongst each other until one of them suddenly stepped forward and removed her hood. Long white hair, thin white brows, and hawk-like eyes that glowed yellow-brown emerged. She was old — older than her grandmother — and therefore definitely more than ninety, but that didn't make her cut any less powerful of a figure. "My name is Aura. I am responsible for the element of air."

For the element of air? Mayla frowned in surprise. "I thought you represented the old magic — the united magic."

A second woman stepped forward. "We would if your ancestors hadn't broken our magic by splitting the stone!" She quickly pulled back the hood and revealed fiery red curls, pale skin, dark blue eyes, and a sullen mouth. She was younger. Mayla guessed around sixty. "My name is Ignatia and thanks to your ancestors, only the magic of fire rests within me."

Only... Mayla refrained from starting an argument. She understood the women's anger even though it was unfair to blame Mayla.

"My name is Agatha and my magic is water." With these words, the third woman stepped forward and lifted her hood. She wore her white-blonde hair in a tight braid, but her facial expression didn't seem as harsh as her hairstyle. She was older than Ignatia but not as old as Aura. She eyed Mayla warily, watching her every reaction as she looked from one to the other in amazement. Four high priestesses, each responsible for a different element. She looked expectantly at Madeleine, who was standing aside as she had from the beginning. She hesitated. Why? What was wrong with her? Why did she stand apart from the others?

Teresa nodded encouragingly at her until she also pushed back her hood without moving closer to Mayla or the other high priestesses. She did this slowly. Oh so slowly, as if still resisting the request to show herself. As the light of the midday sun fell on her face, Mayla blinked in confusion, then astonishment, until she was unable to breathe or think and her eyes widened.

Mayla knew Madeleine had long black hair. No — what surprised her so much were her green eyes. She knew it as well as the prominent chin. She had seen both countless times.

"My name is Madeleine and I am assigned the element of metal."

Mayla's voice trembled. "And, you're...?"

Madeleine took a deep breath, looked down, and when she raised her eyes again, Mayla didn't need any further confirmation. It was clear.

"I'm Tom's mother."

9

A t first, silence filled Mayla's head, and then suddenly the questions started setting off, as if a bomb had exploded. Madeleine was Tom's mother? She hadn't known his mother was still alive. However, she had never asked — and Tom had never said anything about her. Mayla had assumed that the woman had disappeared from his life early on, but she had always thought she'd died, not that she was living as a hermit.

Why hadn't Tom told her that he had met his mother, that she was a high priestess, and that he was working with her? Why hadn't he even confided in her about this?

"He doesn't know."

Irritated, Mayla broke free from her whirlwind of thoughts. Without realizing it, she had been staring at Madeleine, her mouth gaping — and apparently voicing her questions out loud. Or was it so easy to just tell what she was thinking from her facial expressions?

"Tom doesn't know that...?"

Madeleine shook her head. Her face appeared haggard and unfriendly, and there was a bitter twist to her thin lips.

"But you saw each other yesterday in our bedroom. I saw you. He must have noticed the resemblance!"

Madeleine's dark eyebrows twitched for a second, and then her gaze became expressionless again. "That doesn't matter."

It didn't matter? How heartless could a mother be? Mayla put her hands on her hips. "Don't you think he has a right to know?"

"He believes I'm dead, like the rest of the world does. And that's a good thing."

Mayla opened her mouth to argue, but Teresa raised her hand in warning. "You can talk about it later. Now, we have to find Tom."

Mayla turned to her in surprise. "You don't know where he is? I thought you were working together! Does that mean he's with the hunters? With all the pieces of the magic stone?"

Teresa took her hands. "Come, let's sit down and take a few deep breaths, then we'll think about what to do."

Mayla let herself be dragged along. Teresa was right. Still, this was incredible. Through her actions, Madeleine was not only deceiving Tom about his own mother but also cheating Emma out of knowing her grandmother.

While the rush of thoughts in Mayla's mind

couldn't be stopped, Teresa led her to a sitting area in the shadow of the round temple. The others followed and headed for a round table with chairs resembling thrones grouped around it. There were only five places to sit, but this came as no surprise since no one except high priestesses were allowed on the grounds. Before Mayla could commandeer a chair for herself, Teresa raised her hand and a pebble turned into another seat.

She stared at the high priestess's hand in disbelief. "You don't need a wand to perform magic?"

Teresa shook her head. "Our magic is as powerful as that of the founding families."

"If not stronger," Ignatia added. She sat across from Mayla and watched her suspiciously, as if Mayla were planning to attack at any moment. Mayla glanced uncomfortably at the other women and ended up looking at Madeleine. Tom's mother had moved her chair so that she was once again off to the side. Or had the other high priestesses pushed their chairs away from hers? Mayla couldn't tell, but it was clear to her that something separated Madeleine from the other four women.

Blinking, she turned back to Teresa. "I didn't know that. My powers only awakened a few years ago because my grandmother had blocked them. There's a lot I don't know, so please pardon my questions. I didn't mean to be tactless." She took the chocolates out of her handbag and placed them pointedly in the middle of the table. If anything could bridge differences, it was chocolate!

Teresa smiled as she reached for a vanilla truffle. "Thank you, Mayla." She placed it on the table in front of her — Mayla had no idea how she had such self-control — and looked encouragingly at the others. Agatha and Aura also helped themselves to a chocolate, but Ignatia and Madeleine did not. Mayla deliberately ignored this and chose the rum-filled one. It was the perfect answer to all this news. The sweetness of the chocolate paired with the sweet and spicy taste of the rum washed over her frazzled nerves and gave her a moment of peace. She closed her eyes in pleasure only to open them again when she remembered where she was.

"So, you want to unite the stone and fulfill your role as guardians. I have a question about this. Since you are powerful, like the founding witches, wouldn't you become overly powerful with the stone at your side?"

A throbbing vein appeared on Ignatia's forehead and Teresa shot her a look that was impossible to misinterpret.

"Your question is entirely valid, Mayla. As is always the case when power is involved, we need trust. We never intended to bend the world to our will. Our ancestors had the important task of protecting the world of magic and we want to do the same. Once the stone is healed, the magic will flow more strongly again. We will keep it here to protect it. No one knows where this area is — we won't even tell you, and with our protection shield, no one can enter without our permission, so the source of the magic is safe."

A secret world fold. Mayla nodded thoughtfully, and then something occurred to her. "What about the fresh flowers left in front of the small temple? Are they yours?"

Teresa shook her head, a strangely melancholic expression on her round face. "The small offering house out front where the flowers are is located in the publicly accessible world fold, which includes the mountainous area around our temple complex. It is one of many offering houses that were built in various locations that are connected to us and to our important duty. To this day, there are women who remember them and place flowers in front as a sign of gratitude. Some trust that we will hold our protective hand over the world of magic as we once did, without being sure if there are still high priestesses. They have been loyal to us for centuries."

Mayla got goosebumps. She hadn't seen any of these offering houses so far, but perhaps she simply hadn't noticed them because she hadn't known such structures existed. From now on, she would keep her eyes open.

"We would be an additional power alongside the heads of the circles and want to help keep the peace, separate from the head witches. Most importantly, the balance of power will be restored."

Some hunters would be able to use their magic to its full potential, too. Mayla still had doubts. Were there any decisions that didn't involve downsides?

"Where is Tom taking the pieces?"

Teresa leaned back in her chair and folded her hands in her lap. Her skin seemed pale against the dark cloak. "Paris. There are countless public world folds. He's to meet Marianna Lauber in one of them. He took the Fire, Water, and Air stones with him, although we did not agree to place the power in his hands. But we voted and the majority decided to trust him."

All eyes darted to Madeleine, who raised her chin defiantly. "You were watching him, not me. I don't know him."

It felt like a punch to the gut. How could Madeleine be so reserved toward her son? Mayla stared at her in dismay until Madeleine's green eyes locked with hers. They were the same color as Tom's. Mayla held her gaze even though everything inside her screamed to lower her head, but she didn't. Ignatia banged her fist loudly on the table, drawing attention to herself.

"We cannot rule out the possibility that he betrayed us. He falsely gained our trust to obtain the fragments. With the hunters, he will unite the stones. All he cared about was being able to use his magic and perhaps he wanted to give the Metal Circle more power. He felt himself to be superfluous, useless; I saw it in his eyes."

"We don't know that, Ignatia." Teresa's voice remained kind and calm despite Ignatia's outburst. "He seemed extremely trustworthy to me."

Ignatia made a dismissive gesture. "Just as he pretended to work with the hunters, he may have pretended to work with us. He's a chameleon, always has been. He transforms into whoever he needs to be in order to achieve his goals. That hasn't changed. No wonder, given his broken family history..."

Mayla stared at her, stunned. How could she say such a thing about Tom? Before she could address the high priestess, Madeleine straightened up in her chair and glared at Ignatia with hatred.

"Don't you dare talk about him that way!"

Teresa raised her hands placatingly while Mayla stared at Madeleine in disbelief. Now she had defended her son. So she wasn't completely disloyal to him. Why did she behave so distantly? Why did she seem disinterested and annoyed? And why had she never contacted him in all these years? What had happened back then that would explain her actions?

"The time of accusations is behind us, sisters." Teresa raised her index finger in warning. Agatha and Aura remained silent. Did they share Ignatia's view? Who had voted for Tom and who voted against him? "We are glad you have returned to our circle, Madeleine. We can only protect the stone together, so we should find our old unity again."

Ignatia's expression was defiant, as it had been in the beginning, but she kept her biting remarks to herself. Madeleine leaned back in her chair as if none of this mattered to her while Aura and Agatha shifted uncomfortably in their seats.

Now Aura addressed Mayla. "Tell me, Mayla, what happened last night?" Her voice was light and pure. With white hair and yellow-brown eyes, she looked as if she was from another world. From a mystical-magical world — which wasn't far off the mark.

Wait, Mayla was supposed to talk about the night before? Hadn't all that been part of their plan? "You don't know? When exactly did Tom disappear?"

Aura and Teresa exchanged glances and then Aura placed her forearms on the table and leaned forward. "The last time we saw him was after you went to Chateau de Saint Bernard and found the books. Before he brought them to you, we went through them together."

"So, in the meantime, he was with you." Deep in thought, Mayla popped a second chocolate into her mouth.

Teresa shook her head. "Not only you. Before that, he was with the hunters. They demanded to see the remaining stone fragments before telling him the location of the Metal Circle Stone. After we deliberated, we gave him the stones and haven't seen him since."

Mayla raised her dark eyebrows. "He's been with the hunters that long?"

Madeleine spoke, her voice clear and hard. "When did he leave you?"

Mayla went over the past few hours in her mind. It was unbelievable that all of this had happened yesterday. Once again, events were coming to a head. "He brought us the books and then left. He promised he would return that evening and explain everything. When he didn't,

Chief Inspector Georg Stein and I jumped to the chateau. We saw someone running away and gave chase, but then we lost sight of each other just before the forest. When I found Georg again, he was lying unconscious on the ground, holding a small bag that probably contained one of the magic stones. Before I could get Georg and the stone to safety... Tom knocked me out with a stick or some other hard object."

Ignatia jumped up. "He did what?"

Mayla listened, irritated. "Wasn't that part of your plan? So the hunters would trust him and... I don't get involved?"

The high priestesses shook their heads in unison and Mayla's chest tightened.

"He knocked you out?" Teresa straightened up in her throne-like chair, alarmed.

Mayla shook her head in disbelief. "But... he's still not aligned with the hunters. He... didn't... do it on purpose. Not to hurt me. You see, he came back that night. I saw him. He came to make sure nothing had happened to me. He used a healing spell. Otherwise, I would have had to go to the hospital like Georg."

"That wasn't Tom." Madeleine straightened up, her facial features as stern as ever. "That was me."

"You?"

All eyes landed on Madeleine.

"I was searching for you when Tom didn't return to us. I was sure he would contact you."

Mayla's heart skipped a beat. It had been Madeleine? She'd healed them? Not Tom? "Why... didn't he come?" Tears threatened to well up in her eyes, but she held them back. "I thought he..."

Aura stroked her long white hair. "Do you truly think he betrayed us to get the stones?"

"No, no!" Mayla shook her head. "Tom would never work with Marianna Lauber! Never!"

A subtle smile crossed Madeleine's lips, but maybe it had just been Mayla's imagination — the bitter twist to her lips immediately returned. "You know I hardly know him. Nevertheless, I am convinced he would not work with his father's henchmen. He loathed him."

Ignatia raised a red eyebrow mockingly. "As you just admitted, you don't know him, so we cannot rule it out. He also can't use his powers, which pisses him off, as we all know. Or am I wrong about that, Mayla?"

Teresa raised her hands again. "Slow down, sisters. We should find out where Tom and the stones are before we pass judgment on him."

Mayla raised her shoulders quizzically, deliberately ignoring what Ignatia had insinuated. "How are we supposed to do that? He is undetectable. He's like a shadow. The moment you turn on the light because you think you've found him, he's already fading away. He left me a message saying he would take care of everything and I shouldn't worry. I'm sure we won't find him and I'm equally certain he would never betray me or Emma."

"I concur." Teresa gave her a reassuring wink. "Let us follow his trail and reserve judgment for when we know the facts. Remember, sisters, there is too much at stake. When we find the stones, we'll find Tom."

Ignatia crossed her arms over her chest while Agatha and Aura exchanged a glance and nodded.

Mayla peered questioningly at one high priestess after the next. "How do you plan to find the stones?"

Aura smiled pleasantly, countless wrinkles forming around her yellowish-brown eyes and joining with the other lines in her face to form a veritable halo of rays. "The stones are no longer protected by the heads of the circles, so we can find them through a spell."

"You can do that? Then why don't you use a spell like that to find the Metal Circle Stone as well?"

Teresa sighed. "Because that magical stone has not yet been released from the Eisenfels family's protective spell."

"If..." Mayla looked at Madeleine uncomfortably. "If you're Tom's mother, aren't you also a von Eisenfels? Couldn't you find the stone?"

Madeleine shook her head, her lips pressed tightly together. She seemed angrier than before, but Mayla's question was justified, wasn't it? "I am neither a natural von Eisenfels nor was I present when the spell was cast. I don't know that magic, thus I cannot find the stone."

"But the remaining stones were stolen and are with the hunters, which is why you can find the fragments?"

"Right." Teresa pointed to the high priestesses. "Aura can find the Air Circle Stone, Agatha the

Water Circle Stone, and Ignatia the Fire Circle Stone. I can locate the Earth Circle Stone."

So then there was a high priestess connected to each coven's stone. "I see. So what do you need me for?"

The women lowered their heads, seemingly uncomfortable, until Teresa spoke up. "We must make certain... that nothing happens to us, do you understand?"

That was the reason? They feared for their safety, possibly their lives, and that's why they'd sent for Mayla? Stunned, she stared at Teresa, not knowing what to say in response.

"Don't take this the wrong way, we're just as concerned about your safety, it's just that our magic isn't as good for attacks. We are guardians, not fighters. Our special gift is to protect, not to harm."

Incredulous, Mayla shook her head. "How are you going to protect something if you can't defend yourself?"

"We have our spells and they are so powerful on the temple grounds that no one can break them. In other territories, however, what we accomplish with our magic is unpredictable. We may be no match for the hunters' might."

Madeleine stood up. "I'll accompany you, Mayla."

Teresa raised her hand. "No, Madeleine, you know we can't do it without you. We need you."

Madeleine peered down at Teresa with anger in her eyes. "And Emma needs Mayla. I'll accompany her."

Mayla's heart inevitably beat faster as she studied Tom's mother. Had she just heard correctly? Was there a spark of familial love in this woman, after all?

Agatha put her hands together imploringly. "Your place is here, not on the front lines. What do we do if you don't return? How are we supposed to protect the stone?"

"If I don't come back, that means we've failed and there'll be no stone for you to protect. Now, if you'll excuse me, I'll be back as soon as we are ready to leave. She rose, pulled the hood over her head, and hurried away. She ducked into the shadows of the temple so quickly she disappeared within seconds. Had she jumped?

"I don't know if that's a good idea, Teresa," Ignatia interjected, looking suspiciously in the direction Madeleine had gone.

Teresa inhaled deeply. "I don't know either, but Madeleine has a point. If one of us is suited to accompany Mayla, it is her."

10

Mayla remained in the shadow of the round temple. Teresa brought her a carafe of water with ice cubes and lemon slices, along with a glass as well as a bowl of red grapes.

"We are withdrawing to our sacred places in order to find the stones with a spell. We'll be back soon. You can look around, but you are not allowed to enter the temples. Please abide by our rules."

Mayla promised. Although she was eager to learn more about the high priestesses and their work, she would not violate their hospitality by wandering around without permission. She leaned back in the chair. With a wave of her hand, the carafe filled the glass and Mayla sipped the refreshing water. As she snacked on a few grapes, she let her mind wander.

It was unbelievable that she had met Tom's mother and would be setting off with her to find

Tom and the magic stones. Madeleine seemed full of energy and distant. What had happened back then? Had Vincent tried to kill her? Was she running from him? Had he rejected her? Why hadn't she returned to care for her son in all these years? Why did everyone believe she was dead? Why had she left Tom to fend for himself? Had she possibly wanted to protect him? He hadn't said much about the period of time after he'd run away from home. Apart from Mayla, the only woman who could possibly be considered his main contact or confidante was her grandma, Melinda. However, by the time Tom and Melinda met, he had long since reached adulthood.

Would Mayla get something out of Madeleine once they were out together? Where had she disappeared to? Why was she not part of the community of high priestesses? The others had kept their distance from her, just as she had stayed away. Something must have happened. Mayla's curiosity was definitely piqued.

Time passed and she grew more nervous. She shifted restlessly in her chair and peered toward the temples where the four high priestesses had disappeared. What was taking so long? Was the magic that complicated or were the stones not as easy to find as hoped?

When Aura returned, both the grapes and Mayla's chocolates were almost gone. "Am I the first?" The high priestess asked, glancing at the empty chairs around the table in surprise.

Mayla gestured for her to sit next to her. "You

are. Where are the others? Does the spell take that long to perform?"

Aura sat next to her. "Not really, but the hunters placed protection spells over the fragments."

Mayla sat up in her chair, attentive. "Do you think they know you're after the stones?"

The high priestess shook her head and brushed her long hair out of her face. "Nobody knows about us. We are a mystery considered as extinct. We, like united magic, belong to the past."

That sounded exciting, magical, and mystical. Maybe it wasn't such a bad thing that the others were taking longer. Perhaps Aura would answer a few questions for her. She leaned forward confidingly. "What happened when the magic was divided? From your perspective, I mean."

Aura quickly turned her face away. Her pained expression wasn't lost on Mayla. "It's a long story, and one for another day."

Since the high priestess remained silent on the subject, Mayla did not press her. There were plenty of other questions she wanted to try her luck with. "How were you chosen? And at what age?"

Aura smiled. "You are a curious one, aren't you?"

That wasn't an answer. Shoot, why didn't Mayla have detective tactics in her genes? Her manner of interrogation wouldn't be getting her very far.

"It's different for each of us. As you can see, we are different ages. The magic senses when the time has come for one of us to say goodbye and then we use a spell to find a new sister."

Interesting. Before Aura clammed back up, Mayla leaned forward a bit conspiratorially. "And if the woman doesn't want to be a high priestess?"

Aura laughed as if she had asked something extremely stupid. "It's a great honor. No one turns down the opportunity."

Fascinating. But was it true? Mayla was starting to ask the next question when she heard voices behind her. Ignatia and Agatha returned and Aura immediately pressed her lips together. Mayla probably wouldn't get any more information from her. Too bad. But another opportunity would arise.

"Did you find the Air Stone, Aura?" Ignatia asked.

"Yes, but it wasn't easy. Strangely, it is in the Citadel of Besançon, not in a world fold."

Mayla listened. In France again — and this time in the human world? She knew of the citadel, which was a structure in the human world, but had never visited it. What were the hunters planning to do?

Agatha sat next to Aura. "The Water Stone is also there."

They looked expectantly at Ignatia, who nodded in confirmation. Apparently, the three fragments were in the same place. "Now the only question is if Tom hid the stones there or if the hunters are in the citadel with the stones. I'm curious to know where the Earth Stone, the only fragment Tom didn't have in his possession, is."

Mayla grasped the heart-shaped pendant on her necklace and slid it back and forth. "Wait, did I understand correctly? The stones are not in a world fold? So how can they be protected by magic?"

"The fragments rest in a magically protected object, like a box or a chest." Aura turned one of the pebbles into a glass and poured herself a drink from the decanter. "Nevertheless, I also find it astonishing that they are in the humans' world, not ours."

Mayla slipped the pendant under her blouse. "My friends and I believe some hunters, including Marianna Lauber and her colleagues, have probably been hiding in the human world for the last few years. In a world fold, we would have found them long ago."

Ignatia lifted her chin. "I'm curious to see if Tom is with the stones."

The wildest images whirled through Mayla's mind: Tom in chains in an old dungeon, rats scurrying around him, Marianna Lauber holding him captive and torturing him so that he would tell her where they had hidden Emma. Before her fantasies could take over, Teresa returned.

"Sorry, something came up. Is your stone also in France?"

Agatha nodded. "In the Citadel of Besançon."

Ignatia slammed her fist on the table. "So, he betrayed us! I knew it. The stones are all together." Something cracked in the distance and a tree fell over. Even though the priestess had bad-mouthed

Tom, Mayla smiled. Apparently, she wasn't the only adult fire witch with a temper.

Teresa gave Ignatia a warning look before sitting next to Mayla. "We know where your journey is taking you, Mayla. Now it's time to prepare yourself."

Although Mayla was growing more excited, she made a dismissive hand gesture. "I'm pretty good at protective and offensive spells, don't worry."

Teresa shook her head in amusement. "We couldn't teach you that anyway. Our magic follows different rules."

Mayla glanced around questioningly. "What exactly should I do? Bring the stones back to you?"

Aura nodded. "That's the point. The hunters cannot possess them. Additionally, we need to make sure you know what to do in case our enemies are already trying to bring the pieces back together."

Were they too late, for heaven's sake? Mayla sat up. "Do you think they've gotten that far yet?"

Ignatia shook her head, her voice less aggressive than usual. "Not yet. We would have felt it. But since the Earth Stone is with the others, Tom must have given them our stones."

Mayla looked at them one by one, a lump of lead in her stomach. "Why do you think so badly of him?"

Teresa raised her hands soothingly. "We don't think badly of him, but we and our ancestors were often betrayed by the founding families. Several times since the division of magic in 1402, we were promised they would fight with us for the unification of the magic stone, which has not happened to this day. So, I'm sure you can understand our distrust, right?"

Mayla waved her hand. "Of course I can, but people today are not the same as before. And simply because the stones are together doesn't mean they are in the hunters' hands. Tom could have taken the Earth Stone from Marianna and her people and is searching for the Metal Stone. Perhaps he hid the stones in the citadel."

Agatha narrowed her eyes. "Then why didn't he bring the fragments back to us?"

Unfortunately, Mayla didn't know the answer — like so many other things that concerned him. Tom, the mystery. No wonder. He was descended from a high priestess, after all.

"Maybe he had to do it." She just realized that Madeleine had come to the table, her hood pulled low over her face. How long had she been back? "Maybe it was a condition in order for them to trust him. Besides, we agreed we wouldn't judge him until we knew what happened, or am I mistaken?"

An awkward silence followed, which Madeleine took advantage of to wave Mayla over with an authoritative gesture. "Come on, let's get going."

Mayla's heart skipped a beat — whether from anticipation or fear, she couldn't tell. "I thought Teresa would show me what to do if the hunters tried to unite the stones."

"I know what to do, now let's go, Mayla. We

want to get this matter over with quickly so that you don't spend more time in the line of fire that's actually reserved for my sisters." She emphasized the word sisters in a derogatory manner, whereupon the high priestesses exchanged looks that were partly embarrassed and partly outraged.

Mayla stood up. None of the women stopped her. She grabbed Madeleine's outstretched hand and before she could ask where they were going or say goodbye, she lost her footing and the temple landscape began to move. The journey with Tom's mysterious mother was about to begin.

11

Less than a minute later, Mayla and Madeleine landed in a meadow, the constant splashing of a river ringing in their ears. The smell of freshly mown grass filled Mayla's nostrils and she sneezed loudly.

"Hay fever?"

Mayla pulled a tissue out of her purse and wiped her nose. "No, just more of a big city girl."

Madeleine pointed to a hill that rose in front of them. There was a large building that looked like nothing but high walls and watchtowers. Was that the citadel?

"Are the stones up there?"

Madeleine nodded.

Sniffling, Mayla glanced upward. Shoot, another hill to climb! "Isn't there a world fold there that we can jump into?"

"There is one, but it's magically sealed."

"Magically sealed? You mean locked?"

She nodded as Mayla grew increasingly

uneasy. A magically sealed world fold — if they didn't run into any hunters there, Mayla wouldn't have any choice but to eat oatmeal or, preferably, the remaining chocolates. Her heartbeat involuntarily quickened.

Madeleine put her hands on her hips. "We should keep a low profile. Do you have anything to wear over your clothes? Otherwise, Marianna and her rats will recognize you from afar."

Mayla peered into her purse even though she knew there was nothing inside except Emma's stuffed animal, the family photo, and the alarmingly low ration of chocolates. However, she did find sunglasses, which she immediately put on.

Madeleine shook her head sullenly. "That's not enough." From the depths of her cloak, she produced another one, which she held out to Mayla. It was as dark as hers, with a wide hood.

Surprised, Mayla accepted it. Madeleine was certainly prepared. "Thanks." Phew, it was too warm for this time of the year. She could feel drops of sweat forming on her body, but at least she'd remain undetected. She threw it on and was amazed. It felt light and airy as if it held a cooling spell. Wonderful.

Without waiting for Mayla to look up again, Madeleine marched off. She headed toward a narrow trail that wound its way up the mountain through the tall grass. Mayla caught up with her. She wanted to use this opportunity to find out a few things from Tom's mother, but before she could start asking, she ran out of breath.

As expected, Madeleine remained silent. And

so they hardly exchanged a word during the climb even though Mayla had an incredible number of questions on her mind.

When they were halfway there, Mayla put her hands on her hips and panted. "Break."

Madeleine waited, never taking her eyes off the hill or the citadel. Mayla followed her gaze. No one could be seen in the distance, on the wall, or in the watchtowers.

"Keep your head down in case they're watching," Madeleine warned.

"If they're watching, it would be more sensible for us to take regular breaks and enjoy the scenery. Then maybe they'll think we're tourists despite our capes. And a picnic would also keep up appearances. Chocolate?" She held the almost empty box under the nose of her would-be mother-in-law. She didn't expect Madeleine to take one since she had refused in the complex of the high priestesses, but she wanted to be polite.

As expected, Madeleine declined but watched as Mayla selected a vanilla truffle and popped it into her mouth. "You eat chocolates often."

That sounded like a statement, not a question, so Mayla shrugged as she enjoyed the candy. Nothing else gave her so much strength and confidence. When she glanced at the citadel, she no longer felt so relaxed. The gruesome images of Tom's whereabouts and condition resurfaced. "Do you think they're holding him prisoner?"

"We're about to find out." She sounded so indifferent that Mayla could no longer restrain herself.

"Why didn't you let him know you were still alive? Why don't you want to be part of his life?"

Madeleine pressed her lips together. A hard look lingered on her face and her eyes were so deep in the shadow of the hood that the expression in them was indiscernible. "We should move on. Let's go." Without waiting for Mayla to agree, she marched off.

With a sigh, Mayla trudged after her. She wasn't particularly talkative, but to be honest, Mayla hadn't expected anything else. No, that wasn't true. When Madeleine had defended Tom and agreed to accompany her because Emma needed her mother, she believed she might be able to make some kind of breakthrough. Madeleine, though, didn't seem to share her opinion. She hurried up the hill with such determination that Mayla didn't dare ask for another break. But she wanted to believe in the good in her since Madeleine had left to protect Tom. She couldn't imagine anything else.

When they reached the high wall of the citadel, Mayla's heart was racing. No surprise there. She huffed and puffed as softly as possible so as not to draw the hunters' attention or display her poor physical condition in front of Madeleine. At least Mayla quickly recovered in the shadows of the high walls. As soon as she caught her breath, she put her hands on her hips. Thankfully, this time, she didn't have a stitch in her side. Was her body capable of adapting to physical activity after all?

"As far as I know, there is an official entrance." Mayla peered to the sides and pointed down the hill. "There is Besançon, so the main entrance should be in this direction."

Madeleine pointed in the opposite direction, down a narrow path running along the wall. "We'll take the concealed path. Come."

Tom had clearly inherited this command, "Come," from her. Mayla couldn't help but smile. Both were taciturn and the color of their eyes was identical. She wondered what other similarities she would discover. She'd actually hoped spending time with Madeleine would result in interesting conversations and some personal insights. Apparently this was not to be. At least the observations she made were a welcome distraction from her constant worrying about Tom and Emma.

They hurried along the path hugging the wall. It was a narrow, shady path where Mayla constantly felt the need to hold herself at an angle so that her shoulder didn't hit the stone wall while simultaneously making sure not to lose her footing. She kept her eyes cast down so that a careless step wouldn't send her tumbling down the slope and into the bushes.

When Madeleine abruptly stopped, Mayla almost ran into her. The wall hadn't changed, and neither had the steep slope. There wasn't a tree they could climb to gain entry, either. So, why had Tom's mother chosen this spot? "What are you going to do?"

"We're going to fly."

Confused, Mayla stared at her. Fly? "On a broomstick? Won't people see us?"

Madeleine waved her off as she began to rummage through a bag hidden under her cloak. "If they see us at all, they'll blink, rub their eyes, and by then, we'll already be long gone."

"But the hunters won't blink and rub their eyes."

"They won't expect us to come over the wall. We have no other choice. They will certainly be guarding the tourist entrance and they will undoubtedly notice us when we stray off the beaten track. No, it's better if they don't see us in the first place." She pulled a tiny broom out of the bag.

Mayla laughed. How were they both supposed to fit on that tiny thing? Before she could ask, Madeleine put her hand on it and whispered, "Cresce!" In a few seconds, the broom grew until it was the same size as any other flying broom. Amazing. How practical. She would have to remember the trick — why hadn't anyone told her about it? Just think how many boxes of chocolates could be transported in her handbag that way!

"Get on."

Mayla had practiced flying. She had done it often enough with Emma while living on Lesbos. Even if she wasn't completely convinced, she decided to trust Madeleine — after all, the woman had spent years, if not decades, practicing how to hide and not attract attention.

She got on the back confidently and held on to the handle. As Madeleine raised the broom, she felt a sense of happiness that she would have liked to hold onto for a few minutes longer. She enjoyed flying and wished she could do it more often. Before she could fully enjoy it, they landed inside the citadel and back in reality.

The question of why they hadn't flown over the wall with the broom sooner disappeared on her lips. They had landed in the middle of old, tall trees that shielded them from the hunters' eyes.

"Contrahe!" Madeleine whispered, causing the broom to shrink. As she stuffed it in her bag, Mayla studied the buildings on the opposite plateau. In the center was a long main building with smaller outbuildings grouped around it, all made of light-colored stone with red roofs. Countless gray walls stretched across the expanse. What awaited her in this place? Tom? Was he okay? Would they stop Marianna and her people and take the magic stones from them?

"Keep the hood on your head and your eyes down. We want it to take as long as possible for the hunters to discover our presence."

They crept to the tree line and peered into a spacious square where numerous tourists were milling about and wandering in various directions. Mayla watched the crowd, searching for familiar faces, especially a tall man with dark hair. But no one in the crowd was doing anything unusual. "Should we mingle with the tourists first?"

The full expanse of the main building

stretched out before them, and Madeleine pointed to a side entrance. "We'll try that door."

Mayla's gaze wandered over the buildings. Numerous day visitors were streaming inside. Where was the sealed world fold located? Were the hunters truly hiding here, as well as Tom? Her pulse quickened again.

"Are you sure Tom is in the building?"

Madeleine was also observing the citadel visitors. "I don't know where Tom is, but the others detected the stones here. Remember to stay in the shadows and only speak when necessary."

In single file, they crept under the trees and hid in the shadow of the wall as they headed for a small hidden door. It was open — Mayla didn't know if this was because Madeleine had cast a spell or not — and the two were able to slip inside unnoticed.

Mayla coughed. It was dusty and the air was dry. Little light seeped through the windows into the small room where the caretaker's buckets, brooms, ladders, and other tools were stored. The magic stones certainly wouldn't be here... but then again, it was definitely an inconspicuous hiding place.

Instead of searching the room, Madeleine hurried through a narrow door that led to the basement. She stopped briefly, raised her hands, and concentrated. Mayla felt energy moving, magic pulsating. Was this the hidden world fold? Madeleine lowered her hands and beckoned Mayla to follow her through the door, putting her finger to her lips. Mayla nodded and something sparked in her as she crossed the threshold. Power. She stopped in surprise. Entering a world fold had never felt this intense. As she considered this, Madeleine impatiently waved her on.

Mayla crept behind her down the seemingly endless staircase. It grew progressively darker until they could no longer see the steps or anything else. Mayla blew a small flame onto her fingertip so she and Madeleine wouldn't stumble but kept the light dim so it wouldn't reach too far and betray their presence.

They approached a cellar that led into a long hallway. As they entered, Mayla was only just able to stifle a scream. There were barred cells along the sides with unconscious people inside. Many appeared lifeless or on the verge of death.

Mayla rushed to the first cell and tried to open it, but it was locked. The emaciated man lying on the bare stone floor inside did not react as she rattled the bars. His hands and lips were bleeding.

Madeleine stood next to her and leaned forward, her voice barely a whisper. "Come on, we don't have time."

Mayla refused to let go of the bars. Her heart was pounding in her chest. Who were these people in the cells? Marianna Lauber's prisoners? "We have to free these people."

"We don't have the time for that. You know why we're here."

"We can't just leave these prisoners to their fate! A few could already be dead. Look at the woman up front, lying so stiff with her hands stretched out in front of her."

Madeleine took her by the shoulders and turned her toward her. "We'll come back, but we have to find the stones first."

Uncertainly, Mayla allowed Madeleine to pry her remaining fingers from the bars and pull her along. As they hurried down the hallway, Mayla couldn't take her eyes off the prisoners. There were young and old people — luckily no children, but she spotted both men and women. There seemed to be no discernible pattern; rather, it seemed like they'd been thrown together haphazardly. Had they been randomly captured? What were the hunters' plans for them?

"If you can hear me, we will help you. Hang in there!"

No one answered, but perhaps Mayla had spoken too softly. At least, that's what she told herself. She was conflicted as she hurried along next to Madeleine. Tom's mother was right, the stones were important. But so were these people. She vowed to do everything within her power to free the prisoners.

A door appeared at the end of the corridor. Mayla's heart was pounding so hard in the presence of so many victims that she could hardly stand it any longer. It took great strength to look away and focus on the door Madeleine was trying to pull her through. Out of the corner of her eye, she caught sight of the last cell and the man leaning against the bare wall inside. He was sitting hunched over, his head with almost black hair resting on his chest, his arms hanging limply at his sides.

Mayla stopped abruptly, causing Madeleine to also come to a halt. She was about to snap at Mayla when she noticed the man. She stood frozen in front of the cell.

It was Tom.

12

Mayla rushed to the barred door and shook it. "Tom! Tom!"

He didn't react.

She raised her hands to hurl a curse at the locked door, but Madeleine pushed her aside forcefully, placed her hands on the lock, and mumbled something. It clicked and the door swung open. Mayla rushed past her, crouched in front of Tom, and placed her hands on his head. His face looked terrible with bruises lining his jaw, his lip split, and a gash on his forehead.

"Tom, Tom!"

His eyebrows twitched as if he was trying to open his eyes but couldn't. Mayla slapped his cheek, causing his head to flop to the side. For heaven's sake, what had happened to him? She put her hand on his chest. "Sana!" His eyes opened slowly as the yellowish light radiated from her palm and enveloped him. When he recognized her, he was frightened.

"Mayla, what are you doing here? You should..." His eyes closed. As if in slow motion, he touched his forehead. He was overcome with dizziness and his head rocked back and forth.

Mayla peered resolutely at Madeleine. "We have to get him away from here!"

The high priestess was torn. "But the stones..."

Tom gasped. "The hunters. Have. Four... The last one. Missing. Still."

Madeleine stared down at him. Nothing in her bearing indicated that she was looking at her half-dead son. "How do you know they haven't found the last one yet?"

"They would have. Called me. I'm supposed to cast the... spell." He grimaced in pain, but no groan escaped his lips. Why didn't he try to rise and escape? Did he lack the strength? The will?

Mayla tried to pull him up, but she couldn't. He was too heavy. "The stones are important, but Tom is more important. I'll get him out of this hole. As soon as he's safe, I'll come back and help you find the stones." If she couldn't carry him out, she'd have to try to jump from here. She quickly clutched her amulet key as Tom gasped again.

"We can't... jump. Magical. Protected."

"Shoot. Then I'll give you a piggyback ride out of here!"

Madeleine pursed her lips, which deepened the bitter line around her mouth. Then her shoulders sagged slightly and she moved to the other side of Tom. "I'll help you."

Mayla glanced up, both surprised and infinitely grateful. It would definitely have been more challenging to carry Tom on her back through a world fold to the foot of a hill without magic to help her.

Tom gasped for breath. "They will see us..."

Madeleine nodded. "We have to assume that. We will find the stones later."

Relieved, Mayla smiled at her. She was finally allowing her feelings to influence her.

"No, I'm not permitted to..." Tom leaned on his arms, seeming to regain some of his strength. "If I leave, they'll go after Emma."

Mayla's heart sank into her stomach. She stared at him, pale as a sheet. "What? But they can't do that. She's safe with Grandma!"

Tom shook his head. He slowly raised his eyes; there was desperation in them that made Mayla's chest tighten. "They'll find her. Emma is only safe as long as the hunters think I'll perform the spell for them."

Mayla peered angrily at Madeleine, who was hiding her face in the shadow of her hood so that Tom couldn't see her features, before looking back at him. "Maybe they lied to you to blackmail you."

He shook his head. "I know. I saw it. They have ancient magical... spells." He looked Mayla intently in the eyes. "Emma is not safe."

Was that the reason for his behavior? The explanation for why he had knocked her and Georg unconscious? Emma was in great danger? Mayla felt her knees buckling. Madeleine held her tightly so that she didn't collapse on the bare stone floor. She pulled her by her arm to her feet and leaned forward. "If he's right, we have to get Emma to safety first."

Mayla's pulse raced. "But there is no safe place for her."

"Yes, there is. Do you trust me?"

Taking a deep breath, Mayla peered into her eyes, which were in the shadow of the hood and the same green as Tom's. Then she nodded.

"We'll take Tom to the caretaker's room. That's where you'll create a small world fold we can jump from. Can you do that?"

Mayla nodded.

"Okay, let's do it."

They stood on either side of Tom and pulled him to his feet. His knees kept giving out and under his near-dead weight, Mayla struggled to keep from tumbling to the ground with him. Luckily, he hadn't eaten much, otherwise they would never have been able to move him. They walked past the prisoners at a pace that was far too slow. No one responded to Tom's liberation. Not one person shook the bars, shouting, "Take me with you!" All were apathetic or maybe even... dead?

Mayla vowed she would come back and free them as soon as she was able.

By the time they reached the narrow stairs, her forehead was sweaty. Still, she didn't grumble and dragged Tom up the endless steps. He tried his best to lift his feet but he seemed too exhausted, as if Marianna and her people had sapped his physical strength. It took what felt like an eternity to reach the small room in the human world that was outside the hunters' protected area.

They slowly slid Tom to the ground and Mayla raised her hands. Concentrating, she imagined part of the room folding and then unfolding again and thought, *Contrahe mundi!*

A sparkle appeared to shrink the room, which soon expanded back to its full size that only witches could perceive. Would the caretaker notice the room had shrunk?

Madeleine raised her hands and glitter appeared around the new world fold. "I sealed it so only we know of its existence. A little back door into the lion's den. Now come on!"

Mayla pulled Tom back to his feet while Madeleine supported him on the other side. As they entered the tiny world fold, Mayla clutched the amulet key and instinctively chose a place where she and Tom had always felt safe — even with Madeleine at her side, hoping he wouldn't be offended when he found out she had revealed the location.

In her mind, she pictured the abandoned hut and thought, *Perduce nos ad Pyrenaeum desertum!* The ladders, buckets, and dustpans blurred, giving way to a bright summer sky. They landed in the middle of the meadow before the cabin where Tom spent many years of his life and where Mayla had once saved his life — surely that was a good omen!

Mayla raised her hand. With the use of the Vola spell, the door opened and Tom flew inside. He landed on his bed and groaned. Worried, Mayla looked at him until Madeleine clasped her hands. "I'll take care of him. You have to bring

Emma here. Fast."

For a tiny millisecond, Mayla considered if she should trust Madeleine, but then she rushed into the shadow of the hut where the pile of wood was. She mentally summoned Karl, grabbed a log, and turned it into a small doll that looked similar to Emma's. With practiced fingers, she cast a Nuntia spell and told her grandma that Emma should jump here. Melinda had never been there before, but Emma had ben there the previous year with Tom, so she could imagine the place. Luckily, the little one was already able to cast the Perduce spell.

Shortly after she finished, the tip of Karl's tail appeared between the blades of grass and he jumped toward her, meowing.

"Hello, darling, how are you? Did you miss me?" She snuggled with him and then held the doll out to him. "Take this to Emma."

He meowed and looked at her questioningly.

"I know someone might find out, but it's important. Emma has to come here immediately. Every second counts!"

He meowed, licked her finger, and carefully took the doll in his mouth. What appeared in her mind was an image of him handing the doll over to Karamella, since he couldn't find Emma. Mayla nodded.

"That's okay, my darling. Karamella can take it to Emma. But hurry."

With a leap, he landed in the grass and disappeared. Instead of immediately returning to Tom and Madeleine, Mayla remained in the shadow of the cabin for a moment. She gathered her thoughts, mentally prepared herself for what was to come, and took a deep breath. Quickly, one more chocolate — darn it. It was the last one. Hopefully, that wasn't a bad omen. Mayla put it back. She would save it for later. Only heaven knew when she would get a new box, so she should save this last treat... until everything was good again?

Her heart pounded uneasily as she hurried back to the hut. Madeleine was inside and when Mayla entered, she saw the high priestess standing by the bed, leaning over Tom. She had a hand on her chest and the hood had slipped off her head. Her facial expression was so stricken that Mayla got goosebumps. What had happened to this woman that had made her refuse to be with her son even though — Mayla didn't doubt it for a second — she wanted to?

Madeleine jumped when she spotted Mayla. She cleared her throat. Her expression immediately hardened and she looked at Mayla with control, as if she was waiting for Mayla to question her relationship with Tom. Mayla, however, didn't want to pressure her. Madeleine should be willing — but that didn't mean Mayla wouldn't do everything she could to convince this woman to become part of her family.

Mayla pointed questioningly at Tom. "Is he asleep?"

Madeleine nodded. "I also cast a Sana spell on him. Along with yours, it'll be enough. He needs a little rest and then he'll be his old self again."

"That's good."

"Did you send the Nuntia charm?"

Mayla nodded. "Karl is taking it to Emma's spirit animal. I don't know when they'll be here, but I left word that it was urgent."

Madeleine narrowed her eyes. They didn't look hostile or suspicious, more... compassionate? Only then did Mayla notice that she hadn't pulled the hood back over her head. "Are you looking forward to seeing Emma?"

A smile immediately appeared on Mayla's face. "Very much so... I miss her so much. However, I seriously wonder how we can protect her. If Tom believes the hunters are a major threat to Emma, there is a reason. Where are you going to hide her?"

Madeleine lowered her voice. "With the high priestesses."

Mayla glanced up in surprise. "They're on hallowed ground and only a descendant of the high priestesses can enter. Don't you think the others will be angry if you bring a child?"

Madeleine's voice became softer than Mayla had ever heard it before. "Don't you see? Emma is a descendant of the high priestesses."

Emma... Madeleine was right. Her daughter was a descendant of these venerable guardians. She looked up doubtfully. "Do you truly believe she'll be safe there? From the hunters? Given Tom is so scared for her, perhaps... who knows what they're capable of now."

Madeleine peered thoughtfully at Tom. "If he had told us what Marianna was threatening him with, we would have suggested it to him long ago. My sisters know about our relationship and therefore also about Emma."

Had this always been an option? "Why didn't you suggest this to him when you first met? You knew Emma was in danger."

"We didn't know how great of a threat the hunters were, not to mention..." She shrugged awkwardly. "...in order for him to understand why that was possible, I would have had to tell him who... I am." The green of her eyes shimmered. Was she crying? Before Mayla could take a closer look, the telltale shine disappeared, giving way to Madeleine's usual steely gaze — which no longer seemed as indestructible as it had during the hours before.

13

They paced the small hut restlessly. Madeleine hadn't spoken another word and Mayla hadn't gotten any closer to her. It was clear Madeleine needed time. But she wondered what she should do when Tom woke up and Madeleine still kept her lips sealed. Then again, she could worry about that when the time came.

She stepped out into the sun. An eagle circled high in the sky. It was the only tiny shadow moving in the meadow. It was hot — darned hot — so she turned a log into an awning and two others into lounge chairs. As she sat down on one, she felt her tension rising. Where her grandma and Emma? Mayla had noticed several times that Melinda could gather up all her belongings just by pointing her finger. Even if they were doing something exciting, Mayla's message had made the urgency of the situation perfectly clear.

She sat up in the chair, gripped the edge of the

seat, and crossed one leg over the other, bobbing the toe of her sandal up and down restlessly. Had something happened to them? She called out to Karl. Had he given the message to Karamella? Instead of her faithful feline, another black cat appeared and immediately jumped onto Mayla's lap.

Mayla's heartbeat calmed down a little. "Kitty! It's good to see you. Are you here to check on Tom?"

The cat raised her head and meowed, and Mayla placed her forehead against the cat's.

"It's a shame we can't communicate with each other using our minds, but I understand you came to be here for us. Karl will be back soon. It would be helpful if you snuggled with Tom."

Kitty meowed again, jumped off Mayla's lap, and padded into the cabin. As if she were relieving a guard by the sickbed, Madeleine then stepped through the door and held her face in the sun. As pale as she was, she, like Tom, must have spent most of her time indoors — or simply hid her face under the hood.

Madeleine came to her in the shade and sat down on the second lounge chair, but did not lean back and remained on the edge. She eyed Mayla skeptically. "Where are Melinda and Emma?"

Mayla bobbed her foot up and down incessantly. "If only I knew. I hope the hunters haven't already found them. I wish I could find them and..."

The air in front of them began to shimmer and sparkle and in the blink of an eye, Melinda and

Emma were standing before them. Mayla immediately jumped up and hugged her little daughter.

"Emma! How are you?"

"Good, Mommy. Grandma and I did such great things. We were in the forest and even spent the night there. Owls hooted at night and it wasn't just Merlin. But I wasn't afraid. Karamella was with us the entire time. And Grandma showed me new plants."

Mayla held Emma in front of her and inspected her from head to toe. The little one appeared happy, her dark eyes shining. Most importantly, she looked to be unharmed. Thank God. Overjoyed, she hugged her bundle of sunshine to her.

Melinda looked skeptically at Madeleine before turning to Mayla, her voice muffled so Emma wouldn't hear. "You didn't call for us a second too soon. The hunters — they found us. If we hadn't already been on the move..."

The unfinished sentence floated between them. Mayla's heart sank a little and she hugged Emma tightly to her while Melinda glanced around warily.

"I don't think we're safe here. They were able to find us despite my protection. I don't know how it's possible, but their powers... they seem to be figuring them out."

Vigilant, Madeleine stared out over the mountain plain. "That's consistent with what Tom told us. We can't waste any time. "I'm taking Emma to safety now."

Melinda stood protectively in front of Emma, a

deep wrinkle between her white eyebrows. "Safety? Where would that be, if not by her family's side? Who are you, anyway?"

Madeleine hesitated, but Mayla chose the truth. Otherwise, she wouldn't be able to make her grandma and especially Emma understand. She knelt in front of her daughter, took her hand, and pointed at Madeleine. "You know what, my darling? We are incredibly lucky. That woman there, do you know who she is?"

Emma tilted her head, letting her dark curls slide over her shoulders. She put a finger to her lips. "Hmm, her eyes are like Daddy's."

Smart child. Mayla smiled while Melinda stared at Madeleine in disbelief. "Exactly, she has Daddy's eyes because she's his mommy."

Emma widened her eyes and peered at Madeleine with childlike wonder. Her reaction caused a smile to appear on Madeleine's lips and a soft blush tinted her cheeks as she crouched to be at Emma's eye level.

"I am your grandma. My name is Madeleine. I'm looking forward to finally getting to know you."

Melinda shook her head in disbelief. "I thought she was dead. Do you have any proof, Mayla, that what she said is true?"

Mayla watched Madeleine and Emma eyeing each other curiously, both with shy smiles on their faces. "There is no doubt."

Tom's mother reached out to Emma. "Will you come with me, little guardian? I can also show you a few exciting tricks if you're interested."

Uncertain, Emma peered up at Mayla, who squeezed her daughter's hand reassuringly.

"It's okay, my darling. Grandma is going to take you to a magical place where you can learn a lot. She and her sisters will take good care of you."

Melinda frowned at Tom's mother. "Sisters?" But no one responded to her question.

Emma tilted her head again and hesitated, but Mayla couldn't blame her. "May Karamella come with me?"

Madeleine smiled. "Of course. Tell her to follow us. I will make it possible for her."

The little one beamed and closed her eyes. She always did this when communicating with her spirit animal. Meanwhile, Melinda stood by Emma's side, the doubt written all over her face.

"I'm coming with you! I don't want to stir up any conflict, but..."

Mayla pulled her grandma back, gently but firmly. "You can't go, Grandma, Madeleine is taking Emma to a sacred place."

Melinda glanced from her to Madeleine, confused. She didn't like being the one left in the dark. Reluctantly, she placed her hands by her sides, the usual stern crease between her eyebrows. "I don't understand, Mayla. What is going on?"

Madeleine glanced around uneasily and stood up. "They'll be here soon. I'm leaving now, Mayla. Explain to your grandmother what is necessary. You can reach us at any time through Emma's spirit animal." She smiled lovingly at Emma. Mayla would never have believed her to be so tender. At that moment, she realized that this woman would give everything for Emma. And she probably had done the same for Tom back then... "Will you give your mommy another kiss?"

Emma threw her arms around Mayla's neck and Mayla hugged her little star to her. This time it was easier to say goodbye even though she barely knew Madeleine and her sisters. She knew the high priestesses would take good care of her daughter. Emma was one of them and there was no safer place for her at this time.

With a subtle sparkle, Madeleine and Emma disappeared, hand in hand, and Mayla couldn't help but wonder if her little darling would be able to bring down the walls around this woman's heart.

But she didn't have time to think about it. Melinda gripped her shoulders forcefully. "Who was that woman, Mayla? Are you sure she's Tom's mother? And where is this sacred place she is taking Emma? Why can't I enter it?"

Mayla started to answer, but the words caught in her throat. The wind rose up and Mayla and her grandma glanced at each other in alarm. Without a word, they blew a ring of fire around the hut just in time — the next moment, there was a bang.

The hunters. They had arrived.

Marianna Lauber stood in the front, her long black hair wound into a high braid, her red-painted lips twisted into a grin. Her confidence was frightening. Four hunters, just as confident as their leader, stood alongside her. Five wands were pointed at them, causing Mayla and Melinda to move closer together.

"Someone broke our agreement." Marianna walked toward them with long, casual strides. She steadily approached the circle of flames, causing Mayla and Melinda to focus more intently on their protection.

"You won't get Tom!" Mayla shouted.

"Oh, yes, we will." Marianna nodded and the four others approached Melinda. They hurried fearlessly toward the ring of fire, as did Marianna, and crossed it as if the flames were merely an illusion. The fire faded and before Melinda and Mayla could launch an attack spell, they were lifted off their feet. Her grandma flew through the air and landed in the meadow. The four men immediately surrounded her and said some spells so that Melinda lay trembling on the ground as if she were being electrocuted.

Mayla was shocked to see her grandmother lying helpless on the grass while she hung in the air as if a giant had picked her up and was choking her. Marianna pointed her wand at her and cast a spell to cut off her breath. No matter what spell Mayla thought, it didn't work.

"What..." she wheezed, unable to say anything. Panicking, she clutched her throat. It hurt like hell.

"Tom promised he would stay with us and perform the spell so that we would leave Emma alone. And even though he promised he had taken care of you and that you wouldn't bother us anymore, here you are. Standing between Tom and me, annoying as a pesky fly! But I will remedy that. Any final words, mighty fire witch?" Her voice dripped with scorn.

The invisible grip on Mayla's neck loosened and she gasped. "You have no power over him. Emma is safe."

Marianna turned her head and concentrated. The grin on her face disappeared. She glared at Mayla. "Where did you send her?"

"Like I would tell you..."

"Tell me or I'll crush your throat!"

"Never. Do you truly believe I would betray my own child?"

"Then you have chosen your fate." The pressure around her neck increased and her lungs screamed.

Air, I need air.

She wheezed, struggled, and writhed, but she had no chance. The mist settled in her mind as the voices faded and her limbs grew limp.

A voice brought her back from the mist. It was Tom.

"Let her go!"

No. Tom. Don't. She tried to stop him, but no words escaped her throat.

Marianna eased up on the spell around Mayla's neck a little, allowing oxygen to enter her lungs, which she sucked in greedily.

Tom looked at Marianna, undaunted. With his leather jacket slung over his shoulder, he stood there looking as if he hadn't just been too weak to take a single step unaided. "Let her go and I will come with you."

Mayla hung helplessly in the air, unable to speak, so she could do nothing but listen to the conversation.

"How do I know she won't get in our way again? I think we'll do it this way. I'm teaching you a lesson here and now. Mayla will take her last breath and you'll come with us. If you disrupt my plans again, I'll take your daughter. What do you say?"

Tom froze. He didn't know who Madeleine was, what office she held, or that her daughter was truly safe. Mayla used what little air she had left and shouted, "She can't find Emma!"

Marianna snorted and tightened the spell around Mayla's neck. Tom, however, understood. He immediately regained his usual calm.

"Let her go or I won't cast the spell for you."

"I can force you! You know what will happen to you otherwise."

"If Mayla is dead, you will no longer have any power over me. Quite the opposite. If you harm her, not only will I refuse to cast the spell, I will do everything in my power to stop you, you and the entire new circle. That's a promise. Now put her down or you'll find out what I'm really made of."

Uncertainty flickered in Marianna's eyes. "You can't use your powers to attack."

Tom laughed. "I have learned enough from you. Your rats are as stupid as they come. I know how to use my powers."

Mayla glanced at him. Was that true? Could he use all of his magic? So why didn't he do something? Because he wasn't as strong as Marianna and the four hunters combined or because it wasn't true at all?

Marianna hesitated, giving him a searching look. At least, she seemed to believe him. "How do I know you won't betray me? That you'll actually cast the spell for us after I let the annoying fire witch live?"

Seemingly calm, Tom leaned against the door frame and folded his arms over his chest. His leather jacket creaked softly. "I brought you the stones. As you know, I want them to be reunited as much as you do. Only then can I use the full potential of my powers."

"But you didn't bring us the Metal Circle Stone."

"Because I don't know where it is. You, however, do. So, go get it and I will perform the spell."

Marianna looked at Mayla, who was still hanging with her toes over the meadow, her hands on her throat. She had some air, but it wasn't enough. Dizziness threatened to take hold of her, but she fought it with all her strength. She had to stay conscious.

"Come here and take the oath. Otherwise, I will kill her."

Oath? What oath? Mayla flailed her legs. Even though she didn't know what oath they were talking about, she instinctively felt it was not good. But Marianna's powers were extraordinary. She couldn't fight it. She tried to turn her head to check on her grandma, but the angle was not right and all she saw were two hunters staring at the meadow with nasty grins. Those four disgusting men had immobilized the powerful head witch Melinda von Flammenstein. What the hell had the hunters learned in the last few years?

Tom strode toward Marianna, his right hand raised. Gray smoke erupted from his palm and wrapped around his wrist. "I swear on my life not to cast any spell that harms the true members of the new circle."

"No, Tom, stop!" Mayla gasped. Marianna immediately increased the pressure around her neck.

"I want a vow on your daughter's life."

Mayla's eyes widened while Tom remained as composed as if negotiating the rules of a soccer game. He raised his head almost stoically. "Not until you let Mayla down."

Mayla landed on her feet with a thud and collapsed on the meadow, her hands still wrapped around her neck. She couldn't move, let alone use her magic. Glancing upward, she saw Marianna's wand pointed mercilessly at her as Tom amended his vow. What kind of spell was that?

"As long as you and your allies do not harm Mayla or Emma, my family, I will keep my vow. If one of you harms a hair on their heads, it will be considered a breach of contract and it will release me from my oath."

Marianna narrowed her eyes and looked at her men, who were standing over Melinda in the meadow and barely looked up. She deliberated, then flicked her wand. Metal shackles wound around Tom, binding his arms and hands together so tightly that he could no longer cast a spell. She glared condescendingly at Mayla, her voice so quiet that only the two of them could hear her words. "I will not tolerate you following us. I have ways and means to get around the oath, little fire witch, you can be certain of that." She clutched her amulet key, and although she didn't touch Tom or the hunters, they disappeared with her, leaving behind nothing but dark smoke.

14

F inally, Mayla could move again. She immediately jumped to her feet. Tom, Marianna, and the four hunters had disappeared. Only her grandmother was still lying in the meadow, unmoving. Mayla ran to her and knelt beside her. She was lying half on her stomach. Mayla turned her on her side and brushed her disheveled curls out of her face.

"Grandma... Grandma, wake up."

Melinda didn't respond. There was sweat on her face even though her body felt ice cold. What had the hunters done to her? She looked like the prisoners in the citadel. Powerless, not all there, and frighteningly lifeless. Was it the same spell?

"Grandma... Grandma..."

Melinda, however, didn't move. Mayla felt her pulse. It was weak but regular. Trembling, she raised her hands to Melinda's chest. "Sana!" Yellow light emanated from her palms and enveloped her grandma like a blanket, but even that didn't wake her. Mayla wasn't strong enough. Madeleine had also cast the Sana spell on Tom, which was probably the only reason why he'd gotten back on his feet so quickly.

Tom...

The hunters had blackmailed him with Emma. That's why he had been so distant and hadn't told her anything. Before she started worrying about him again, she focused on her grandma. "I'm taking you to a hospital. Don't worry, Grandma. Listen, I'll take care of you. Everything will be okay." She didn't know if Melinda was even aware of her in her condition, but the possibility was there. So, just in case, her grandma should know she wasn't alone and that Mayla was looking after her.

Without further ado, she grasped her amulet key and gripped Melinda's hand. "Perduce nos in valetudinarium lapidis Mariae!"

The green meadow and the bright blue sky disappeared, but the surrounding area was bathed in bright light. The first things Mayla noticed were the white walls and frantic voices. They had ended up in the middle of the emergency room. A healer immediately approached them, waved his wand, and Melinda floated onto one of the stretchers in the hallway.

"My grandma was..."

He was already turning his back on her. "Registration is over there."

"But I..."

He casually pointed to a sign on the wall that said "Registration" in thick red letters and a red arrow pointing down the hallway to the left. Before setting off, Mayla glanced back one last time at her grandmother, who was lying quietly on the gurney and didn't seem to be in danger of dying.

She reached a spacious room with far too many chairs. God, she hoped she wouldn't have to wait too long. At least most of the seats were unoccupied. She saw a few older people sitting together patting each other's hands and a mother with a child who had a bandaged arm. Since there was no one waiting in front of the registration counter, Mayla walked right up to it. Behind it was a plump woman who smiled good-naturedly and left the paperwork to the pen that leisurely filled out a few forms.

"Welcome to the Marienstein City Hospital, what can I do for you?" Her smile was genuine, which reassured Mayla, but she still spoke nervously.

"My grandma back there was knocked to the ground by four hunters. I don't know what they did to her. They are new spells, or rather old ones. I've never seen someone overpower my grandma so easily."

The receptionist nodded sympathetically and listened calmly, as if in the background there weren't beds being moved around frantically and patients flying through the corridors, followed by healers engaged in loud discussions. The receptionist was the calm in the eye of the storm and it felt incredibly comforting. She was such a good listener that Mayla would have loved to tell her everything that had happened over the past few days as well as her entire life story. But Mayla stopped herself and only mentioned the bare essentials.

"Do you have any idea what magic affected your grandmother? How old is she? I also need her name for the registration, darling."

Mayla drummed her fingertips on the counter impatiently. "Her name is Melinda von Flammenstein and..."

The receptionist stood up abruptly, her eyes wide. "Melinda von Flammenstein, the head witch of the Fire Circle? She was knocked out by four hunters? Why didn't you say that straight away? Where is she?"

Mayla led her to her grandmother, whereupon the receptionist gave a signal and several healers gathered around Melinda.

"Melinda von Flammenstein? That's impossible. Who can defeat such a powerful witch? Take her to treatment room two. Stat!" Ignoring Mayla, they pushed the bed past her down the long hallway before disappearing into the depths of the hospital, the receptionist right alongside them. Mayla remained behind, speechless. She just stood there, staring down the white hallway until the realization dawned on her that her grandma was in good hands. When Violett had brought Georg here, he'd been treated by competent doctors. Were the two of them still in one of the wards? Mayla was briefly tempted to use a search spell to locate them when Karl appeared in front of her and rubbed up against her legs, meowing.

She bent down and stroked his back. "Hello, darling, what are you doing here?"

An image appeared in her mind. It was the hut in the Pyrenees from which she had just come.

Mayla frowned. "Should I go back? Did something happen?"

He meowed and she patted him on the head. The feeling he sent her wasn't urgent, but it was something important.

"Thanks, I'll jump right back." She peered down the bright corridor one last time, but there was no sign of her grandmother. The healers would take good care of her. Breathing in deeply, she grasped the amulet key and thought, *Perduce me ad Pyrenaeum desertum!*

She landed in the meadow in front of the cabin and looked around cautiously. If she were in danger, Karl would never have sent her there. Still, it was second nature to expect an attack whenever she landed somewhere. But nothing was around her but oppressive summer heat. There was no trace of the cat, though she heard meowing inside the hut. She knew that cat's voice.

"Kitty?" Tom's spirit animal was still there?

She rushed into the little cabin. It took a moment for her eyes to adjust to the darkness since the shutters were closed. After blinking a few times, she recognized Kitty sitting on the bed with a box of chocolates in front of her.

Mayla's mouth dropped open. Touched, she put her hand to her chest. "Chocolates? You're the best." She rushed to the bed and stroked Kitty's back, at which point the faithful cat stretched out her forehead and Mayla pressed it against her own. She loved these moments. Even though Kitty wasn't her spirit animal, they both shared a deep bond, love, and a sense of belonging. Mayla knew she could always rely on her.

Kitty meowed and nudged the box with her nose.

Mayla laughed. "You're right, I need one right away." She scratched the back of Kitty's neck and pushed the lid aside. One truffle was lined up after another — white chocolate, dark chocolate, with coconut flakes and pistachio nibs, or plain. Poetry. Only the truffle in the middle seemed different.

She looked at Kitty knowingly. "A message from Tom?"

Kitty meowed and curled up next to Mayla's hip as if she understood that the message was private, but also didn't want to leave Mayla alone. Such a sensitive animal.

She turned away from her animal friend's shiny black fur and reached for the large fake chocolate. So, Tom had brought the chocolate for her. He certainly knew how to wrap her around his finger.

She slowly brought the fake treat to her lips and hesitated — not because she was afraid of what Tom had to say — no. As soon as she had listened to the message, Tom would disappear again and she would not be able to view the message again.

She took a deep breath and held the message to her lips. "Te aperi!"

The truffle swelled until it broke open and

Tom appeared in the middle, growing to his normal height. His gaze was warm, his hand extended as if he were imagining her sitting in front of him and as if he could take her hand while she listened to the message.

"Mayla, I'm sorry for what happened. I'm sorry for what I did. I should have let you in on everything from the beginning. Believe me, I never meant to harm you. But they blackmailed me. If I don't do as they say, they will kill you. Their powers are superior and they can even use them to attack. However, they need me to cast the spell that will unite the stones. They need me because I am a descendant of the von Eisenfels family and the ancient magic is united within me. That's my only leverage."

He paused and looked up. There were voices in the background that sounded familiar. Was that her grandma and Madeleine? And herself and... Emma? Had Tom recorded the message while they were at the cabin and he was lying inside? He looked up wistfully, as if he were looking through the door outside. Did he feel compelled to go to his daughter? Before Mayla could think about it any further, he continued.

"The hunters don't know the location of the Metal Circle Stone. They're searching for it, but they have no clue other than the locket you luckily found before Marianna. That is our only chance. You must find the stone before they do. When the time comes, I'll retrieve the remaining four stones."

A bang sounded. That was the moment Marianna had appeared with the hunters. Once again, Mayla thought she felt the pressure around her neck as the huntress choked her with a spell. She grabbed her throat instinctively.

Startled, Tom glanced up and then looked at Mayla. "Go to Julie Martin, she can help you. She and her allies are on our side. And get the locket. I'm convinced it holds the answer to where the magic stone is hidden." He hesitated, apparently staring at the door before he looked her directly into her eyes, as if he were actually sitting in front of her. "I love you, never forget that." The next moment, the message popped off and Tom was gone.

Mayla inhaled deeply, her hand landing on Kitty, and she petted the cat, lost in thought. Her warmth calmed her as did her soft purring, so she sat on the bed absent-mindedly and deliberated.

Tom told her to get the locket. Hopefully, Anna had found it at Donnersberg Castle. How long had she been gone? Mayla peered outside. It was late afternoon. Where had the day gone?

Her stomach growled. She urgently needed to eat something before making any further decisions. She wanted to eat the chocolates, but she would overdo it and wipe out the supply again in no time. So she treated herself to the last one from the package in her handbag and replaced it with Tom's box. How sweet of him to have left her a supply along with the message. Love was...

Oh, Tom. Why hadn't he admitted the truth straight away? Who knew what could have been prevented...

Mayla took a deep breath, stroked Kitty's back, and then went to the well behind the house. She was so parched that her tongue stuck to the roof of her mouth. After quenching her thirst and refreshing herself, she sat on the grass. She grabbed a buttercup and cast a Nuntia spell. Hopefully, Anna was ready. She desperately wanted to talk to her. Before she called on Karl to deliver the message, she quickly picked another buttercup and cast a Nuntia spell for Emma. After all, the little one was with people she didn't know and she shouldn't be afraid.

Karl's tail appeared between the tall blades of grass and then the cute little guy jumped straight into Mayla's arms. Purring, he ran his little head along Mayla's hands and kneaded her legs.

"Sweetheart, what would I do without you... Can you take this message to Karamella and this one to Anna?"

He meowed. It still sounded high-pitched even though he was no longer a kitten.

"Thank you, my darling." She ruffled his fur before he carefully took the flowers in his mouth and bounded off through the meadow.

Mayla leaned against the well, remaining in the shade for a while. Even though everything inside her was at full throttle, she needed a short break. She felt drained. Having something more than a chocolate for a meal wasn't a bad idea, but of course, Tom had nothing but ingredients for sticky oatmeal in the cabin. Why hadn't they stocked supplies over the years? That wouldn't happen again. Simply because one adventure was over didn't mean the rest of her life would be safe and free of stress. She vowed she would prepare so that she would never have to cook oatmeal again.

Weary, she entered the hut, poured water, added a handful of oats and a good portion of sugar to the pot, and padded back outside. She lit a small fire and cooked herself a late lunch. Gruel. How low had she sunk?

While the pot was simmering, she thought about her grandmother. How long would it take her to get back on her feet? Would the healers in the hospital cure her as quickly as Madeleine and Mayla had managed to cure Tom together?

A little later, the food was ready. Back when she and Tom hadn't been a couple yet, they had also eaten oatmeal. As she shoved spoonful after spoonful into her mouth, she thought about him. Contrary to her expectations, the oatmeal didn't sit like lead in her stomach — rather, it warmed her from the inside as if Tom were with her, holding her hand.

When the pot was empty, she glanced inside in disbelief. Unbelievable. She had finished the entire pot and she'd found the meal surprisingly agreeable. A smile played across her lips but there was a tingle of melancholy, too. She stood up.

A quick spell took care of the dishes, returning them clean to the cupboard while Mayla sat in one of the lounge chairs in the shade. She actually shouldn't have felt safe there anymore — after all, the hunters had been there and had seriously injured her grandma and taken Tom. Nevertheless, the cabin and the meadow with a view of the mountains gave her a sense of peace and strength. She felt Tom's presence with every breath, probably because he had spent so many years of his life in this place.

It took a while until Karl returned. Mayla was startled awake. She had dozed off, which was no surprise given the heat and all the excitement.

"Did you deliver the messages, my darling?"

He didn't answer because there was a small marble in his mouth. He placed it on her lap and meowed.

"A message? From Emma?"

Karl meowed again and an image of Anna appeared in her mind.

Her shoulders sagged in disappointment. She would have liked to see her daughter, but a message from Anna was actually better.

"Thanks, Karl, you did a great job." She stroked his little head before putting the marble to her lips. "Te aperi!"

The marble grew larger and larger until Anna appeared.

"I need a little time, but we can meet at the agreed-upon location in half an hour. If that no longer suits you, send me another message. See you later."

Mayla nodded even if Anna couldn't see it. The image of the earth witch popped and disappeared as Mayla leaned back in the lounge chair. The break was a relief and helped her to clear her thoughts.

What was Emma doing? Had the high priestesses told her who they were and that Emma was descended from them? Or would they just play with her until the danger passed? How she would have loved to jump there, but Madeleine hadn't told her the location. Mayla smiled as she remembered how Madeleine had reacted to Emma and how loving she had been toward her. What had happened back then that made her turn her back on life and Tom? How would Tom react if he found out who she was? And would he ever forgive her for not being there for him?

The questions were piling up and before she knew it, half an hour had passed. Mayla made the deck chairs and the awning disappear. She clutched the amulet key, extremely excited to see what Anna had discovered. Hopefully, Anna's research would lead somewhere, and hopefully, Tom was okay. And hopefully, they'd find him before he was cursed back into that frighteningly lethargic state again.

15

W hen Mayla landed at the von Eisenfels property, Anna was already there. She had tidied up the room, restoring the bookcases to their upright position along with the rest of the furniture. A few books and small figurines lay unsorted on the shelves.

Anna was sitting on a piece of upholstered furniture with her hands folded in her lap. When she saw Mayla, she immediately jumped up. "Mayla, great. Let's talk somewhere else." And before Mayla had really gotten a chance to settle in, Anna grabbed her hands and jumped with her into the forest. It wasn't the same spot where they'd brewed the potion that morning, but Mayla instinctively knew they weren't far from it.

Anna gave her a searching look and folded her arms over her chest. "What happened?"

Mayla was tempted to reply, "What didn't happen?" Instead, she summarized how

Madeleine had come to her and what happened afterward.

"She's a high priestess? They actually still exist? Unbelievable, I had no idea." She stroked her cheek thoughtfully.

Mayla shrugged. "Apparently, nobody knows. They live in seclusion, only a few hope or suspect they still exist. No one knows for sure, let alone how to get to them. That's why Emma is safe with them."

Anna put her hands in the pockets of her pants and stared off into the forest. "So, Tom has been recaptured? It's unbelievable what the hunters are capable of. God knows they've been busy these last few years, damn it." She looked at Mayla, a deep crease lining her forehead. "And what have we done? Wasted time searching for them, without success."

Mayla understood her frustration. She felt no different. At least Anna hadn't enjoyed a lengthy beach vacation with the family but had set out with her friends to do something about their adversaries.

"You found some hunters and they ended up in prison. Time wasn't wasted."

Anna snorted and glanced at the treetops before turning back to Mayla. "So, Tom wants us to find the Metal Circle Stone? And for that, he says we need the locket?"

"That's what he said in his message. Do you have it with you?"

Anna shook her head slowly. "It's no longer there. Angelika seemed suspicious, which was why I didn't ask her about it. If I had known how important it was, I would have searched for it longer. However, I found something interesting in the library."

Mayla listened. "Tell me."

Anna lowered her voice even though they were in a world fold where Mayla did not feel the presence of other witches. "The woman in the locket, Charlotte de Bourgogne, was a noble witch. You remember that was the woman in the locket."

Mayla's heart beat faster, hoping that Anna's findings would help them. "I remember. She was a member of the noble family that supported the von Eisenfelses back then. What did you find out?"

Anna leaned forward. "Haven't you wondered why the locket with her image was hidden in another family's grave?"

"You're right." Frowning, Mayla recalled the events. She'd found it in the Mont Saint Michel cemetery. What was the name of the family on the grave? Marchand. And below it, a list of names of the people buried in the family grave: Caroline, Jean-Léon, Chantal, Valérie, and Raoul. A rose was engraved next to it.

Mayla tapped her chin. "The Marchand family... do they have anything to do with this? Have you read anything about them?"

"I did." Anna peered off into the distance again, unaware of how much she was trying Mayla's patience. Mayla was about to ask more questions when Anna finally continued. "The family had no magical powers."

Mayla listened. "Not witches? Then why was the locket at the gravesite?"

"I asked myself the same thing. And I wondered why the death of the family was mentioned in a chronicle about the von Eisenfelses."

This was getting more and more confusing. "What did you find out about the deaths of the Marchand family?"

"The entire family died in a fire in 1815. Despite an extensive investigation, the police had no leads. The burned bodies lay in the house on Mont Saint Michel, but the house itself showed no signs of fire — and there were no pyres or other signs of fire nearby.

"That's why Marianna decided to look for the locket at the family grave." Mayla sat on a tree stump, lost in thought. "Do you think we should check the family home?"

Anna shook her head. "Another family lives there now, not a witch among them. I already looked into that."

Okay, so this wasn't promising. Mayla folded her hands in her lap and leaned forward. "Was there anything in the book about why this was mentioned in the chronicles? Are you assuming the von Eisenfelses killed the Marchand family?"

Anna crouched next to Mayla and rested her forearms on her knees. "Yes, apparently there was an affair between a von Eisenfels daughter and one of the Marchands' sons. Raoul, if I remember correctly. Elektra von Eisenfels, the head of the family at the time, didn't like it at all. To both punish the Marchand family and teach her grand-daughter a lesson, she wiped out the entire family. To do this, she used a fire spell that even our police officers couldn't link to her. For the investigating police, the possibility that she had a hand in it remained just a rumor."

An ill-fated love à la Romeo and Juliet, except that magical powers were involved. "How tragic."

"That must be why Marianna was searching for the necklace at the gravesite. The question is why Vincent or Bertha hid the locket there." She sighed heavily. "So Tom believes we can use it to find the last magic stone, right?"

Mayla nodded. "And since Marianna has been hunting for it, she seems to know that too — or at least has a hunch. Do you have any idea who at Donnersberg Castle might have taken it? Angelika, perhaps?"

Anna shrugged. "If only I knew. Violett and Angelika were the first to examine it closely. Have you asked your friend yet?"

She shook her head. "But I will, right away. Are you coming with me?"

Anna hesitated.

Mayla reached out to her. "You can trust them. Violett and Georg are on our side."

"But he's a police officer."

Mayla remembered Anna's story about what had happened to her after her parents had been murdered by the hunters. She had only briefly mentioned that the police had not turned out to be her friends or supporters, but quite the opposite. Tom had saved her from the worst and then taken her to the outcasts, where she'd been safe. That was why her loyalty to Tom was unshakable — and her distrust of the police more pronounced than that of the other former outcasts.

Mayla placed a sympathetic hand on hers. "Anna, I trust Georg. You know you can, too. You've known Violett for a long time and she's never betrayed your trust, right? So, what do you say?" She smiled encouragingly at her.

Anna furrowed her brows and then took Mayla's hand even though she didn't seem particularly happy about it. "All right, I'll come with you."

Mayla breathed a sigh of relief. Anna was a great help to her and it felt right to integrate her into her team of friends. Not wanting to take a chance that she'd back out, Mayla quickly grasped the amulet key and thought, *Perduce nos in domum Violettae!*

The lush green of the forest disappeared and gave way to the brightly colored interior of Violett's place. The red sofa was empty, as was the dining table in the room leading to the kitchen. Yellow candles and a small bouquet of sunflowers stood on it, waiting to be admired. There was no trace of her friends.

"Violett?"

Frowning, Mayla let go of Anna's hand and walked toward the stairs that led to the upper floor where the bedrooms and bathroom were located. Maybe they were resting.

"Violett? Georg?"

Nobody answered. She hurried up the stairs

and searched the upper floor, but the two were nowhere to be found. Disappointed, she went back downstairs to Anna, who was casually looking at the photographs on the wall that showed Violett in various places around the world. Her friend had traveled a lot throughout her life and based on the pictures, she had even traveled with her parents. As Mayla came down, Anna turned to her and raised an eyebrow quizzically.

Mayla shrugged. "They aren't here. They're probably still at the hospital. Hopefully that doesn't mean there's something seriously wrong with Georg." She stared sadly into space.

"Do you want to go to the hospital?"

Mayla deliberated. "I could, and then also visit my grandma. Then again, I don't want to waste too much time. We urgently need to find the last stone — and we need to free the other prisoners in the citadel too, not to mention Tom."

Anna clenched her hands in determination. "Then I will jump to Donnersberg Castle again. I'll find the locket and return with it."

Mayla nodded. "Good idea." Anna's commitment and strength were admirable, and also contagious. It would have never occurred to her to feel sorry for herself or to hang her head in Anna's presence, which was why she felt stronger and more hopeful when she was around her.

The earth witch tilted her head questioningly. "What are you going to do in the meantime?"

She thought for a moment. "I will try to contact Madeleine. Maybe she can help us. I didn't ask her about the locket and she doesn't know we're trying to find the last magic stone. Up until now, we only planned to retrieve the other four stones from the hunters."

"Okay. I'll send you a message as soon as I have the necklace or know where it is. See you later."

"Until later. Oh, and Anna?"

The earth witch raised her eyebrows questioningly.

"Watch out for yourself."

A brief twitch at the corners of her mouth revealed the smile Anna had hiding inside "You too, fire witch." She disappeared as she spoke these words, leaving only fine glitter behind.

HOPING that her friends would return before she left the house, Mayla cast the Nuntia spell for Madeleine in Violett's kitchen. Next, she put a chocolate in her mouth, letting it slowly melt on her tongue as she sat at the dining table. Waiting wasn't her strong suit, but she had no other choice. Hopefully, Madeleine would reply quickly.

A yawn escaped her. Exhausted, she stretched out on the chair as best she could. She looked around the dining room wearily and spotted a set of baby bibs on the counter. She smiled. Violett was expecting her first child. Hopefully, she would be able to enjoy the remaining months unharried and with no further escapades.

The wind picked up and the next moment, a crow landed on the table. Mayla flinched and jumped up. She remembered all too well how Vincent von Eisenfels's crow had followed her everywhere. Then again, it couldn't be his spirit animal. But it didn't look like Violett's crow either.

Get a hold of yourself, Mayla, it's only a spirit animal. Although her heart was beating faster, she leaned closer and did her best to make her voice sound confident and calm. "Hi, who are you?"

The crow cawed loudly, then tapped at a pebble on the dining table. Both were the same light brown color, which was why Mayla hadn't noticed it.

"Oh, is that a message? I thank you."

The crow cawed again as Mayla grabbed the stone and brought it to her lips. "Te aperi!"

The stone swelled until a woman in a dark cloak appeared in its center. It was Madeleine.

"We'll meet in five minutes at the von Eisenfels family's country estate in southern England." No greeting, no "Your daughter is okay." Without another word, the message popped and Madeleine disappeared. And when Mayla looked up, so had the crow.

16

M ayla didn't hesitate for a second. She quickly wrote Violett a message asking her to contact her and placed it on the dining room table. Then she closed her hand around the amulet key, imagined the room where she had met Madeleine and which was much tidier than before thanks to Anna, and jumped to the estate in southern England. When she touched the carpet with her heels, Madeleine was sitting in one of the armchairs, holding an elf figurine in her hands. When she noticed Mayla, she placed the statue on a side table and approached her.

With her heart pounding, Mayla asked the all-important question. "How is Emma?"

"Everything is fine, but we should talk elsewhere. Come."

When Mayla took her hand, the room disappeared and they landed on a coast somewhere. A strong wind was blowing, causing strands of

Mayla's hair to escape the clip at the back of her head and whirl around her face. She tucked them behind her ears and glanced around. Surging water crashed loudly against the rocks at their feet and the pink color on the horizon heralded the sunset. Not far from the cliffs was a simple wooden hut so similar to Tom's in the Pyrenees that Mayla had to smile. Like mother, like son...

As soon as Mayla had hastily looked around, she spoke up again. "Is Emma feeling well? Did she cry?"

Madeleine shook her head and her pinched mouth softened. "My sisters are looking after her lovingly and Emma feels at home. She senses she is among her equals. She's an inquisitive child."

Smiling, Mayla nodded. Yes, she was. She couldn't wait to experience her daughter's thirst for knowledge again. She sighed. "It's good you took her away. The hunters showed up less than five minutes later. Luckily, Marianna couldn't find you. That's why she took Tom with her. He bound himself to them, vowing he would not perform any spells that harm the hunters."

"Damn him..." Madeleine clenched her hand.

"He had no choice. Otherwise, Marianna would have... strangled me." Once again, Mayla thought she felt the cold pressure around her neck that had robbed her of the ability to breathe.

Tom's mother shook her head. "That's not what I mean. He should have talked to me sooner. I could have hidden Emma from the beginning."

Mayla pressed her hands against her sides, struggling to control her temper. "Maybe you should have been honest with him from the start, then he might have considered the possibility."

Madeleine's eyes darkened and she hurried toward the hut. With a wave of her hand, a stone turned into a hanging swing that was so wide Mayla could sit next to her without it being awkward — which Mayla did. The cushions were soft. They rocked back and forth wordlessly.

As the sun began to sink into the sea, Mayla took a breath, about to ask about the locket and the magic stone when Madeleine suddenly started speaking.

"I'm so ashamed I let him down."

Mayla quickly shut her mouth. She folded her hands in her lap and waited even though impatience raged within her.

"Everyone thought I was dead. My sisters know I almost was. Vincent, he... At first, he was charming and incredibly eloquent, and he was unreasonably good-looking. He impressed me with his knowledge and abilities, so much so, I..." She laughed bitterly, "...considered him almost a god. He bewitched me, courted me, and gained my trust through a lot of patience."

"Were you already a high priestess then?"

Madeleine nodded. "I became one early on, as did Ignatia. We weren't even sixteen when we were accepted into the Sisterhood of the High Priestesses. It's actually unusual for us to lead a normal life with a husband and children, maybe even grandchildren and great-grandchildren, but the rules don't specifically prohibit it."

Tom's mother shrugged and stared out at the

vastness of the horizon. Mayla also kept her eyes on the sea, which was wild and slapping loudly against the cliffs. Although elemental forces were at work, the rushing and splashing of the water had a calming effect.

"They warned me, but I wouldn't listen. The von Eisenfels family did not have a good reputation in the eyes of many people. However, since my element is also metal, I always felt connected to them. The day Vincent proposed to me, I confided in him."

Mayla listened in surprise. She had assumed that the guardians were not allowed to tell anyone about their task. "He knew you were a high priestess?"

"Yes, apparently even before then, but I didn't want to believe it. My sisters warned me, but I wouldn't listen. I thought it was envy because they were facing lonely lives."

That was understandable, especially because Madeleine had been so young. "Did you even want to be a high priestess?"

Madeleine nodded. "My great-aunt was one before me, which was why I was introduced early. It is a great honor and an important task, if not the most important one. But I didn't want to miss the chance to have children and a family of my own, which is why I accepted Vincent's proposal."

Mayla nodded. She could imagine how conflicted she must have been. She probably would have made the same choice.

"I was young and naive, less than twenty years

old, and he guided and influenced me in a way that I didn't understand for a long time. It was only when I met Bertha that I started to become suspicious. She looked at me in a way that sent shivers down my spine. Today, I believe she urged him to enter the union with me in order to strengthen the family's power. She was the one who discovered who my great-aunt was. I didn't want to rule out the possibility that Bertha had a hand in her death so that I could become the next high priestess before Vincent married me. But I could never prove it."

Madeleine folded her hands in her lap and bowed her head. "When Valerius — I mean Tom — was born, my task seemed complete. Although they were disappointed that there was no daughter, the offspring was born. They gave Tom all their attention even though Vincent continued to visit me at night. I think Bertha never gave up hope of having a female heir."

A crow cawed loudly. The bird came out of nowhere and sat on Madeleine's shoulder. The animal gently rubbed its head along her cheek. When Mayla looked at Madeleine, she saw a tear glistening in her eyelashes. The priestess wiped it away with the back of her hand.

"I heard them trying to indoctrinate Tom before he even learned to speak. They repeatedly railed against the other witches, especially the founding families, and portrayed the von Eisenfelses as victims. They emphasized that this had to change and that they were obliged to avenge the injustice. It was terrible. Whenever I could, I took him into my room, which I tried to make cheerful and warm."

Mayla didn't have to ask what room it was. It was the room that stood out from all the others and where she had met both Anna and Madeleine on several occasions.

"At one point, they denied me access to him. It was a bad time. Moreover, I was rarely permitted to leave the property. Vincent was monitoring me, which was why I couldn't take a single step without being watched. And God forbid if I were to violate one of his orders." She kneaded her hands in her lap. She seemed insecure and vulnerable, nothing like the distant, bitter, strange woman Mayla had met.

"I found a loophole and was able to contact my sisters. They advised me to take Tom and come to them. They wanted to hide him and promised me that it was their duty to protect him. Since he was a boy he couldn't become a guardian of the stone and was not allowed to enter our temples, but they wanted to consider him one of them and create a place where I could live safely with him. So I had a plan, but Bertha found out. She put a curse on me and told me that if I ever tried to kidnap the family heir again, he would suffer bitterly. I don't know if she would have truly hurt Tom, but at that moment, I believed her."

Mayla nodded sympathetically. Just as Madeleine had allowed herself to be blackmailed with Tom, Emma had been used as leverage against Tom. "And then you left?"

Madeleine shook her head. "I couldn't leave

Tom behind. I loved him more than anything. My sisters urged me to get to safety, but I couldn't. When Vincent found out about my and Tom's attempt to escape shortly afterward, things grew really ugly. He..." Her voice trailed off. "He tried to kill me and... he almost succeeded. I was lying half-dead on the beach on the southern English coast. He must have hoped that I would be washed away with the waves and never play a role in Tom's life again. To this day, I don't know how I managed to muster enough strength to run away before he could return. The following weeks were a complete blank. I don't know where I was or who helped me."

Madeleine fell silent and Mayla let the story sink in. It was unbelievable what this woman had faced. It must have been unbearable when she'd discovered the trap she had fallen into and realized she couldn't save her son. When Mayla looked to the side, she saw another tear on her cheek.

"I know it doesn't explain why I didn't go to Tom. But..." She raised her eyes and looked at Mayla, completely vulnerable. "...I was so incredibly scared. Of Vincent, of Bertha, and then of Tom, who would harshly judge the woman who left him as a child. I... didn't know how to be there for him, imagined he would be better off if I stayed away from him... and from my sisters too. Ignatia was angry, not without reason, because I had revealed a few secrets. And I was ashamed in front of everyone who knew about my past. That's why I lived in secret, not even allowing myself to watch

Tom from a distance. I... did so many things wrong."

Mayla put her hand on Madeleine's and smiled encouragingly at her. "Everybody makes mistakes. It's never too late to try to make amends."

Madeleine shook her head. "Tom will never forgive me. I wouldn't either."

"Maybe you should, though. Perhaps you ought to make peace with the past. And if you're a good grandma to Emma, little by little, you'll sneak your way into Tom's heart."

Madeleine stared at Mayla in disbelief. "You want... me to be part of your life even though...?"

Mayla nodded. Tom would also have a say. As far as she was concerned, there was no reason to exclude Madeleine. She meant what she had said. "Everyone makes mistakes. I know that all too well. Show Tom that we can rely on you, show me, and show your sisters. It's not too late, Madeleine, I'm sure of it."

And then Madeleine did something Mayla never expected. This strong, forbidding woman leaned against Mayla's shoulder and began to cry.

17

Although Mayla was upset after hearing the story, she wrapped her arm around Madeleine and supported her until Tom's mother regained her composure and sat up. She wiped away her tears with the back of her hand.

"Sorry, Mayla." Her tone was cooler again, although not as distant as Mayla was accustomed to. "We didn't meet to discuss my life story. Let's get down to business. Tom is back in the hands of the hunters and we have to find the last magic stone. Knowing Bertha, she did not tell Vincent where she hid it, let alone any of her followers. She didn't trust anyone. In the end, she pulled all the strings. She was the kind of witch you read about in storybooks."

Mayla considered. "Do you have an idea how we can find the stone? Or figure out why the locket is important?"

"Maybe Tom picked up something over time

when he was little or later. He was as good at sneaking around and living in secret as I was." Madeleine gave it some thought. "Your friend Anna is trying to get the necklace, but maybe you can tell me something about it in the meantime. Did you notice anything unusual about it?"

A crow landed in front of them. Mayla only noticed it in passing. It must have been Madeleine's spirit animal. But her mother-in-law looked up suspiciously. "Who is this? Your spirit animal is a cat, right?"

"Oh, it's not yours?" Mayla eyed the animal warily until she noticed the slightly bent beak. "Merkur... This is my friend Violett's crow."

Merkur put a chocolate in Mayla's hands, which unfortunately was another fake. A message from Violett.

"Thank you." Mayla brought the truffle to her lips. "Te aperi!"

A few moments later, Violett was standing before them. Her cheeks were flushed, her red hair disheveled, and she appeared tired. "Mayla, I was in the hospital until now. Georg is doing better, but he has to stay overnight for observation." Violett wiped her nose, the tip of which was suspiciously red. Her friend had been crying. It broke Mayla's heart that she couldn't be there for her, but Violett was tough. Mayla decided that as soon as things were back to normal, she would plan a great weekend with her. "I'm home now, but I want to go to sleep early. If there's anything else, you'll have to hurry. Otherwise, I'll speak to you tomorrow."

Mayla quickly picked up a stone from the ground and turned it into a message spell. "You look tired, Violett. Don't worry, and sleep well. Georg will be better tomorrow. I just have a quick question. Can you tell me where Charlotte de Bourgogne's locket is? Hugs!" She handed the stone to Merkur, who immediately spread his wings and disappeared into the evening sky.

While they waited for Violett's answer, she and Madeleine didn't speak. They enjoyed the peace, the calm before the storm, before Violett's reply revealed their next move, which would ensure there would be no further rest.

The time until Merkur returned passed both far too quickly and far too slowly. Mayla was itching to free Tom and get Emma back. At the same time, she was afraid of what lay ahead when it came to stealing the magic stones from the hunters and once again facing Marianna's incredible powers.

When Merkur appeared in front of the pink evening sky and flew toward them, she felt relief and anxiety simultaneously. Torn between her feelings, Mayla watched the black bird as he again dropped a fake chocolate on the table in front of her. God, couldn't Violett use other things for the message spells? This made every single truffle unusable. How could she be so heartless?

She picked up the sacrificial chocolate remorsefully and held it to her mouth. "Te aperi!"

Violett appeared in front of her again, yawning loudly. She stretched her arms above her head and blinked lazily. "I gave the locket to Pierre because he is the most knowledgeable about French history. He wanted to compare it to an illustration in one of his books. As far as I know, he brought it back to Donnersberg Castle without finding out anything worth mentioning. If you have anything else on your mind, let me know — but please not before breakfast!" She yawned again and disappeared.

"Who is Pierre?" Madeleine asked.

"Pierre Dubois. He belongs to the Inner Circle of former outcasts. If he returned the necklace, Angelika and Artus von Donnersberg will have it in their possession — and then Anna will be able to locate it. For us, though, that means we have to wait even longer."

Madeleine stood up. "On the contrary. We are searching for clues as to how the locket can help us. And to do this we need to go to the place where Bertha spent most of her life. The hotel in Frankfurt."

The thought sent a shudder through Mayla. The last time she had been there was when they had battled Bertha and Vincent — and she and Tom had almost died in the process. The fact that they also were going there at dusk didn't make her any happier. But Madeleine was right. Sitting around doing nothing was out of the question. They had to act.

"Very well." She held out her hand invitingly, and Madeleine took it. Maybe it was just her imagination, but somehow her grip felt tighter, more familiar... now they felt more like allies than before.

"Perduce nos in domum Berthae!"

When they landed in the deserted reception room, it was as dark as it had been five years before when Mayla had landed there with Georg. A shiver ran up her spine as she looked around the abandoned building. Although the inn had been doing well, Bertha's death and the revelation of who she truly had been had deterred any enterprising individuals from reopening the hotel. And so it seemed to Mayla like a journey through time. Everything was in its place, the curtains were drawn, cobwebs covered the chairs and tables in the breakfast room, and a thick layer of dust covered the floorboards and the stairs leading up to the rooms.

Madeleine stepped forward boldly, unable to hide how uncomfortable she felt. "Do you know this area?"

Mayla pointed into the breakfast room. "There is an additional world fold in that room that leads to a linden grove. That's where she united the ancient magic, which is why Tom and Emma have it."

"Then we should take a closer look at that place. It seems suitable as a hiding place, don't you think?"

Did Mayla have a choice? She would have loved to never set foot in that old, abandoned place again, but if there was a clue to the stone's whereabouts or even the stone itself... She reached for her box of chocolates and pulled out a rum ball that she popped into her mouth. With her lips closed, she relished the bittersweet taste to the fullest before she opened her eyes again. She held the box out to Madeleine. "Would you like one?"

Madeleine said no and raised her hands. "Te aperi, munde contracte!" Evidently, she didn't want to waste any more time. Mayla watched as the chairs and tables moved to the sides to make way for a forest. Like the first time, it was fascinating to see a world fold opening up. They were standing on the floor. Not two steps away, the wooden floorboards abruptly stopped and gave way to a leafy ground. A damp forest scent that hadn't been there before filled their nostrils.

"Wow, I had no idea." Madeleine glanced at Mayla. "Are you ready?" Clearly, the question was purely rhetorical because Madeleine hurried off before Mayla could even take the breath to answer.

Mayla followed, an uneasy feeling in her chest. Her footsteps rustled as she stepped onto the forest floor. After a few meters, the linden grove stretched out before them, with the old cathedral on the top of the hill.

"What kind of magical place is this?" Madeleine asked, quickening her pace.

Mayla struggled to keep up with her, but she gritted her teeth, determined not to let a woman nearing sixty leave her behind.

The closer they got to the ruins, the more awestruck Madeleine's gaze became. After circling the stone structure and reaching the entrance, they stopped. Mayla also let her eyes wander over the high, glassless windows and ancient stones. The sight was definitely impressive, but images from before kept popping into her mind — from when Karl's life had been in danger and Bertha had suddenly appeared in the shadows behind Vincent. She thought she heard the voices of her adversaries, Vincent's ugly laugh and Bertha's raspy voice, as if their spirits remained in this deserted place.

"Are you coming?" Madeleine's tone was surprisingly empathetic.

Mayla squared her shoulders. "Of course, two sets of eyes are better than one."

They entered the entrance side by side. This time, no fog lingered. Yet the air within the walls was different from that in the forest even though the cathedral had no roof. It was oppressive and magical at the same time. There was an immediate sense that there was more to this place than typical ruins. Who had built the massive structure? And, when?

They walked reverently toward the altar. The bowls Bertha had used five years before were still there.

"Do any of the hunters know about this place?"

Mayla considered the question. "Eduardo de Luca was here at the time, but I didn't notice anyone else."

"We should be careful and remain vigilant." Madeleine gently ran her fingers over the altar, then raised her head and took a deep breath. "This place is ancient and important."

Although Mayla also believed this, she looked at Madeleine curiously. Maybe she knew more.

"The High Priestesses may have used it long,

long ago. I feel the magic in the stones. It is similar to mine. Bertha chose the location for a reason. I wonder how she found it when my sisters and ancestors obviously couldn't. No one has ever spoken to me of this cathedral."

"Her powers were unbelievable."

Madeleine nodded. "That was her. All those years, I wondered who would ever be able to stand up to that woman." She gave Mayla an admiring look.

Mayla raised her hands defensively. "Our strength wasn't enough. Ultimately, it was Bertha herself, or rather her pride that caused her downfall. Because she used the ancient magic to its full extent even though she wasn't born with it, that power cost her her life."

Madeleine crossed her arms over her chest. "Then it wasn't only her pride but also her impatience, considering what you said about Marianna's powers and those of her allies."

Mayla shuddered. "A blessing in disguise, I would say. Still, I'm wondering how we're going to stop Marianna. She's not as powerful as Bertha, but her energy is even greater than my grandma's."

Deep in thought, Madeleine raised her eyes to the pink evening sky that flashed between the mighty linden tree crowns. "We will succeed, together with my sisters. And Emma."

Mayla frowned. "What does my daughter have to do with this? If you think I'll let her stand up to Marianna..."

"Mayla?" It was Anna's voice. It had come from outside the cathedral.

"Anna?" Surprised, Mayla stared at the entrance, where her second ally appeared a moment later, holding the locket in her outstretched right hand. "You found it?" Excited, Mayla hurried toward her. "That's wonderful. How did you know we were here?"

"Karl brought me here. I wanted to send you a Nuntia charm, but instead of delivering the candle stub, Robin, my cat, led me to Karl, who in turn led us to you. He obviously knew that time was of the essence."

Madeleine took a big stride forward from behind Mayla and Anna narrowed her eyes skeptically. "You're Tom's mother, one of the last high priestesses?"

Madeleine gave Mayla a disgruntled sideways glance. "Did you tell her everything?"

Undaunted, Mayla met her accusing gaze. "Everything that was necessary. Anna is my ally. She has always been loyal to Tom and we can trust her. I would stake my life on her."

Anna glanced up in surprise. The corner of her mouth twitched slightly, but she quickly changed the subject. "Here is the locket. How does it help us?"

"Did Angelika just give it to you?"

Anna shook her head. "No, it was a happy coincidence. Pierre asked me if I could take a closer look, knowing I have access to libraries most witches will never hear of. He had previously taken the necklace with him to do his own research but didn't discover anything new. I jumped at the chance and promised to do what I could."

Mayla breathed a sigh of relief. What a happy coincidence. Meanwhile, Madeleine inspected the piece of gold jewelry. The top cover was decorated with tendrils and curlicues. "Can I take a closer look?"

She handed it to her, even though it was clear in the way she held herself that she remained skeptical. Madeleine snapped open the lid, revealing the portrait of the deceased noble-woman. Madeleine jumped back in surprise, causing the medallion to slip from her hand and land with a metallic clank on a stone. Anna quickly bent down for it while Mayla put her hand on Madeleine's shoulder. "What's wrong? Do you know her?"

Paler than usual, Madeleine nodded. "That's not Charlotte de Bourgogne."

Mayla frowned. "How can you be so sure? We compared her picture to an illustration in a book about the family. We were all relatively certain, weren't we, Anna?"

The earth witch shook her head back and forth uneasily, not taking her eyes off Madeleine. "Who do you think she is?"

"That is Elektra von Eisenfels."

Mayla frowned quizzically. Elektra von Eisen-fels... Then she remembered. She stared in alarm at Anna, who also remembered. "Wasn't that the von Eisenfels high witch who killed the Marchand family?"

While Madeleine nodded slowly, Mayla

hunched her shoulders, shivering. Together with Anna, she bent over the portrait again. She didn't see much resemblance to Bertha, Vincent, or Tom, but the image was incredibly tiny. Wait, didn't that woman also have an imperious chin? And her hair was probably black —at least that's what it looked like in the black-and-white picture. However, these few clues weren't enough to prove beyond a doubt she was a member of the von Eisenfels family.

Anna raised her head. "Why are you so certain?"

Madeleine hesitated. It seemed as if she were freezing under her thick cloak. "I saw her image. I will never forget it. It was on the day..." She looked at Mayla with vulnerability in her green eyes that inevitably reminded Mayla of Tom. "...she punished me because I wanted to run away with Tom. She took me into a room I had never entered before and never found again. As you know, all the heads of the von Eisenfels family are painted in oil on the walls in the hallways. Except Elektra. Her portrait was hanging in this secret room."

Mayla felt a shiver. "Are you absolutely certain?"

Madeleine nodded. "The woman in the picture is Elektra von Eisenfels."

18

Madeleine turned a fallen linden leaf into a chair and sat in it while Mayla and Anna stared at the image.

Anna pointed to the old piece of jewelry. "If this is a von Eisenfels family heirloom, then it will more than likely help us find the missing stone."

Mayla nodded, then remembered something. "That's why Tom wanted me to get it. He must have recognized Elektra. Why didn't he tell us? We wouldn't have given up the locket at all."

Anna tapped her forearm with her fingers thoughtfully. "Wasn't John with you when you found it?"

Mayla shook her head hesitantly until she remembered clearly. "No, not until later. Only Georg, Tom, and I went to Mont Saint Michel."

Madeleine peered out the high windows of the cathedral. "Maybe he didn't recognize the portrait. Shortly after my punishment, Bertha left the property and, as I mentioned before, the portrait hung in her secret room."

Mayla touched her forehead in disbelief. "Do you think she took it?"

Madeleine shrugged. "I guess so. We'll probably find it either in the hotel or here. Or she had other hiding places."

"Which is what we have to assume," Anna added.

Mayla scanned the cathedral carefully. "Let's search this place. Maybe we'll find the hiding spot."

The other two nodded and immediately went to work. But they soon discovered that apart from the altar where the old bowls lay, there were no other objects or furniture in the ruins. They felt the ground and tried to use search spells to find hiding places, but they discovered nothing. Disillusioned, they regrouped.

"So, now what?" Anna asked, lifting her perfectly plucked eyebrows. These facial expressions used to intimidate Mayla, but now she realized that Anna seemed skeptical and strict most of the time even though her heart was loyal and sincere.

"I'm still convinced we can find something here or in the hotel." Madeleine waved her hand at the surroundings. "After all, she spent the last few years in the hotel and was the only one to use this world fold. Where, if not here, would she hide something so valuable?"

Mayla glanced around indecisively. "I understand what you mean. Let's just search the world fold outside the cathedral. Maybe we'll find something."

Anna pointed to the sky. Twilight was gradually falling over the forest. "Let's get started, it's growing dark."

Without a moment's hesitation, they hurried out of the cathedral into the linden grove and glanced around warily.

"It's best if we split up," Madeleine suggested.

Goosebumps shot up Mayla's arms. The forest didn't seem dark and threatening, but it was growing darker and they were in a world fold where Bertha had lived for many years of her life. That was enough to impart an oppressive feeling. Before she could voice her misgivings, Anna and Madeleine agreed.

"Whoever finds something calls the others. Otherwise, we'll meet back at the hotel. I'm heading that way." And without waiting, Anna trudged off in the northern direction.

"I'm going this way." Madeleine also didn't wait for Mayla's reaction and headed east.

Shaking her head, Mayla watched the two. They weren't the perfect team players, but at least they were helping. She looked pensively from west to south and chose a path in between. The previous year's leaves crackled beneath her heels as she took one step after another. It gradually became darker and before long, she would be in total darkness. It would be better if she hurried, especially since it would be difficult to find anything in the dark.

The forest didn't change. One linden tree came

after the next with various bushes growing between. After she had walked for a while, the hill headed down again and she saw the other side of Bertha's breakfast room not too far away. Apparently the hidden world fold was not particularly large. She wandered over the slope, searching between the linden trees for another place to stay or a hiding place, a hut or a cave, but she discovered nothing. The trees weren't growing especially densely so her view was relatively clear, but there was nothing unusual to be found.

Bertha had probably only used the ancient magic of the cathedral to unite the magic. She had likely spent many years looking for a place like this. And then when she'd found it, she purchased the hotel so that she alone could access the hidden world fold. If Madeleine's suspicions were right and this site had once ben used by the high priestesses and then sealed, Bertha's powers must have been extraordinary even then, considering she was able to break through the high priestesses' protection. It was probably a good thing Madeleine hadn't escaped with Tom when he was a child. It seemed like there was a high probability that Bertha could have located the place protected by the high priestesses. Who knows what would have happened to Tom and Madeleine...

Mayla strolled onward without a word from Madeleine or Anna and saw the spot at the hotel where they were supposed to meet. Suddenly, a scream shattered the silence.

Mayla listened in alarm. The scream had come from the forest, quite high up on the hill. Without thinking, she ran. She rushed up the small hill and spotted movement to her left. It was Madeleine. Then it must have been Anna who screamed.

Madeleine looked at her without saying a word. They hurried uphill until the cathedral rose before them and they heard voices.

"Where did she go, damn it?"

Madeleine peered questioningly at Mayla, who merely shrugged. She hadn't recognized the voice.

"She can't be far, I saw her." Mayla's jaw dropped. That was Marianna Lauber who had spoken. "Hunter," Mayla mouthed distinctly, and Madeleine nodded in understanding. She beckoned her closer, so Mayla crept toward her, careful to only step on dirt, not dry leaves.

"Did you check the cathedral yet? What kind of place is this anyway? I don't recognize it." Marianna couldn't be far, given how loud her voice had sounded.

"This is where she reunited the ancient magic back then."

Mayla paled. She knew that voice, especially with the Italian accent. Eduardo de Luca. So the two were in cahoots.

"Quaere Annam!" the Italian shouted suddenly, whereupon Mayla saw glitter darting through the forest and disappearing in the direction of Bertha's hotel. Judging by the crackling, Marianna and Eduardo were following the spell down the hill.

Mayla glanced uneasily at Madeleine, who pointed to a few bushes they could hide behind as they moved down toward the hotel. Madeleine pointed her finger at her feet and closed her eyes briefly. She probably cast something like the Obsurdesce spell. Incredible. Mayla had no idea it could be used outside of buildings and shared with other witches. As they continued to hurry, it didn't matter where they stepped, their footfalls made no sound.

They rushed as quickly as they could back to the hotel where, according to Eduardo's magic, Anna had run once the hunters had discovered her. But what were Marianna and Eduardo doing here? How had they found their trail?

"We need to get the locket. Quickly, before she runs off with it!" they heard Marianna's imperious voice exclaim.

Madeleine and Mayla exchanged an alarmed look. Had the hunters found Anna with the spell that had brought them there, or had they tracked the locket? Was there a tracking spell on either of them? Or was it the same spell that allowed Marianna to find Emma anywhere, anytime, before the high priestesses had hidden her?

"Even if she runs, you can easily find her again," said Eduardo, which made Mayla panic.

"But I don't feel like chasing the stupid goose halfway around the world!" Marianna's voice was so shrill it cracked. Hopefully, that meant things weren't going according to plan.

Eduardo cursed and the sounds of his footfalls stopped. "Damn, she's not here anymore! The spell isn't going anywhere. She must have jumped with an amulet key."

Mayla beckoned Madeleine over and took her hand. Wordlessly, she grabbed her amulet key and jumped with Tom's mother into the forest near the Polish border. She imagined the place where the wicker chair that Mayla had conjured up after Anna left probably was probably still to be found. This forest was Anna's refuge and the earth witch would know that from now on, Mayla would always search for her there first.

They landed on pine needles and Anna immediately rushed toward them.

"Thank goodness, here you are. You found me. The hunters were there. Sorry for fleeing, but they're after the locket and I didn't know how to warn you. That's why I screamed as loud as I could. Did you see the hunters?"

Mayla nodded frantically. "Yes, they can either locate you or the necklace. We're not safe here or anywhere in the world."

Madeleine held out her hand to Anna while still holding onto Mayla. "Come on, I can hide us."

Anna hesitated for a heartbeat, then took the final step toward Madeleine and put her hand in hers and Mayla's. A sparkle wandered through the forest as Madeleine thought the spell. While the trees began to change around them, three people appeared among the linden trees and hurled a malediction at them. The flash of red seemed the only constant in the swirl of colors. It hissed toward them unchecked. Mayla sensed the heat when the forest disappeared along with the red light and they landed in the temple grounds of the high priestesses.

As if they had set off a silent alarm, Teresa and Ignatia immediately rushed toward them from the shadows of the temples. "What are you doing here?"

Ignatia snorted. "Madeleine, you didn't seriously bring another witch here who has no place on our hallowed ground." She pointed accusingly at Anna, who glanced around with furrowed brows. The area was bathed in twilight and the outlines of the ancient temples were silhouetted against the dark blue evening sky, which led the earth witch to let out an impressed whistle.

"We had no choice." Madeleine held out her hand to Anna, who then slipped the locket into her hand. "The hunters can find us anywhere, and only here are we safe from them." She held the necklace under the noses of the two high priestesses, but Ignatia didn't look at it.

"How long will this place remain safe if more and more unauthorized people come? The protection will crumble if there are too many, not to mention that our existence must remain a secret."

Teresa ignored Ignatia's accusations and examined the locket as best she could in the twilight. "What is this piece of jewelry?"

"Tom told me we can use it to find the Metal Circle Stone." Mayla looked over Teresa's shoulders, but she didn't see any of the other high priestesses or her daughter. "Where is Emma? Is she okay? Is she truly safe with you if we remain? Or is it true what Ignatia says? If so, I'll jump immediately. I'd rather be on the run all night than have anything happen to Emma."

Teresa placed a hand reassuringly on Mayla's. "We can protect you tonight. But tomorrow you should leave."

"Are you certain?"

"Well, since our missing sister is by our side, definitely." She smiled kindly at Madeleine. "Emma is fine, but she misses her grandma."

Madeleine's mouth twitched. "Where is she?"

"She's resting in the Temple of Power. I had a feeling the place was good for her."

Mayla's pulse quickened. "Why? What do you mean? Isn't she feeling well? Is she dizzy or crying?"

Madeleine and Teresa exchanged a look until Madeleine turned to her and placed the locket in her hand. "Don't worry, Mayla. Unfortunately, you can't go to her, but I will check on her. If she is awake, I'll bring her. Make yourselves comfortable." With those words, she disappeared into the shadows of the temple.

Mayla wanted to rush after her to see her daughter, but instead crossed her arms over her chest.

"Emma is fine, Mayla. Don't worry." With a wave of her hand, Teresa transformed a few rough stones into comfortable beds full of pillows and blankets, reminiscent of ancient campsites. A canopy appeared above them. Out of the darkness — probably from the high priestesses' kitchen — a carafe of fresh water and a bowl of grapes appeared.

Mayla and Anna sat restlessly on the beds while Teresa disappeared into the shadows of the temple to talk to her sisters.

"Can we trust them?" Anna whispered as soon as she believed they were unobserved.

"They are protecting my daughter. I can hardly trust them more."

"Why are they protecting her?"

Mayla yawned. Gradually, the adrenaline drained from her veins. "Because she's one of them."

Anna didn't reply. She quietly stretched out on her bed, though she didn't put down her wand.

19

Mayla was dead tired and wanted to stretch out on the plump cushions and doze off. But she was eager to hear what Madeleine would say when she returned, even though her inner voice whispered that Emma was probably asleep and she wouldn't be able to hug her little star for yet another night.

Anna seemed to feel the same way. She yawned loudly and sat upright again — probably to stay more alert for the conversation. "What do we do tomorrow?" She asked, yawning again.

In response to the question, Mayla raised her shoulders, though the gesture was barely visible in the encroaching night. In the distance, a few fires burned in bowls, casting a flickering glow over the temple grounds. "We need a plan before we jump out of here. Perhaps the high priestesses can help us find the Metal Stone. Otherwise, I say we jump back to the citadel, grab Tom and the remaining stones, and work with him to search for the last missing fragment."

"Get Tom before the stone? The hunters will be hot on our heels."

"Won't they be anyway?" Mayla sounded more relaxed than she felt. The thought of being followed by Marianna and her people the next morning made her uneasy. Although... "The hunters came after us for the locket, right?"

Anna nodded. "Correct."

"And they didn't see Madeleine or me, just... you."

Anna sat up even straighter on her bed with her back against the headboard. "You mean they'll come after me, not the medallion."

"Exactly. When Eduardo cast the tracking spell, he used your name. I clearly heard it. Maybe they'll do the same tomorrow."

Anna snapped her fingers. "You're right. They can't locate the necklace. Otherwise, Marianna would have found it on the grave before you. They will be searching for me. Consequently, our paths will part at dawn. I'll distract them."

Mayla hesitantly turned to her. "It is too dangerous for you alone."

"I'll decide for myself what is too dangerous for me, fire witch. I'm wondering, though, how did they know I had the locket with me? Do you think Pierre...?" She left the insinuation unspoken.

Mayla shook her head resolutely. "I don't believe that. Another traitor in the castle? Why should Pierre work with the hunters? No, I don't want to believe it. There must be another explanation."

"You're so naive!"

"No, I'm not, I simply trust the people who fought alongside me against Vincent and Bertha."

Anna snorted. "Then why did you flee Donnersberg Castle and never return?"

"Because they disappointed me. They turned on Tom, suspected him despite everything he did back then. Of course, that doesn't mean they're working with the hunters, rather, they accused him of what society has been accusing them of all these years, dang it!" Even though there was more on the tip of her tongue, she swallowed the rebukes. She didn't want to lose faith in her true allies. And she didn't want to rail against them either.

"You can say whatever you want, but with all due respect, please enlighten me; how did the hunters know Pierre gave me the locket at Donnersberg Castle?"

Mayla bit her bottom lip. She had no idea. "Has anyone been watching you? Who knew you were at the castle?"

Anna thought about it. "I saw everyone from the Inner Circle when I was there, even John and Andrew. It wasn't exactly obvious when Pierre gave me the necklace, but we were alone in the library at the time."

"John and Andrew?" Could it be? "I don't suppose those two would have gone over to the hunters, no matter how stupid they acted, would they?"

"Absolutely. Maybe... we're thinking too small."

Madeleine approached and interrupted their musings. "They found the locket because of the pulsating magic within it."

Frowning, Mayla and Anna glanced up. "I'm sorry, what?"

"Metal energy is hidden inside the locket. Marianna must have observed this trace of magic. She obviously didn't dare go to Donnersberg Castle to get the necklace, but when she noticed someone was moving through the world folds with the locket, they followed its trail."

Anna mumbled something in Polish. "So, no more traitors at Donnersberg Castle?"

"Then why didn't Marianna find the necklace at the gravesite straight away?" Mayla asked, voicing her earlier thought.

"Because she can't pinpoint it exactly."

Interesting. Luckily, this confirmed Mayla's belief that none of her former allies had actually betrayed her. "How is Emma?"

"She's sleeping. She's fine. Karamella is snuggled up by her side and will tell her we were here tonight looking after her. She'll be happy about that."

Mayla nodded and swallowed. It was disconcerting to know that her daughter was not far away in a temple that she was not allowed to enter. She resolutely turned back to her musings — there was no faster way to get her daughter back. "We were discussing the fact that after the hunters surprised us in the world fold, they were looking for Anna, not the necklace."

Madeleine nodded. "So, tomorrow Anna wants to serve as the bait and be hunted?"

"That's the plan. It'll give you time to find the stone."

"Not a bad idea. I'll cast a spell with my sisters to make it look like there's still metal energy near you. If it works, the hunters will chase you and hardly pay any attention to us." Madeleine peered thoughtfully at Anna. "Still, it's quite dangerous alone. Are you sure there is no one who will fight alongside you in case the hunters surround you?"

Anna hesitated.

"What about Susana and Nora, your best friends?" Mayla interjected.

"I don't want to put them in danger."

Mayla tilted her head. "If it were the other way around, wouldn't you want them to tell you?"

Anna didn't reply. While she deliberated, Mayla turned to Madeleine. "Can you use your high priestess powers to at least pinpoint where the Metal Circle is?"

She shook her head. "Bertha's protection covers it. If she wasn't dead, there would be no way for us to find the stone. But with her death, her powers aren't as strong. In any case, it's surprising it continues even though she's dead. Normally, every spell expires as soon as you take your last breath. In short — no, I can't locate the stone. Didn't Tom tell you how we should use the necklace?"

Resigned, Mayla shrugged. "He didn't and I have no idea. "That's why I think we should free Tom tomorrow morning before the hunters expect us, grab the stones, and search for the last fragment together."

Madeleine chuckled. "You do have moxie. Do you know what you're doing?"

Obviously, she knew how crazy it sounded. "What choice do we have?"

Madeleine rocked her head back and forth thoughtfully. "I'm afraid you're right. What about you, Anna? Feel like playing the decoy who lures the lions away from their den for us?"

"Naturally. You can count on me."

Mayla's voice was merely a whisper. "Will you let Susana and Nora know?"

Anna stretched and closed her eyes. "We'll see tomorrow."

Mayla would have preferred to send a message spell to Anna's friends on her own, but it wasn't her place to make that decision.

"You should sleep, Mayla. Tomorrow will be demanding for all of us."

Grateful for the suggestion, Mayla slid her head onto her pillow. Tomorrow, she would free Tom. Tomorrow, she would face Marianna and her immense powers. Tomorrow, this madness would hopefully end. Then she would visit her grandmother, whom the healers had hopefully been able to help, in the hospital.

She closed her eyes and imagined herself sitting by her daughter's bed the following evening, stroking her dark curls and being able to tell her, "Everything is fine again, my darling."

SOMEONE SHOOK Mayla's shoulder and she stirred sluggishly. "What?"

"Get up, time to move."

Mayla sat up sleepily. It was pitch black out, with no visible sign of dawn anywhere. Madeleine placed a lantern next to the bed and lit it. Otherwise, Mayla would not have seen the hand in front of her eyes. The glow illuminated Madeleine's face. She seemed tired. Had she even slept?

Mayla stretched. "Isn't it a bit early?"

Madeleine held a cup under her nose and the smell of freshly brewed coffee invigorated her senses.

"Thank heavens, it smells amazing."

"Should we jump at the same time?" Anna asked.

"I think that's the most sensible thing to do." Madeleine dug into Mayla's handbag and held the box of chocolates under her nose. "Do you need anything else to wake up?"

Mayla yawned. "Thanks, that's perfect." She sipped her coffee, which was wonderfully strong. Perhaps a little more milk, but she certainly wasn't going to complain. "Did you tell Susana and Nora?"

When Anna nodded, Mayla smiled. "Good decision, Anna. Anything else and they would have resented you."

"You sound just like them. We meet in ten minutes. Can you be ready by then?"

Madeleine shot a questioning look at Mayla, who yawned again and stretched. "Sure, I'm more than ready. Today, I'm getting my family back. But first, I have to freshen up. Is there somewhere I can splash my face with some cold water?"

Madeleine pointed into the darkness. "There's a fountain over there."

A fountain... Better than nothing. Mayla set off into the darkness with the coffee and chocolates in hand. A little later, she returned to the others, refreshed. She'd drunk her coffee, eaten the truffle, and she was ready for action. "How should we proceed, Madeleine? Are we jumping straight into the little world fold in the citadel?"

"I wanted to suggest that too. The hunters don't know it exists — unless they discovered it by accident."

"Positive thinking never hurt. So, are you ready, Anna?"

The earth witch nodded and handed Mayla the locket to take along. Once they freed Tom, they would be able to search for the Metal Circle Stone together. She considered putting it in her purse, right under the chocolates and the jewelry box from Tom's nightstand but then decided against it. She attached it to the chain around her neck along with the protective amulet and said goodbye to Anna. "Thank you for helping Tom and me. But please, if you have any concerns, you don't have to follow through. I bet if you jump to Donnersberg Castle, everyone will support you against Marianna."

Anna waved a hand dismissively. Her mouth twitched, as if she wanted to smile. "Thank you, fire witch, though I would never abandon a good plan out of fear. Good luck."

They clutched their amulet keys simultaneously, with just the small candle in the lantern providing light as they looked into each other's eyes and thought the necessary spells. As the glitter appeared and the darkness began to spin around them, the sun's first rays illuminated the eastern sky with a subtle glow. It seemed to Mayla like the long-awaited glimmer of hope on a dark horizon.

When she landed next to Madeleine in the tiny world fold in the citadel, she was met with absolute darkness. They stood still for a moment and listened. Nothing was to be heard.

"I hope Tom is still here," Mayla whispered.

"You don't have to whisper just yet. They don't see the world fold, so they can't hear us. And, yes, I hope so too, but they probably didn't return him to the same cell."

Mayla suspected that too. "Let's wait a moment so they can track Anna."

"Okay, but no more than five minutes. We should take advantage of the early hour. They certainly won't be expecting us at this time."

Mayla chuckled half-heartedly. "Even I wouldn't expect anything at this hour." She yawned again, the last bit of sleepiness leaving her lips, and straightened her shoulders. Even though her heart was filled with trepidation, she would give her all today and fight for her happiness.

Time flew by. The five minutes passed in a heartbeat. Still, they heard nothing. Who knew where the hunters usually stayed?

"Ready?" Madeleine asked.

Mayla nodded, blew a small flame onto her fingertip, and together they crossed the magical threshold. They crept to the stairs leading to the basement and stole down the many steps. As they entered the basement, they looked around. To the sides, like last time, there was one inhumane cell next to another, all occupied by the same apparently lifeless figures as the day before. Again, no one responded to them or the dim light. How Mayla would have liked to free them all straightaway, but Madeleine would have used too much energy to crack the metal charms on each lock. In addition, neither of them had enough strength to carry everyone out or heal them, let alone take on Marianna and the hunters afterward. Still, Mayla was wracked by a guilty conscience while they passed the rows of prisoners.

As they approached the back door, she couldn't help but hold her breath. Was Tom in the last cell again? As soon as she was able to see into the partitioned area, Mayla let out a sigh of relief. Tom wasn't there. Was that good or bad? On the one hand, he wouldn't be so weak and battered, maybe even tortured, again, but on the other, it meant they had to find him in the depths of this old building. Where had Marianna taken him? To a hidden room in this area or a completely different location?

"I'm sure they're hiding somewhere around here," Madeleine said, answering her unspoken question, keeping her voice quiet. "The stones are here, my sisters and I made sure of that before we left. And Marianna will not stray far from the stones or Tom, who is the insurance she needs to unite the fragments."

"Why doesn't she do it herself? As a member of the Metal Circle, the ancient magic is also united in her."

Madeleine didn't reply. Instead, she put her finger to her lips in warning, and Mayla blew out the flame on the tip of her finger. Had Madeleine heard something? She listened intently in the darkness. She heard no sound, no voices, no footfalls, or anything else. She peered questioningly at Tom's mother, whose outline was so dim in the darkness that Mayla couldn't see her facial expression. Madeleine took her by the hand and slowly pulled her along. Okay, she obviously wanted to go through the door. Hopefully, it wouldn't open into a brightly lit room — otherwise, they'd be instantly spotted.

Mayla waited with bated breath as Madeleine slowly pushed the door open. It wasn't locked, but it creaked softly. Madeleine immediately stopped moving. When no one responded, she carefully pushed it further. With every inch the door opened, Mayla relaxed. If candles were burning in the room or hallway behind it, the light would have reached them by now, and if their enemies had been there, they would have had to defend themselves against various curses by now.

They peered cautiously into the darkness beyond when Madeleine clasped her hand again and brought her lips closer to Mayla's ear, her voice merely a whisper. How she could see so well in the darkness was a mystery to Mayla, but maybe her eyes were trained to see in the dark.

"Let's try to open a hidden fold. Even if the stones aren't in one, Marianna and her people are certainly hiding in one, otherwise the operators of the citadel would have noticed them long ago. The barren basement, however, doesn't look like it meets their standards."

Mayla squeezed Madeleine's hand to show her approval. She closed her eyes and thought, *Te aperi, munde contracte!*

Maybe it was her imagination, but she thought she saw a subtle sparkle floating across the room before the dark space expanded, light flooded in — and a deafening alarm went off.

20

The shrill sound of the alarm pierced through the basement, causing Mayla and Madeleine to recoil and hide in the shadows. Before they attracted attention, Mayla raised her hands and thought, *Averto!* while imagining noisy footfalls scurrying away in the opposite direction. At that moment, a man in his mid-twenties jumped up from an armchair with its back facing them. Mayla didn't recognize him. He scanned the room before hurrying after the footsteps.

Madeleine quickly cast a Tutare spell on them, causing the alarm to fade away, making it seem as if the intruder had fled, leaving no one else in the room. When the man was swallowed by the darkness, they had a moment to examine the newly discovered fold.

In front of them was a room lit brightly by candles on the walls. But it was unoccupied. There was another armchair next to the first one, but no one was sitting in it. Presumably, the man was a guard.

The room appeared to be an anteroom. In the back, the cellar continued just as they had seen before, with doors leading off to the sides in the direction the guard had gone.

Madeleine and Mayla looked at each other indecisively.

"Let's use a tracking spell." Mayla raised her hands, thinking, *Quaere Tomem!* A sparkle erupted from her fingertips and raced toward one of the doors. Without hesitating for a moment, they chased after it. Madeleine remained focused on keeping the Tutare spell over them to prevent the alarm spell from going off again, which impeded their progress. They needed to remain unnoticed, because otherwise Anna's distraction and the danger it put her in were pointless.

They cautiously pushed open the door that the search spell had disappeared through and found themselves in another room that resembled a hallway. Again, more doors. Hopefully, they wouldn't get lost searching for Tom. The room wasn't as brightly lit as the previous one. A three-armed candelabra stood on a table in the middle that had a few chairs around it. Nobody was there. Strange. The hiding place seemed deserted. Or was it because of the time of day? Or had most of the hunters taken off after Anna?

The subtle glitter of the search spell led toward a door at the far end of the room, which they also passed through. They entered a dark corridor. Glancing sideways at Madeleine, Mayla noticed how her expression appeared strained. It clearly was taking a great deal of strength to maintain the Tutare spell over them.

"Shall I relieve you?"

Madeleine squinted down the hall. "That would be good. I bet one of the next doors will be locked and my magic will open it effortlessly, and more quietly than yours."

Mayla closed her eyes and imagined a bluish shield around them, hiding their presence from the Motus Indica spell. Back when she and Tom had freed Georg from von Wickert's custody, she was the one who had cast the spell. The knowledge that she had succeeded before gave her courage. She thought, *Tutare!* and a sturdy protective shield joined Madeleine's.

"I'm dropping my spell now."

Highly focused, Mayla nodded. When Madeleine's shield fell and still no alarm sounded, she relaxed. It was much easier for her than it had been with Tom. Was it because her powers had grown or was it because Tom wasn't distracting her with his presence? Instead, her heart raced dangerously as she imagined what Marianna might have done to him. *Stay calm, stay calm.* They would soon find him and free him.

When Madeleine started moving, Mayla remained behind her. The corridor was too narrow for them to walk side by side. Plus, Madeleine was the one who had to act quickly if they ran into someone.

The corridor seemed endless and they breathed a sigh of relief when they finally reached a door. The glitter paused in front of it for a moment before disappearing through the dark wood. As expected, the door was secured by a large lock as well as magical protection. Madeleine unlocked it easily, which caused Mayla to hesitate.

"Could it be a trap?"

"I don't think so. They don't know I'm helping you, which is why they haven't reinforced the metal spells. Lucky for us — it should stay that way. According to Marianna, Tom is the only one on our side who can cast metal spells."

"That's right," Mayla whispered, listening intently while Madeleine cautiously opened the door. Even if the argument was sound, she expected an attack at any moment. Yet once again she was met with nothing but dim light as the door swung open softly without squeaking. Instead of finding a prison cell with Tom lying on hard earth, they were in a spacious library.

The walls were paneled with dark wood and there were rows of shelves in carved wood that was just as dark. Even the floor was covered with dark wooden floorboards. Whoever worked in or created this room had put a lot of care into the interior design. A small oil lamp stood on a bureau against the far wall where no one was sitting. However, the open notebook and the quiet shuffling of footsteps indicated someone was in the room. Was it Tom?

There was no longer any sign of the search

spell. That meant Tom had to be in this room. Mayla wanted to call out for him, but it was clear it would only draw unnecessary attention to them. Side by side, they entered the room that exuded a gloomy atmosphere in part because of the dark interior, but for other reasons, too.

The faint shuffling approached, so Madeleine raised her hands, ready to cast a spell. When they peered into the hallway where the footfalls were coming from, Madeleine dropped her hands and instead crept forward. Confused, Mayla followed and spotted a woman who was carrying a stack of books under her arm while she placed them back on the shelves. She walked hunched over, as if the weight of the world was on her shoulders. Her long skirt dragged along the wooden floor and her movements seemed tired and weak. Her back was to them, so Mayla couldn't see her face, especially since Madeleine was squatting between the book-shelves. Who was she? Since she worked behind a locked door, did that mean she was a prisoner?

When she heard their footsteps, the woman glanced up. Before Mayla could even see the face, she felt as if she knew this person. Something about her seemed familiar. As soon as she saw the tired but familiar eyes, her heart sank and she was only able to maintain the protective spell with difficulty.

It was Sarah, Emma's teacher.

"What are you doing here?" Mayla asked angrily, while Madeleine stood next to her with a wide stance. She didn't ask who it was. Apparently, she had been watching Tom, Emma, and Mayla lately and therefore knew how this woman felt about Emma.

Tears came to the teacher's eyes. "She forced me. I didn't want to help her, but she has Leonie and Theodor. I had no choice."

While Sarah began to cry, Mayla's brain raced at record speed. It was Sarah who had planted the bug on her, who had told the hunters that she and Tom were engaged, and who had allowed Emma to be almost kidnapped. Mayla had to restrain herself from wringing the woman's neck right then. She struggled to keep her voice down so that she didn't shout across the cellar. "What do they have to do with the hunters?"

"My father did a lot of research on ancient magic before he died. I had to give them a list of all the ancient books he had in his possession."

"Did you just work at the kindergarten to spy on us?"

The teacher dropped her shoulders. "Yes, actually, I'm a librarian. I'm sorry, I didn't mean for anyone to get hurt. When I refused to comply with their demands, they kidnapped my family."

"Your family? Do you mean your children?"

Sarah's shoulders shook. "No, my sister and her husband. They are all I have left since our father died."

Mayla swallowed. She wanted to judge this woman and curse her, but she felt a little sympathetic. "When did that happen?"

"That summer before Emma had her visitation day."

Mayla shook her head in disbelief as the

pieces of the puzzle came together in her mind. "We chose the kindergarten closest to the Fire Circle headquarters for Emma. Like most other fire witches. And because there are witches among the hunters who were once fire witches, they guessed where we would send Emma."

Sarah nodded. She seemed miserable. "I am so sorry. I didn't want anything to happen, but I didn't have the guts to object. What choice did I have?"

"Dang it, you could have confided in my grandma! As a fire witch, you know how strong she is. We all would have helped you."

Sarah raised her hands in despair. "That's easy to say, but Marianna Lauber threatened to cut my sister and her husband's throats if I spoke a word of it to anyone."

"How long have you been trapped here?" Madeleine asked.

The teacher raised her shoulders uncertainly. "Immediately after Emma's kidnapping failed and it became clear she would not return to the kindergarten."

Shoot. Everything inside Mayla clamored to charge this woman, to convict her in the highest court, but she couldn't lose her head. Despite her unbridled anger, she remembered that the tracking spell had brought them here. "You are not alone. Where's Tom?"

"Tom? Your fiancé?" She frowned. "I haven't seen him since the last time I saw you."

What? But the search spell... She looked questioningly at Madeleine when an intrusive laugh erupted behind her and someone clapped loudly. Surprised, they spun around. Marianna Lauber was standing in the doorway with a shockingly large number of hunters in the hallway behind her.

"Bravo, how far you have come. Did you truly believe I would just let you wander through my lair and free someone who swore an oath to me?"

"Where's Tom?" Mayla shouted. At the same time, she concentrated more than ever on the protective shield that no longer had to protect her from the alarm spell but from an attack by her enemies.

Marianna laughed loudly. "You'll never see him again!"

Mayla's face dropped. Her pulse faltered. "What did you do to him?"

"I didn't do anything to him, it's just that he... well... he swore an oath to me. Little tip: That part you did not hear."

Her heart was beating faster and faster, panicked and desperate. Where was Tom? She forced herself to breathe calmly and remain composed on the outside. She couldn't let herself be upset, especially because of the protective spell. "What do you mean?"

Marianna wrapped her long braid around her finger and watched Mayla. She clearly enjoyed having the upper hand. Her voice became play-fully cute, as if she were talking to a dimwitted child. "Didn't he tell you that? I thought you two wanted to get married."

"Stop toying with me and tell us what you mean!"

"Speaking of us, who is the veiled one?" Marianna curiously watched Madeleine, who had previously held back and was now calmly putting her hands down as if there was nothing to fear.

"My name is completely irrelevant. Mayla asked you where Tom is!"

Marianna's gaze grew suspicious. She turned her head to peer under Madeleine's hood. "Are you the one breaking my metal spells? Are you a traitor?" She took a step forward and raised her wand. A bolt of lightning shot out of it and struck the protective shield. Mayla gritted her teeth to hold her own against the huntress when it suddenly became easier. She dared to look to the side and saw that not only Madeleine had raised her hands but also Emma's teacher, who was pointing her wand at the hunters.

Marianna's expression hardened. Unrelenting, she observed Sarah as she stepped naturally alongside Mayla. "You are the traitor? Are you sure you want to stand against me?"

Sarah pressed her lips together. Was she going to stab them in the back and cast a spell on them? But she stood her ground, looked Marianna in the eyes, and strengthened her defense. "An injustice remains an injustice. I'm no longer standing on the sidelines!"

Marianna laughed, but it didn't sound as smug as before. "You realize your sister and her husband will pay for your decision, right? I need someone else to practice the new spell that supposedly makes anyone talk. You know which one I mean, right? The one that made the old herbalist collapse last week. He's been lying in the cellar like a corpse ever since. Maybe I should take one of the two. What do you think? Is that a good idea?"

Mayla's anger boiled over and before she knew it, she dropped her shield, stormed out from behind the protection spells of the other two, pointed her hands at the hunters, and roared, "Animo linquatur!"

A beam shot from her fingertips. Before their opponents could put up a defense, the spell hit some of them full force, causing them to fall to the ground unconscious as the others dove to the sides.

As if they had agreed on the course of action, Madeleine, Sarah, and Mayla simultaneously ran past the surprised hunters and back into the corridor. They closed the door behind them and Madeleine quickly sealed it with a metal charm. The hunters would have no problem solving it, but it was better than nothing and it bought them a few minutes. Precious minutes.

"Run, run!" Madeleine urged, already sensing the counter spell on the other side of the door.

They dashed through the dark corridor back into the hallway where no one had been the last time, but now four hunters were standing watch behind the door. Caught off guard by their appearance, they hesitated as Mayla and Sarah burst into the room. A fight broke out and curses flew through the room. Mayla gritted her teeth and tried to position herself so that her enemies weren't looking in the direction where Madeleine was protecting the door. A shiny red malediction shot through her shield and whizzed a hair's breadth past her head. Sarah did her best to support Mayla but her spells were far too weak. Finally, Madeleine joined in. The hunters didn't notice as she raised her hands and cast a powerful metal spell on them, causing the three to fall unconscious to the ground.

They quickly rushed past them as a fourth hunter leaped out from behind the chairs. As he hurled a curse at her, Mayla shook the last door they had to go through. Dang it. It was locked. The hunter's red flash missed her by a few millimeters and he immediately fired another attack spell. Finally, Madeleine came running. They stood in front of her to buy her time. Sarah sent up a protective shield, but one volley by the hunter destroyed it and Sarah was hit in the stomach. She arched painfully and Mayla slipped an arm under her armpit and around her back.

"Tutare!" she shouted.

A hissing malediction shook her shield as Madeleine placed her hands on the doorknob and broke the spell. Thank God Marianna and her people didn't know Mayla had a metal witch on her side, but now the advantage was lost.

Madeleine pushed open the door and Mayla, with Sarah in tow, dashed into the last room in the secret world fold.

"Let's try to jump!" Mayla shouted, but Sarah shook her head.

"It won't work. The entire fold is sealed, even for the hunters."

Without hesitating, Madeleine hurried to Sarah's other side and helped Mayla support her. They crossed the last room and rushed back into the hallway that led past the prison cells to get to their own secret world fold.

On the way, Sarah raised her eyes, scanning the inmates in the cells. Suddenly, she screamed, "Leonie!" Her strength returned and she rushed toward a cell were a woman not even forty years old lay, leaning against the wall, her chin resting on her chest. She didn't move.

"We have to move on!" Madeleine urged, but Sarah pointed to the cell.

"That is my sister and I'm not leaving without her."

Cursing, Madeleine rushed over, put her hands on the lock, and the door burst open. None of them could say where Sarah's remaining strength came from as she pulled her unconscious sister from the cell. Mayla helped support her and Madeleine ran ahead up the stairs to open the secret world fold.

"They're over there!" They heard Marianna's voice as they slammed the door to the basement stairs behind them and entered the tiny fold in the caretaker's room. Hearing the footsteps of their pursuers on the stairs, Mayla's pulse raced, but she remained focused.

Madeleine grasped the amulet key and

reached out to Mayla, who was still touching Sarah and her sister. As soon as everyone had entered the fold, the rug was ripped out from under them, the cleaning buckets and ladders swirling until the shouts and footfalls of the hunters faded away.

21

They ended up in a deserted forest that seemed unfamiliar to Mayla at first glance. The sun illuminated the surrounding maple trees with its first rays and a squirrel scurried up a wide trunk, but nothing else moved.

Exhausted, Mayla slid Leonie onto the moss and Sarah collapsed to her knees next to her. She was white as a sheet and holding her midriff.

"Let me see," Mayla urged, but Sarah wouldn't hear of it.

"We have to take care of Leonie first. Her heart-beat is irregular." Panicking, she felt the pulse in her sister's neck. "What did the hunters do to her? What kind of magic is this?"

Madeleine crouched next to her. "Probably the same one they used on Tom. Let's cast the healing spell together, Mayla."

Mayla nodded and held her hands next to Madeleine's over Leonie's body. They closed their eyes and thought *Sana!* and a yellowish-white light enveloped the weakened woman's body. Her eyelids fluttered and she groaned, but she didn't awaken.

"What is wrong with her?"

Mayla felt for the pulse inside Leonie's wrist. "She needs time to recover, her heart is beating steadily. It's best we get you to a hospital."

Madeleine stopped Mayla before she could grasp her amulet key and turned to Sarah. "First, tell us everything that might help us!" She pushed back the hood a little and her austere expression appeared, causing the woman who had impersonated a teacher to shrink back.

"I'll tell you everything I know."

And she did. As Sarah had said in the library, the hunters had noticed her because of her father's studies and although Sarah was merely a librarian at the Ulmen City Library, the hunters had forced her to help them, leading Sarah to become involved with Marianna and her coven. Lowering her eyes in shame, she repeated how she had gained Mayla's trust, hid the bug in her blouse, and looked the other way when Emma had run into the forest. Mayla's heart filled with pain as if she were reliving it all: The fear for her child and the panic when she realized they were being spied on and no longer safe in their own home.

Impatient, Madeleine intervened. "That's important, but first and foremost, we need to know where Tom is. Did you hear the hunters talking about him?"

"They didn't mention him, but I did overhear two of them strengthening the spell outside my door. They talked about needing to create an additional hideout. Someone had escaped and they were taking him to Paris so that he wouldn't slip through their fingers again."

Paris? Mayla paled. "That city is huge! How are we supposed to find him there? I'm not trusting a search spell again anytime soon. How could Marianna have fooled it?"

"The hunters have powers you cannot imagine. There are ancient spells that have rightly been forgotten." Sarah wrapped her arms around herself. It was obvious how uncomfortable she felt.

Madeleine snorted. "Let me guess, you helped them learn those old incantations."

Her cheeks flushed and Sarah lowered her gaze. "I... I... I didn't mean to."

Leonie groaned. Restless, she tossed her head back and forth. Had the hunters harmed her more than Tom? Had they truly tested old curses on her like they had the other prisoners?

Sarah felt her forehead, panicked. "My sister must get to a hospital."

Mayla took her hand. "We'll take you, but please think some more. Is there anything the hunters said that might help us? A direction, an arrondissement? Anything to narrow down the search?"

Sarah vigorously shook her head, her eyes fixed on Leonie. "Please, my sister needs to see a doctor."

Mayla nodded resignedly. "I'll take you to Frankfurt immediately." If they hesitated any longer, they would be no better than Marianna and her people. Without waiting one second more, she linked arms with Madeleine and grasped the amulet key while her other hand rested on Sarah, who in turn held her sister in her arms. Mayla concentrated on the spell and the maple trees spun around her and a few moments later, they landed in the sterile emergency room of Frankfurt's Marienstein Hospital.

A healer appeared out of nowhere, just like when Mayla had been there with her grandmother, and placed Leonie on a gurney. Sarah shouted a thank you over her shoulder before rushing off to check in. Perplexed, Mayla and Madeleine looked at each other.

"Now what? Where do we look in Paris?"

Mayla closed her eyes. She wanted to use the time in the hospital to ask about her grandma and Georg, but they were pressed for time. She had to follow through with Madeleine now. She finally came up with an idea for how they could proceed and leaned forward so no one could overhear their conversation. "Can we jump to your sisters?"

Madeleine frowned. "You know the protection..."

Shoot, Mayla had forgotten about that. If she stayed there, the high priestesses might no longer be able to protect Emma. She quickly rethought her plan. "Okay, then you jump alone. In the meantime, I will inform the police about the hideout in the citadel. When they hear about the prisoners as well as the hunters, the officers will storm the basement with the cells and all the world folds within the old walls in the next hour. That will force Marianna to move the stones so the police don't accidentally discover them. I bet she takes them to where Tom is being held — after all, he's supposed to cast the spell that unites the fragments."

Madeleine clapped her hands together. "Good idea. My sisters and I will keep an eye on the stones. Once they arrive at the new location, we'll know Tom's whereabouts."

Mayla nodded. "We'll keep in touch through the Nuntia spell, okay?"

Suddenly, warmth filled Madeleine's eyes. "Thank you for your loyalty to my son and for supporting me and my sisters. You are a special witch, Mayla von Flammenstein."

Sheepishly, Mayla glanced down and fished the box of chocolates out of her bag. She held the package out to Tom's mother, who took a vanilla truffle, winked at her, and jumped away.

Mayla smiled and treated herself to a marzipan-filled truffle, which she enjoyed with her usual solemnity while clutching the amulet key and thinking, *Perduce me in domum Violetttae!*

When she landed in her friend's living room, Violett was drowsily descending the stairs. Startled, she cried out and cowered until she recognized Mayla. She clutched her chest.

"Mayla, have you lost your mind? What are you doing here so early? And the emphasis is on

you and early, in case there was any misunder-
standing."

She hugged her friend happily. "Please inform
the police about a hunters' lair where an incredible number of witches are being held captive.
They are testing ancient spells on them."

Violett's gray eyes widened. "What? That's
terrible! Where?"

"In France, in the Besançon Citadel. They're
being held captive in the basement in a sealed
world fold."

"How terrible. Why don't you inform the
police?"

"Because they would detain me and question
me about Tom. You know, about the stolen stones."

Violett looked at her warily. "And you don't
have time for that because...?" She hadn't been
able to fool her friend in a long time.

"Tom was also trapped in the citadel, but now
the hunters have taken him elsewhere."

"Let me guess, you are going there to free him?"
Mayla nodded.

"Alone? That's far too dangerous! Mayla,
come on."

"I'm not alone. I have unexpected rein-
forcements."

"Who would that be?"

She was running out of time. She trusted
Violett, but still it was important for the high
priestesses' involvement to remain unknown for
the time being. Besides, if she started talking
about Madeleine and her sisters now, Violett
wouldn't make it to the station before ten o'clock

— and by then, the hunters would be ruthlessly hunting down Anna and the locket. Anna. That was an idea.

"Anna is on my side. She's helping me." That wasn't even a lie, but it wasn't the entire truth. Still, Mayla grew nervous. Don't look up and to the left, don't look up and to the left.

"Anna Nowak? Seriously?" Violett shook her head. "Well, she has always been loyal to Tom. Only you and her... You two weren't exactly great friends, were you?"

"No, but she's helping me anyway and I am grateful for that. She's a great witch." And Mayla didn't have to lie about that. She withstood Violett's scrutiny, even as her friend's expression darkened.

"Don't forget, I won't give up my place as best friend so easily."

Mayla chuckled. "I'm glad to hear it. We created a small world fold in the caretaker's room just outside the sealed one. The police can use it to get there quickly and undetected. So, can you please inform the police as soon as possible?"

"Before breakfast?"

Mayla thought a spell, causing bread to fly out of the box along with a knife from a drawer that cut two thick slices and generously spread butter on them. As soon as a hearty portion of ham landed on it, the sandwiches flew to Mayla, who held them under Violett's nose. "Food to go!"

Violett rolled her eyes. "Okay, but then you owe me a favor, promise?"

"I promise."

"Be happy Georg has to stay in the hospital for a few days. He'd give you a piece of his mind. But best of all, I'll be able to use the amulet key from the station." Violett winked at her and took a bite of the sandwich, which smelled truly delicious. As Mayla watched her take every bite, she nodded toward the kitchen. "Help yourself. In the fridge is the cream cheese you like so much. And you can reheat the coffee that's still in the pot."

Mayla didn't have to be told twice — besides, she had to wait until Madeleine told her where the hunters were taking the stones. What could be better than spending the time fortifying herself for what lay ahead?

As she settled on the comfortable red couch with her breakfast, all the thoughts came flooding back to her and her stomach lurched. Luckily, she'd eaten a slice of bread. Overwhelmed by worries, she wouldn't be able to get anything else down. Her soul cried out for Tom. She missed him, his closeness, his smell, just everything about him. And obviously, Emma. They were such a great team, a family of her own, just when she had given up on ever having one. Her heart bled without them and she wanted nothing more than to lead a perfectly typical family life, even if life would probably never be completely normal.

She sipped the coffee and treated herself to a nougat chocolate, which mixed wonderfully with the coffee and put a gentle smile on her lips. Violett had left more than half an hour ago. Presumably, since she hadn't returned yet, the police officers were keeping her at the station for more information. She would tell the truth — that Mayla had sent her because she'd discovered the prison and that Tom had been held there but had been removed. There was no reason to hide it. On the contrary, it would show that neither she nor Tom were working for the other side.

When would the longed-for news from Madeleine finally come? Karl appeared and Mayla jumped up. The little one mewed and rubbed up against her legs.

"Do you have a message for me, little one?"

He meowed and she sensed he merely wanted to be there for her. Sighing, she bent down and stroked his velvety black fur.

"Thanks, Karl. You always sense when I'm restless. I'm so glad I have such a great spirit animal." She picked him up in her arms, sat back down on the couch, and cuddled with him. Karl purred and rubbed her cheek with his tiny head. His presence gave her patience and strength, as usual. She stroked his head absentmindedly while he kneaded her lap.

Out of the blue, a crow flew across the living room and dropped a small pebble onto the couch next to Mayla before it perched on the back of the chair and looked at her curiously.

"Well, finally. Thank you, dear crow!" She really needed to ask Madeleine the name of her spirit animal. She quickly picked up the stone and as she brought it to her lips she thought, *Te aperi!*

Madeleine immediately appeared before her. "Your plan worked. They are in Paris, near Notre

Dame Cathedral. I'm waiting for you in the world fold there. See you soon."

Was that why Mayla, Tom, and Georg had immediately encountered their enemies in Paris when they'd landed on Pont Neuf? Because Marianna and her people were roaming the area?

Mayla's pulse raced as she mechanically pushed Karl off her lap, clutched the amulet key, and imagined the ancient church in Paris.

Tom, I'm coming.

"Perduce me in locum Notre Dame!"

22

S he had never jumped into this world fold before, but she knew the huge cathedral and the magic required, which was why a few moments later she landed directly in front of the imposing entrance to Notre Dame. Mayla tilted her head back to view the top of the famous structure as goosebumps overtook her. This church was special.

Madeleine immediately approached, her face hidden under her hood even though there was no other witch in the tiny world fold.

"Are the stones in the cathedral?"

Tom's mother shook her head. "This time they're using a world fold as a hiding place, and according to our search spell, it's south of the area. Come on, there's no time to waste." She was already storming out of the fold and around the cathedral, with Mayla trailing her.

Before Mayla could ask where this second fold

was, Madeleine stopped and looked around discreetly. The people streaming by were so preoccupied with themselves that they barely gave them a second look. They stared at their smartphones while magic was taking place right before their eyes. Had Mayla been this oblivious before?

Although passersby ignored them, Mayla and Madeleine raised their hands as inconspicuously as possible to cast the spell. They concentrated and it seemed like an eternity before a vertical crack appeared in the air. A dazzling light materialized through it. As people, cars, and buildings were pushed to the sides, a world they hadn't expected was revealed before them.

They heard leaves rustling in the wind and smelled spruce needles and pine cones. In front of them stretched an immense ancient forest.

Judging by Madeleine's expression, she hadn't known what to expect either.

Stunned, Mayla stared at the forest. "Do you think we need a protection spell? So no alarm sounds again?"

Madeleine shook her head, which was barely noticeable with the hood. "I don't think they can cast a spell over such a large area, but we should play it safe. They aren't expecting us. They aren't expecting anyone, and it should stay that way."

'Tutare!' Mayla thought. A shimmering, bluish shield spread over them like a dome. At the same time, they took a big step into the world fold so that no mere mortals would notice the magical shimmer. When their feet hit the ground, they paused for a moment. No alarm went off.

Mayla relaxed but kept her protective shield up. Just to be safe. The element of surprise was on their side and it had to stay that way. Marianna and her fellow hunters knew nothing about the high priestesses. They had no idea Mayla was able to find the hiding place where the magical stones were. They needed to keep this advantage.

They crept forward while crouching down because even if they didn't set off an alarm, they could still be seen or heard. The further they progressed, the faster their steps became, and since they didn't meet a single human soul, they grew more anxious. Or was it more appropriate to say that they didn't meet a single witch soul?

"Are you sure this is the right place?" Her voice was merely a whisper even though they had heard no one else.

Madeleine pointed between ancient oak trees. "It's getting brighter ahead. Maybe that's where we'll find what we're searching for."

Mayla crept behind her, avoiding any of the previous year's dried leaves and concentrating on the protective shield. Following their intuition, they moved in the direction where the forest grew brighter. What was there? A simple clearing? A hut like the one Georg had been held prisoner in by the disgusting von Wickert? Or possibly another von Eisenfels family country estate?

As they approached where the trees ended, they slowed. Before leaving the shelter of the trees, they stood awestruck in the shadows. There was no simple clearing in front of them, no hut or country estate as Mayla had expected — no, it was a small town that they saw before them.

A simple wall stretched around the area, but it couldn't have been intended for defensive purposes since it was no higher than Mayla's chest. Behind it stood countless houses, most of them with two stories. Some stood alone while others were lined up wall-to-wall. Their late medieval, half-timbered architectural style was reminiscent of the world fold in Frankfurt, into which Mayla had stumbled on her first day as a witch. Consequently, the world fold and this witch village had to have been in existence for several hundred years.

Stunned, Mayla stared at Madeleine, who appeared as surprised as she was. "A village?"

Madeleine pointed at the front gate, which stood open, with crowds of people streaming in and out. "Apparently, we don't need a protection spell. Just look at all the witches in this world fold."

Mayla nodded hesitantly. She carefully allowed the shimmering blue shield to fizzle out and listened. When no alarm sounded, she let out a sigh of relief. "Now what? Should we just walk in? Or do you think we'll stand out?"

"I think we can risk it. To be on the safe side, pull the hood over your head so the hunters don't recognize you."

Mayla swallowed as she pulled her hood low over her forehead. "Do you think all the witches in town are hunters?"

"They definitely belong to the Metal Circle because I was able to open the fold, but since it remains hidden from others, it could be a secret world fold reserved only for the von Eisenfels coven.

Mayla shivered and shrugged. "So, we just walk in?"

"Right, that's where we're going." Madeleine adjusted her hood, linked arms with Mayla, and strolled onward.

"Won't they recognize us?"

"I'm trying to obscure your fire magic with mine, and you need to conceal your power. Hide it within yourself. Don't let it mingle with other people's magic and we might remain undetected."

"Might?"

They were already on the wide path that snaked toward the city gate, and encountered the first metal wizards. A man who magically made a farm cart move behind him looked at her. He raised his left hand and Mayla was about to raise her hands in defense when the man simply lifted his hat and subtly bowed. "Good morning, ladies."

Mayla was speechless and Madeleine gave him a friendly nod. "Good morning to you too."

Mayla glanced around in disbelief. She had expected a horde of bloodthirsty hunters, but instead, she found herself face to face with mothers and their children laughing happily, men young and old greeting them in a friendly manner, and scores of merchants chatting cheerfully as they carted their wares to town.

She lowered her voice, a little ashamed of her question, but she needed clarification. "I thought only hunters supported the von Eisenfels family."

Madeleine shook her head. "No, this coven has been around as long as yours. These people have done nothing wrong except that they carry the same magic as the von Eisenfels family."

"I had no idea. Why aren't they represented within the police department or at the big council meetings when all the head witches meet?"

"Because the constant strife between the founding families forces them to live in seclusion. I'm sure you remember. For a long time, no one knew about the existence of the Metal Circle."

She knew the biases that all witches had against the von Eisenfels family. However, according to history, not all members of the family were tyrants. When she considered how the Metal Circle's members had been forced to live for centuries simply because there had been squabbles, Mayla understood why some von Eisenfelses railed and fought other covens. It simply wasn't fair.

"Once you and your sisters reunite the stones, will these people fare better?"

"I don't know, but I sure hope so. When the witches see that metal energy is not inevitably bad, but represents a fraction of the original magic, perhaps it will wake some of them up. In any case, it is important for the power to be distributed and for my sisters and I to take on the task of ensuring that the magic continues. This is a first step toward equality."

They were approaching the city gate, so they paused their conversation. Curious, they entered the secret city, where they heard the calls of barkers and the chattering of the residents. Apparently, Mayla and Madeleine were on the main road. There were a few shops on each side: a cheesemaker, a bookstore, a post office, a clothing store and... Mayla clapped her hands. A confectionery!

She was now convinced these witches couldn't be bad. Mayla pulled Madeleine to the shop, where she was immediately won over by its lavish display of chocolates. She happily entered the shop before Madeleine could stop her. A woman with blonde curly hair wearing an old-fashioned apron greeted her warmly, beaming from ear to ear, causing Mayla to finally warm up to the people of this city.

"Welcome to Diana's Chocolate Dream. We have some delicious specialties that you are welcome to try. Do you know what you want?" She smiled, showing her bright white teeth.

"We don't have time for this," Madeleine whispered, but Mayla wouldn't be deterred from her plan. There was always time for chocolate and if not, you had to make the time!

"Thank you, I would like to try one of your specialties."

The lady beamed happily. "This is chocolate peppermint cream, and our late summer hit is white chocolate with stracciatella filling. It's a bit like ice cream. Try it."

Mayla's eyes widened as she happily reached

for the late summer hit. She took in a deep breath, closing her eyes so she could focus on the scent. She ignored Madeleine's jabs in her side and savored the moment to the fullest before she happily shoved the truffle into her mouth. The chocolate with the cream filling and the chocolate chips mixed together created a flavor explosion and she let out a contented "Mmmmmm. Phenomenal! I'll take a box of those."

"Very good." The saleswoman ran to the back of the storeroom and returned shortly afterward with a package with a dark satin bow tied around it. How festive.

Mayla paid and asked as casually as possible, "Have you noticed anything lately?"

The lady placed the bill in the cash register and handed Mayla the change. "What do you mean?"

Madeleine nudged her again, but Mayla was not to be fazed. A woman who conjured up such delicious chocolates was not conspiring with Marianna Lauber and helping with her machinations. "Was there perhaps a loud argument or have some shady characters been lurking about?"

Madeleine rolled her eyes, which Mayla could see even from under the hood. Did she believe her question was too obvious?

The saleswoman tapped her finger on the counter. "Now that you mention it, maybe half an hour ago, a horde of frustrated young wizards arrived in town." She sighed. "I understand that the young men are angry, but violence is not the solution."

Madeleine suddenly stopped jabbing her in the side and turned her attention to the saleswoman. "Do you know where they went?"

"Probably around the cemetery again, near the city park, you know. Tell me, what do you want from them?"

Mayla bit her lip. Before she could serve up an unconvincing lie, Madeleine smiled at the saleswoman. "A friend of ours had her shop door demolished. It's not the first time, so we thought you might have seen something."

The saleswoman nodded sadly. "It's a shame how they sometimes take out their frustrations on us. I just wish these young people would finally realize that there's no point in it. We will never be equal members in the witch world."

Her words pained Mayla. The lady's previously radiant face now looked completely disillusioned and her blonde curls drooped as if they had suddenly lost their bounce.

Mayla swore to herself that by the time she was head witch of the Fire Circle, ideally even before that, she would do everything to ensure that these people were welcomed as impartially and openly as all the other witches. She patted her hand sympathetically. "I haven't given up hope that one day things will get better. Until then, why not have a truffle, it will cheer you up."

A smile crossed the saleswoman's pale face, and the stunning radiance was quick to reappear. "You're right, you should never give up hope, but keep your chocolates for yourself. I am, after all, at the source. Have a nice day."

Once they were on the street, Madeleine pulled her near. "Good idea to sound out the saleswoman. I wonder if that was your main intention when you entered the store or was it the opportunity to replenish your supply?"

Mayla simply winked at her and put the box in her purse. Then she looked ahead and to the sides, but all she saw were the lines of half-timbered houses and lots of people — nothing unusual. "Where's the cemetery?"

Madeleine pointed to a sign with a rose vine winding around it. "That way."

They turned left and walked down an alley until they reached a large park bordered by a cemetery. Mayla scanned the area. "Where could they have hidden Tom?"

Madeleine discreetly pointed to a chapel located on the border between the cemetery. In front of it were two young men sitting on the ground, dozing in the shade of the building and the surrounding fir trees. "Probably in there, along with the stones."

"Do you feel their presence?"

Madeleine shook her head. "Unfortunately, no. As I said, Bertha's protection still conceals the metal stone, but it's the only structure and these guys are loitering in front of it. That can't be a coincidence."

Mayla linked arms with Madeleine and strolled closer to the building as casually as possible, at which point the men raised their heads and watched them warily.

"What are you doing here?"

Mayla deliberated feverishly as Madeleine passed the two of them unfazed. "I'm sure we're allowed to visit our dead mother and grandmother!"

Without paying attention to these presumed hunters, Madeleine led Mayla into the cemetery and purposefully walked to a gravestone in one of the middle rows. They knelt down. Instead of looking closer at the epigraph, Mayla peered past the wide stone toward the chapel. Not a single sound emanated from it. There was probably a spell on the building that blocked any noise.

As soon as they were no longer under the watchful gaze of the guards, Mayla was able to take a longer look at the chapel. The dark stone building was small enough to hold a maximum of fifty people. In addition to the front door where the hunters were standing watch, there was a single large window on one side. The panes, however, were made of dark glass so it wasn't possible to see inside.

"Do you think Marianna is in there too?"

"I don't know."

Mayla glanced over the gravestone. The two men could not be seen from where they were kneeling. "How are we supposed to get in without putting the whole city on alert?"

"We have to lure the hunters away."

Mayla grew more anxious. "How are we supposed to do that? Do you want me to be the decoy?"

Madeleine hesitated. Oh God, was that actually the plan? But then Mayla gritted her teeth. If it was necessary, then so be it. They had to free Tom and retrieve the stones. Since she didn't have any other ideas and they were running out of time, she wasn't going to back down.

"Fine, I'll do it!"

Madeleine put her hand on her back. "Are you certain? I don't know how the townspeople will react. Even if they don't think the hunters are not behaving properly, they will stand with their own kind, not a fire witch who comes from a founding family."

Until recently, it had been an advantage to belong to one of the founding families. When the heck had that changed?

"I know, unfortunately, I don't have a better idea. Will you be able to free Tom without my help?"

A determined look came over Madeleine's face. "You can count on it."

Hopefully, she'd be able to do it. Mayla wouldn't lose her optimism in the final moments. "All right, I'll walk back. As soon as they watch me pass by, I will discreetly pull down the hood. I bet they'll recognize me straight away."

"And then an alarm will sound through the town and everyone will come looking for you while I grab Tom and the stones. You just have to give me enough time. Preferably, fifteen minutes if possible."

Mayla pressed her lips together. "Sounds easy." She chuckled uneasily and the corners of Madeleine's mouth twitched.

"Do you have one of those chocolates for me?"

Grinning, Mayla reached into her bag and pulled out the new box. "Here, take one."

Madeleine reached for it and waited until Mayla had also chosen one and inhaled deeply. "Here's to our success!" She pretended to toast Mayla with the truffle, following her example, before they slowly savored them.

"Nothing can go wrong now." Mayla placed the box in her bag and stood up. Waiting any longer would only make her more anxious. "Where do we meet?"

Madeleine pondered a moment. "In my old room at the country estate in southern England, or in the forest where I spoke to you. As soon as Tom is on the run, they will be hunting him, just as they are hunting Anna at the moment. We may only have five minutes at each location."

Mayla nodded, then remembered something. "How are we supposed to find the Metal Circle Stone while they're chasing us?"

"We'll think of something. First, we need Tom and the other fragments. One step at a time."

"Okay. Are you ready?"

"More than ready."

"Great, see you soon." Even though Mayla's knees were trembling, she started walking. She tried to add some spring to her gait so as not to immediately arouse the guards' suspicions. Moving slowly toward the chapel, she clutched her purse tightly. It would be unimaginable if she were to lose her provisions and the beautiful photo of the family at the beach. Without further ado, she dug around for the picture and when she found it, she pulled it out enough so that she could look at it. A smile played across her lips as she greedily drank in Emma's happy beaming face and Tom's subtle smile.

I'll get our happiness back, I promise you that!

23

C lutching the handle of her purse tightly, she strolled by the chapel. The two men immediately stirred from their sleepy state and watched her suspiciously. Mayla waited before lifting the hood since she was still too close to the chapel.

She continued walking even though her heart was beating so fast that it seemed the hunters must have been able to hear it. To be on the safe side, she turned to them so they would remain suspicious. Good thing, because they were already starting to relax. But when they felt Mayla's eyes on them, they sat up abruptly. They watched warily as Mayla approached the street and shook her head, the hood slipping down as if by accident. Her dark hair, which she wore pinned up at the back of her head as usual, shone in the light of the morning sun. Seemingly frightened, she turned her head, and a cry rang out, making her feel simultaneously triumphant and stunned.

"That's Mayla von Flammenstein! A fire witch!"

She glanced back, seemingly surprised, which reassured the hunters that they were correct. They jumped to their feet and rushed after her. Mayla dashed off too. She wanted to grab the amulet key and flee immediately, but she had to give Madeleine at least ten minutes.

Her pursuers were catching up. Okay, five minutes had to be enough. Shoot! Why didn't she have athletic genes? Mayla scurried through the streets, the first of the curious townspeople watching her. As the men chased her, the people's murmurs grew.

"Who is that? Why are those two chasing her?"

"She's a fire witch! She belongs to the founding family!" the hunters shouted, and the people's stunned expressions turned to suspicion and anger. For heaven's sake, would two minutes be enough for Madeleine?

She rushed through the city, which no longer seemed so idyllic but rather like a pure threat. The first malediction hurtled after her and she was only able to deflect it at the last moment. *Tutare!* she thought, and a shimmering bluish shield appeared around her. The next curse bounced off, but the trembling in her arms revealed how much stronger the hunters had grown.

The residents didn't stop the two men, but at least they didn't join them as Mayla headed straight for the city gate. The main shopping thoroughfare was busy, so she slowed down and fought her way through the crowd. Still, less than two minutes had passed since the men had begun the pursuit.

"Stop her, she's a fire witch!" the two shouted.

Everyone knew at a glance that they were talking about Mayla. Not only was she wearing a long cloak, but she was also fleeing the city as if chased by the devil. Although some verbal curses and threatening fists followed in her wake, no one stopped her or aided the hunters. Apparently, their behavior was tolerated but not supported.

All it took was a glance over her shoulder to tell her the men were getting closer. At least they weren't hurling curses at her. Mayla was relieved when she realized that they didn't want to hurt any of the residents or visitors to the city.

How much time had passed? Could she jump now? "Aaaaahhhh!" Her protective shield was penetrated and a weakened curse hit her in the back. Her vision went black. Panicking, she reached for her amulet key, but it was still too early. She wrapped her fingers around it and darted into a side street. If she left the city, there wouldn't be much protection from her pursuers, who would then unleash even more maledictions on her.

She hurried into a narrow alley where there were fewer people and shops. Before she could take shelter behind a wooden shack, she heard the two men's footfalls.

"She's over there!"

Mayla picked up the pace and hunted for a hiding place. God, how long could this last? She spotted an intersection and rushed around the corner — not a second too soon, because a glowing red curse whizzed by her. Shoot. She gritted her teeth and kept moving. She dived around another corner and was lost. Going back was not an option because another bolt zipped by, missing her by only a few centimeters.

She should have looked at the clock. How long had she been distracting her pursuers? While she speculated, she headed down another alley. There was nobody around, only a few workshops lined up in a row with no customers or sellers in sight. She wanted to speed up and looked ahead, but she had to slow down. A wall was blocking her way. Brick upon brick so high she wouldn't be able to climb it. Could she fly over with the Vola spell? No, it was too high, but charming out the stones, like Tom always did, might work.

Mayla imagined individual stones protruding from the wall like steps and thought, *Commove!* A scraping sound indicated the spell was working, but the hunters were already entering the alley, and because there was no one there but Mayla, they fired a barrage of maledictions at her. Before she could grasp the first stone, a burning spell hit her hand. She quickly pulled it back as another curse hit her in the back.

She doubled over in pain. From now on, Madeleine and Tom would have to manage on their own. As she tried to stay calm, everything in front of her blurred, and her legs felt paralyzed. She fell forward onto the street and before she could use the amulet key, her chin scraped the asphalt, and everything went black.

MAYLA FLINCHED as a hand touched her forehead. "Shhh... Lie still."

Realizing she was being spoken to politely, she turned to the side and opened her eyes. She was lying on a sofa with a man she had never seen before leaning over her. His straight brown hair was neatly combed to one side and his glasses gave him a well-mannered appearance. He wore work clothes that were slightly dirty but well cared for. Was he a hunter? But he was probably a bit too old for that. Still, her heart pounded in alarm.

"Calm down. You're safe."

Confused, Mayla blinked and sat up. "Where am I?"

"In my house." The stranger tried to push her gently back onto the couch. There was no question he had the strength for it, but she wouldn't allow it, which he respected.

"Who are you?"

"Winfried Hoppmann, a local carpenter, a pleasure to meet you. You must be Mayla von Flammenstein, if I heard the angry shouts on the street correctly."

Mayla nodded and looked down at herself. Her hands were free, as were her legs, and no magical chains encircled her body. She glanced up in disbelief. Except for the carpenter, there was no one in the room, which appeared to be a typical living room that merely lacked a bit of color. The sofa, armchair, and table were all a similar boring brown, the walls were white, and the ceiling light was plain — probably because the interior design lacked the feminine touch.

"Where are the men who were chasing me?"

"They ran back. The young, overzealous people thought you managed to jump with your amulet key."

"The hunters believe...? Wait a minute, I collapsed on the street." She frowned skeptically. "Did you help me?"

A subtle smile appeared on the gentleman's thin lips. "Of course."

"Why?"

"When injustice happens, one shouldn't turn away."

Mayla swallowed. "Thank you, that was very... very nice of you. How did you manage it?"

The gentleman chuckled mysteriously. "Let's say I paid attention in school and remembered some spells that many people regard as unimportant."

"Okay..." She casually felt the chain around her neck, which held two important things. When she felt the locket and the amulet key, she breathed a sigh of relief. He hadn't robbed her, probably hadn't even searched her. He'd simply helped her. She eyed the carpenter uncertainly. "And now...I can just go?"

"Naturally, but I would strongly recommend you get some rest because even though I healed the curse that incapacitated you, your body needs it."

"It'll get that when this is all over." Mayla swung her legs off the sofa and pushed herself up.

She swayed momentarily before she felt steady on her feet. "Thank you. And I promise I won't turn away when injustice happens." She waved her hand toward the city. "I had no idea so many of you live in secret. I will do everything I can to improve your situation and that of the other metal witches."

The man's eyes seemed to light up. "Then I guess I saved the life of the right witch."

Mayla grinned. "Can you tell me how long I was unconscious?"

He glanced at the simple wall clock. "Maybe fifteen minutes."

Oh, shoot. "Thanks. Goodbye." Without another word, she grabbed the amulet key and jumped to the estate in southern England. To be on the safe side, she didn't land in Madeleine's room, but in the hallway in front of it. Which was a good idea because she immediately heard the excited voices of her enemies.

"Damn, we missed her."

Next, she heard Marianna Lauber's shrill voice. "How could you let him get away? I would like to teach you all a lesson that you will never forget." Something clinked. She'd probably thrown something made of glass on the floor.

Someone spoke up, stuttering. Was Marianna's power so superior that the others were afraid of her? Or was it merely her self-confidence that got her that rank?

"We had enough metal spells on the chapel that he could not have broken down the door without assistance. Someone beside him who can also cast metal spells had to have helped. And that person is extremely powerful."

That meant their advantage was gone. The hunters knew someone with superior metal power was on their side. At least they didn't know about the high priestesses yet.

Before Marianna and her people noticed Mayla, she clutched the amulet key and imagined the forest where she and Madeleine had first spoken. She had to hurry before the hunters located Tom again. The dark hallway of the mansion spun before her eyes and she lifted upward before landing on soft moss. There were trees all around, but that wasn't what made her gasp. There he was in the middle of the forest, not five steps from her.

Tom.

When he turned to her, tears welled up in her eyes. He opened his arms and in a few long strides, she was standing in front of him. She threw herself against his chest, ignoring Madeleine, who was standing next to him watching. Tom. Her heart beat faster as she breathed in his scent. When she lifted her head and peered into his green eyes, her stomach did wild flips. His lips fell on hers and a tremor traveled through her body as she pressed herself closer to him. How much she had missed him, his closeness, his lips. She would have preferred to never let go of him again, but the impatience Madeleine radiated was significant. She broke away from him reluctantly and turned to the high priestess. "Fantastic, you made it. Do you also have the magic stones?"

"No, we didn't find them. The guards came back quicker than expected, so we had to escape."

Mayla clenched her hand. "Darn!"

"What took you so long?" Madeleine asked as Tom quickly ran his hands over her. While he stroked her back, she flinched at his touch and his dark brows furrowed.

"You're injured. What happened?"

Mayla smiled. He cared about her, her needs, and her well-being. And there was no longer anything hidden in his gaze. They were finally playing on the same team again. "I'm okay, let's talk about it later. How can we find your circle's magic stone?"

He flinched almost imperceptibly when she said "your circle." But she was no longer thinking about the threatening von Eisenfels family, but rather the people who had to live in secret, like the saleswoman in the confectionery and the carpenter who may have saved her life. There was nothing wrong with belonging to the Metal Circle. He should be proud of it.

"Do you have the locket?" His deep voice... How much she had missed it. It was as dark and rough as ever.

"I do." She pulled up the chain of the amulet key she had attached the locket to and retrieved it from beneath her cloak. "What do we have to do?"

Tom hesitated and glanced at Madeleine. Judging by his expression, he still had no idea who she was — and this was the worst possible time to reveal it to him. Marianna and her men could show up at any moment.

"We can trust her. She and her sisters are hiding Emma."

Tom nodded slowly before turning back to Mayla. "We have to go to our house on the Rhine. I hid something there that will help us."

Mayla frowned. "What do you mean?"

"Your ring." He took her hand and stroked the engagement ring on her finger. "It's part of an ensemble that my father once gave my mother."

Mayla smiled. "I know. And look what I have with me." She reached into her purse and pulled out the case she had found in Tom's nightstand.

He laughed softly. "Your jewelry-sniffing nose is just as good as your chocolate-sniffing nose."

Mayla grinned. "So it seems. So, how does the jewelry help us?"

When Tom opened the box, Madeleine stiffened, but he didn't notice. "My mother couldn't take it with her when she left because my father had placed a protection spell on it. I've been wondering about it all these years. I mean, the jewelry is beautiful but not particularly valuable."

"Probably because it's been in the family for a long time," Mayla speculated, but Tom waved it off.

"That's true. Still, when he noticed my mother was trying to leave, why did he put a protection spell on it but didn't lift it even though she had long since died?"

Mayla looked uncomfortably at Madeleine, who was standing stock still next to Tom. She shook her head almost imperceptibly, so Mayla bit her tongue. "What do you think?"

"Because there is magic hidden within them that will help us find the magic stone."

Mayla stared at the necklace and earrings in disbelief. The bluish-black tourmaline sparkled in the morning light that peeked through the tree canopy. "How does it work? What role does the locket play?"

"We have to go to southern England and find Elektra's secret room."

"Elektra?" Mayla frowned. He knew about her? "So, you recognized her picture in the locket after all."

"I wasn't sure, but now I am. The necklace is part of this ensemble... look. The tendrils on the lid are also on the earrings and the way the jewelry was cut matches every detail. They will help us retrieve the magic stone."

The air around them began to swirl. The hunters were coming.

"Quickly, before they catch us." Mayla clasped Madeleine and Tom's hands and thought, *Perduce nos ad scopulos Rheni!*

Before their adversaries materialized in front of them, the forest turned and they landed on the cliffs where she had hidden with Tom and Georg for so long. The view of the Rhine was as breath-taking as ever and the forest seemed unchanged. Was the small inn where she had stayed with Georg still down there?

Shaking her head, Madeleine scanned the area. "What are we doing here? We have to go to the estate in southern England."

Mayla raised her hands placatingly. "We have

to wait. Just before I jumped here, Marianna and her men were there. Perhaps those who followed us were the advance team and there are still a few hunters on the property. We don't want them to think we're going back there."

Tom stroked his chin. His stubble longer than usual. "You're right. It's best for us to jump to a few other places. Maybe we'll get lucky and they'll follow our magic trail. That will buy us some time. By the time we arrive in southern England, we'll have diverted their attention and maybe even gained a few precious minutes before they show up there. Every moment counts."

Madeleine tilted her head and the hood slipped slightly from her head. She immediately pulled it back in place, as if afraid of being recognized by Tom. "They can't track me. I'll jump to southern England. You distract them while I search for the secret room. Once I find it, I will summon you with a Nuntia spell."

Tom folded his sinewy arms over his chest, his wary eyes on Madeleine. "What do you mean they can't track you? Because you're a high priestess?"

He suspected something. Suddenly, his attitude changed. He seemed tense, alert. It wasn't right that he had no idea who the woman in front of him was.

Madeleine didn't look him in the eyes. Was she thinking the same thing as Mayla? "Exactly, my sisters' protection conceals me. They can find you, but not me or Emma while she is in the care of my sisters."

Tom narrowed his eyes skeptically. "Why didn't

you tell me earlier that you could protect Emma? You could have hidden her and Mayla. And all of this would have been less nerve-wracking and I wouldn't have had to swear an oath. Marianna only had control over me because she threatened to kill my family."

Mayla placed a soothing hand on Tom's arm, but it was Madeleine who answered.

"For Mayla, the protection only works for a short while."

Tom's expression grew more suspicious. "Why?"

Suddenly, Madeleine pushed the hood off her head and looked directly at Tom. She was shorter than he was, although she clearly towered over Mayla. Suddenly, her expression grew vulnerable. "Emma is descended from the high priestesses."

He froze. His breathing was so slow that Mayla could barely feel it under the hand she had against his back. He stared at Madeleine wordlessly. Why didn't he say anything?

"Tom?" Mayla stroked his back. He didn't react. As the air began to crackle and swirl, Mayla slid her hand under his folded arms until she could grasp his right hand. They had to leave before their pursuers caught them, but neither Madeleine nor Tom moved. She couldn't jump with him without either of them saying something to clarify the matter!

When Tom finally spoke, his voice was suspicious. "Who are you?"

The hunters materialized, so Mayla grabbed the protective amulet and cast the spell that took them to safety. Madeleine did the same. Mayla thought she owed Tom an answer, but as she was lifted off her feet, she heard her whisper, clear and distinct, as if she were whispering in their ears.

"I am your mother."

24

T hey landed in the Pyrenees at Tom's hut. The hiding place was no longer safe since the hunters had already tracked them down there once. Nevertheless, it was the first place that popped into Mayla's mind after the cliffs above the Rhine. When their feet landed on the grass, Tom's expression remained frozen. He didn't move. The morning sun was in a cloudless sky, causing Tom to cast a long shadow across the meadow. A motionless shadow that Mayla quickly turned to.

"Tom, she's telling the truth. She is your mother and therefore Emma's grandmother. That's why the high priestesses can protect our daughter. I just found out yesterday. I would have told you when we freed you from the citadel, but everything happened so fast and I couldn't reveal anything in front of Marianna. Our trump card was that Madeleine could cast metal magic without landing on the hunters' radar." She wrapped her arms around him and he finally moved.

"It's okay, Mayla. If anyone needs to apologize, it's me. I should have told you the truth from the beginning, but the hunters threatened to kill you and the high priestesses forbade me from telling you about them. I only worked with them to save Emma. When I had to strike you, Marianna was watching. She already knew the tracking spell that would allow her to find Emma. I hit you as lightly as I could without making her suspicious. I'm truly sorry."

Mayla smiled. "You've never talked so much in one go."

He grinned contritely. "You're usually the one who has a lot to say." His expression turned serious again. His mother seemed to be back on his mind.

"Do you want to talk about it? She's nice and she's sorry she left. I think she wants to explain it to you herself."

Tom simply nodded, brushing the matter aside. "We'll worry about that later. Now, it's time to find the last magic stone. Uh, I have to tell you something, Mayla."

Suddenly, she remembered Marianna's words. The vow... "What did you promise Marianna?"

"I swore to her that if she had all five fragments, I would come to her and cast the spell that would reunite the magic stones. And..." He paused and looked at her. And — oh God, there was regret in his eyes. Her heart clenched, but she had to know. Now. Immediately. She couldn't take it any longer.

"And?"

"That spell, she won't cast it herself since it is dangerous. Actually, it's not dangerous, that's the wrong word, but it's beyond our powers. It's an ancient magic spell."

Mayla's heart beat in panic. "What do you mean by that? Obviously Marianna can use her powers unreservedly without dying. Why doesn't she do it herself?"

"She can use some of her powers, but not her full potential. To do this, she regularly swallows a few drops of a potion, just like the other hunters. The spell for the reunification is too powerful; it would kill her as it did Bertha and Vincent. And that spell, it..."

His gaze made Mayla's throat tighten.

"It's going to kill you?"

Tom shrugged in resignation.

"No, Tom, then you won't cast that spell. You can't do that. Nobody can ask that of you."

"I have no choice. The oath is binding."

"Why the hell did you even make that damn vow?"

"Because they threatened to take Emma and make her cast the spell."

Mayla's heart faltered. "And they already have four stones?"

"Yes, that's why we really need to find the Metal Circle Stone before them."

Her eyes welled up and a tear ran down her cheek. She wiped it away with the back of her hand. "No, Tom. That can't be. We'll find another way."

"There isn't one. Our only option is to prevent Marianna from ever obtaining the fifth stone. That's why we have to find it before she does and take it to the high priestesses for safekeeping. Then, we will do everything possible to take the other four stones from her."

"Then let's do that. Tom, we'll prevent it. I won't let her take you away from me. Nobody is allowed to do that."

Tom chuckled softly. How much she had missed that laugh. The air in front of them began to spin, so Tom clutched his amulet key. "Ready to travel the world?"

"Will you promise to stay with me?"

"I will, Mayla." He leaned down to her and as his lips touched hers, her heels lifted off the grass. She barely noticed the swirling colors around her as she concentrated on his deep kiss, his heart so close to hers. Sighing, she fell into his embrace.

They landed on soft ground and hearing a loud noise, Mayla reluctantly pulled her lips from Tom's. She glanced up in surprise as warm rays pelted her skin. There was sand beneath their shoes and a seemingly endless sea in front of them. Or was it simply another lake?

"Where are we?"

"Welcome to Italy. I would love to take you for coffee and breakfast... unfortunately, I'm afraid the hunters won't give us that much time."

Mayla smiled. Italy. How long had it been since she had last been here? She loved this country. She gazed longingly at the Mediterranean, its waves crashing onto the beach, which was conspicuously empty for the end of August. Obviously, they were in a world fold. "Where exactly in Italy are we?"

"On the Adriatic."

Mayla wistfully inhaled the wild scent of the sea. The salty air felt good and she closed her eyes happily. When she opened them again, she nodded at him. "Let's not wait for the hunters to arrive. We'll jump first to confuse them."

"Your wish is my command." He grasped the amulet key again and intertwined his fingers with hers. Just holding his hand gave her confidence. She breathed a sigh of relief. Even though Tom was pessimistic, she was hopeful that luck was on their side.

The beach, the sea, and the sand began to spin. Mayla kept her eyes open and was amazed when they landed on a high peak in the middle of a large mountain range. "The Alps?"

"No, still Italy. I thought it would be good if they thought we were here searching for the last stone."

"What mountain are we standing on, if not the foothills of the Alps?"

"Obviously, on one that only witches know about. It's called La Bramosia, which means 'longing.' It was named for the view it offers and the longing that inevitably takes hold of you. The world fold was created thousands of years ago."

Mayla smiled. She understood all too well. The sea glittered in the far distance and individual villas stood on the slopes of the rocky massif, but were far enough apart so that everyone could enjoy their peace and quiet. She wouldn't have minded living here as well.

Before she could enjoy the view any longer, she lost her footing and the wonderful landscape began to spin. Next, they landed in a typical Italian landscape. Wide fields, isolated country houses, few people.

"Tuscany?"

Tom nodded as a raven flew overhead. Tom glanced up suspiciously, but Mayla raised her hand and a small pebble landed in it.

"That is Madeleine's spirit animal. Te aperi!"

Madeleine appeared before them, her voice lowered as if she feared being overheard. "Come quickly, I found it. Meet me on the stairs to the west wing."

Mayla frowned quizzically, but Tom nodded. He knew where that was. She squeezed his hand tightly, wishing they could prolong the jumping trip around Italy when the colorful landscape began to turn and they ended up in a dark hallway. In front of them stretched a marble staircase that led to the second story. Madeleine was leaning against the wall, her face carefully concealed under the hood. Nevertheless, they immediately noticed her index finger pressed to her lips in warning. Were the hunters still in the house? Mayla peered behind her, but she didn't hear any footsteps or voices.

Madeleine motioned for them to follow her upstairs. Mayla tiptoed up the steps beside Tom.

Not a word or gesture revealed what there was between Tom and Madeleine and what they urgently needed to talk about. If Mayla had any lingering doubts about their relationship, they vanished at that moment.

Halfway up the stairs, Madeleine stopped and pointed to an oil painting. It didn't show a von Eisenfels ancestor, which was suspicious, but rather a country house on the edge of a forest that Mayla had never seen before. Mayla frowned, but Tom nodded in understanding and reached into her purse. He dug out the box and pulled out an earring, which he placed on a spot in the house — specifically, on a stained glass window that had the same pattern as the jewelry. Mayla's eyes widened in surprise.

With the earring resting on the lines of the stained glass window, Tom closed his eyes and a red light appeared. It was impossible to say whether it came from his hand or from the earring itself. The next moment, the picture swung to the side, revealing a narrow door with a lock that opened with a soft click.

One after the other, they crept into the dark room, and Mayla blew a flame onto her fingertip. Madeleine silently slid the door shut and whispered, "I bet there's magic surrounding the office so that no sound escapes. But Bertha is long gone, so it's strange that the room is still undetectable. But who knows if that also applies to the Obsurdesce spell."

Tom watched his mother for a moment longer than necessary and then, as if he had caught himself, quickly turned and began to search the antique desk that stood in a corner and was piled high with scrolls, inkwells, and quills. Bertha had never been tidy.

Mayla marveled at the dark wood-paneled walls with only a single portrait hanging above the small fireplace. It was the same woman whose face was depicted in the locket.

Elektra von Eisenfels.

Madeleine stood next to her, also looking at the portrait. "Even though this is Elektra's secret room, Bertha continued to use it. She took me here once." The memory made her shudder. "That's the only reason I was able to find it, I think. And as her direct descendant, Tom was the only one who could open the space. My magic wasn't enough."

Tom looked at her for a brief moment, his expression unfathomable, before turning back to the scrolls.

"What about the jewelry?" Mayla stared at the box in her hand. "Do you think the hunters can follow us into the room without the earring?"

Madeleine shrugged. "I don't think so, but we shouldn't risk it. Do you have the necklace with you?"

Mayla fished the chain out from under her blouse and unfastened it. She held it out to Madeleine with a questioning look in her eyes while Tom quietly closed a drawer that apparently held nothing of interest in it. Then, he examined the portrait. "The locket matches the jewelry we used to open the office. The image is of the woman whose office we are in. It's clear that Bertha emulated her, studied her spells, and spent a lot of time in this room. Who knows how many times she was here when I was a little boy and thought there was no one in the house except my father and a few servants."

Madeleine nodded while Mayla thought. "Perhaps there is a protective spell on the stone as well as on the door and we can use the locket to remove it."

Loud footfalls were heard. "Where are they?" someone shouted.

Mayla's heart sank into her stomach. The hunters. They had found them.

"Quickly now." They scattered and Mayla felt the walls and every single crack between the floorboards as Tom slipped the necklace into his pocket and turned to the rest of the desk while Madeleine began searching a shelf she had missed. No one found anything unusual. Mayla opened the drawers of a dresser that contained ingredients for potions, mortars, tweezers, pipettes, and other utensils. However, there was no clue as to the whereabouts of the stone. At a loss, she approached the portrait from which Elektra von Eisenfels smirked mockingly at her. Acting on a hunch, she reached out to Tom. "Give me the locket."

Tom set the scrolls he had been skimming back on the desk and pulled the necklace out of his pocket. "Did you spot something?"

Mayla opened it and tilted her head. Her eyes moved from the portrait in the painting to the one in the locket. "Look, the hairstyle is identical, the necklace is the same, and the dress collar in the locket matches the one in the painting. It's the same picture."

Madeleine went to the door. Judging from the noise and voices, more and more hunters were gathering behind it.

"Use the search spell again. They must be here somewhere!" Marianna's commanding voice seeped through the door, which suddenly seemed far too insecure to Mayla.

Madeleine kept her arms raised in case the hunters somehow managed to break the protection. A spell swelled from her fingertips and settled over the door. "Hurry up!"

With a sinking feeling in the pit of her stomach, Mayla turned from the door and back to the portrait. She pointed to the necklace Elektra wore around her neck. The pendant was mostly hidden under the collar of the dress, but wasn't it... "Look, Tom, in the picture, isn't that the same locket that we're holding?"

Tom frowned and stepped closer. "You're right."

Without thinking, Mayla wanted to press the necklace against the painting, exactly where Elektra wore the medallion, but she was too short and couldn't reach it. Tom took the piece of jewelry from her. In any case, it would take his magic to break Bertha's protection. He pressed it to the painting and concentrated, closing his eyes, but nothing happened. He was about to remove his hand when Mayla stopped him.

"Don't give up. You can do it. The stone must be hidden there."

Tom inhaled deeply and closed his eyes again. As the door splintered, a lock clicked and the painting swung to the side.

"They're coming!" Madeleine shouted. "Tutare!" With this, a shield appeared.

"Just a moment." Mayla stood on her tiptoes, but she couldn't reach the safe-like space that opened up behind the oil portrait. Tom, however, had long since reached his hand inside. Next to a thick book, possibly the family's grimoire, he discovered the small stone, which looked so unre-markable that one had to wonder why such a fuss was made over such a tiny, simple object. As soon as Tom picked up the stone, it began to glow red.

"They're in here!" Marianna shouted, raising her hands and shattering Madeleine's protection with a single spell. Madeleine leaped toward them, grabbed Mayla's hand, and began to jump as curses were hurled at them. Someone caught Mayla's cloak and pulled her back, breaking her grasp on Madeleine. A spell was cast, causing the room to spin slower, and Mayla and Tom landed back on the floor until everything stood still.

There was no trace of Madeleine, but the hunters stood before them with Marianna in front. And she laughed nastily.

"You won't escape me again!"

25

M ayla raised her hand and together with Tom, they created a protective shield. Marianna shattered the barrier with a single blow.

"Animus..." Mayla began, but before she could render her enemies unconscious or before Tom could grasp his amulet key, magical chains bound their hands and arms, tightening around their bodies. Marianna placed a shield around them, causing any spells to bounce off the dome. The chains, however, penetrated the protective spell and none other than Marianna herself held the ends firmly.

Mayla's pulse was racing, but at least Tom was with her. Though she was afraid of Marianna's power, she wouldn't show that to the hunters. She stood with her bonds as gracefully as possible.

Marianna looked down at her scornfully. "I'm telling you, you won't escape me again. The game is over. Where is the stone?"

Tom raised an eyebrow. "What stone?"

Hate blazed in Marianna's eyes. "You're trying my patience, stupid von Eisenfels!" Aren't you concerned with preserving your family's legacy?"

Mayla glanced discreetly at his hands, which were tightly fastened against his body. Luckily, she hadn't spotted the red glowing stone. Had he given it to Madeleine in time? A feeling of exhilaration shot through Mayla. The fifth stone was safe. She lifted her chin more courageously. "His family's legacy is not limited to Vincent and Bertha."

"Don't call her Bertha! Her name was Valentina Victoria, the victorious, which is what she will be in the end!" Marianna turned her back to them. "Take them to a secure place!"

"But the citadel was raided," one of the hunters replied.

"Then put them in some abandoned ruins."

"Shouldn't we just kill her?" another asked, eyeing Mayla with hatred.

Marianna gave Mayla a weary glance over her shoulder. "You can do whatever you want with her. She's completely irrelevant to me."

When Tom answered, his voice was calm. "If you kill her, I'll refuse to cast the spell. Remember the oath I swore and the conditions attached to it."

Marianna turned swiftly and came as close to them as the protective dome would allow. "If you break your vow, it's not only death that awaits you — no, it will be painful and last forever." She laughed arrogantly, but Tom's expression remained impassive.

"If you kill her, I'll refuse to cast the spell — that was also part of the oath and you know it."

"And you know full well that you have no other choice! Get them out of my sight!" She handed the ends of the chains to one of the hunters. The room began to move around them again, the painting of Elektra spinning rapidly in circles, seeming to taunt them until they ended up in a dark basement. It smelled musty, the air was humid, and daylight barely penetrated the small window.

Mayla pressed herself anxiously against Tom. Did the hunters want to kill her? But the three young men who had brought them pointed their wands not at Mayla, but at the wall, and then there formed a thick iron ring that was firmly anchored in the masonry. With another spell, they bound the magical chain to it and then turned toward them arrogantly. "Make yourselves comfortable." Snickering, they disappeared with an innocent sparkle.

Mayla immediately tried to use her magic to remove the restraints, to at least to remove the chains from the ring, but it was futile. Tom, on the other hand, remained completely still.

"Aren't you going to at least try to free us?"

He shook his head. "It is pointless. I told you before that they drink a potion that lets them use ancient magic. Their strength far exceeds ours."

"What kind of potion is it?"

"I'm not sure how they brew it, but they use the blood of witches from all four covens. This fools the old magic into thinking they have the ancient magic physically within them, which is why they can use it to a limited extent without dying."

"That's why Marianna is so strong?"

"Exactly, still, they can't fully use their powers."

"Which doesn't help us much if they're already more powerful than us."

Tom didn't reply.

Mayla tilted her head back to look at him. "What do we do now?"

"Keep calm and don't talk too much." He nodded upward. Shoot, were they being listened to?

Mayla bit her tongue. There was so much to talk about, so many things she wanted to get off her chest in case this truly was the end. Marianna planned to leave her to the hunters and Tom would die casting the impending spell. As long as the high priestesses protected Emma and the stones, they were safe, but she certainly didn't want to spend her best years in this hole.

Luckily, Madeleine had been able to jump with the magic stone. She was probably with her sisters now and the five of them were discussing how they could rescue her and Tom. Surely that was the case!

Or would they focus their efforts on retrieving the other four magic stones? To what extent were they loyal to her and Tom? Weren't they both just two small cogs in the great structure called fate?

The high priestesses' goals were clear. They wanted all the fragments in their possession so they could reunite them and guard the source of magic. What role did Mayla and Tom play? At least Emma mattered to them. As a direct descendant of a high priestess, born with ancient magic, she would become a powerful guardian of the stones. But Mayla wanted to witness that, damn it. She wanted to be a part of her daughter's life, wanted to watch her grow up, make friends, see her shape her future, and go her own way — because for Mayla, there was no question that Emma would do that. She was a smart girl who knew what was important. And she was loving and good.

She raised her head resolutely. She wasn't that pessimistic and just because she was stuck in a dank basement didn't mean she would be. Tom was close enough that she could smell his warmth and familiar scent. At least he was with her again.

Time passed and no one came. Mayla's tongue was now stuck to the roof of her mouth, but her opponents clearly didn't care about how she was doing. They had sat down next to each other on the cold floor and were leaning against each other's backs. This allowed them to touch hands, which comforted Mayla slightly. She was dozing off when the air in front of them shifted and in the next moment, two hunters were standing in front of them.

"What happens now?" Tom demanded.

Nobody answered. Instead, they released the magical bonds from the ring and pulled them up. Before Mayla could steady herself, the musty basement room began to spin and a glaring bright light blinded her. As her feet landed on a hard surface, she squeezed her eyes shut until she adjusted to the brightness. Amazed, she looked around.

Tall temples, similar to those of ancient times, rose into the sky. Was this the high priestesses' secret world fold? But this one was different. She also didn't see Emma or any of the sisters, nor the round temple where she had sat and consulted with the women. Was this another sacred place of the guardians? Were there several?

Marianna emerged from the shadows of a long, rectangular temple, her face twisted into a smug grin. Goodness, why did she look so happy?

"You are lucky. I have been offered a trade. Obviously your allies don't know how worthless you are compared to the magic stones."

Mayla listened. "I'm sorry, what? A swap?"

"Yes, who would have thought. Your life for the last magic stone. Isn't that a phenomenal trade? Everyone will be happy."

What? It couldn't be true. Mayla looked at Tom, who appeared more composed than she felt. The high priestesses knew nothing of the oath he had made. Once Marianna had all five fragments, he had to go with her and cast the spell that would likely cost him his life.

Mayla forced herself with all her might to remain calm. Madeleine and her sisters had to have a plan, otherwise, they would never have gotten involved. Right? Agitated, Mayla yanked on the chains. Unsuccessfully.

"Patience, little fire witch, you'll soon be free again." Marianna turned her back to her.

Tom had his eyes closed. Why hadn't Madeleine said who she was sooner? Emma would have been safe and Tom would never have sworn the oath. Would have, could have, should have, darn it! It couldn't be changed now. There had to be a way out. A chance for both of them.

Pleased, Marianna looked around. "I suggested this place. It is an old holy place that Valentina Victoria von Eisenfels showed me. Here, our magic can be unleashed unchecked. No matter how many show up, they stand no chance against us." She laughed smugly.

This meant they were not on the same grounds where Emma was being protected. Apparently, the high priestesses had more than one of these sacred world folds and Bertha had been searching for them back then. Were these and the one at the hotel the only two she'd known about?

The air in front of them began to move until a cloaked figure materialized. Although she was wearing a loose cloak and hid her face in the shadows of the hood, Mayla immediately recognized her. It was Madeleine. She was standing so far away that Marianna wouldn't have recognized the resemblance to Tom even if she could catch a glimpse of her face. There was a protective shield around her and in her hand, she held the small stone that glowed red under her touch.

"I have what you want, stranger," Marianna

called over to her. "Now give me the stone so we can make the exchange."

"I will give you the last fragment. What good is it to you when Tom stole the other four?"

"We have long since acquired the other magic stones. And now that our power far exceeds yours, I'll be so kind as to show it to you." She reached into her pocket and pulled out a silk scarf. When she unrolled it, there were the four magical stones of the Fire Circle, the Air Circle, the Water Circle, and the Earth Circle. Mayla's heart beat faster and faster. All five fragments were in the same place.

"Bring me the stone!" Marianna demanded.

Tom's mother squared her shoulders. "I'll walk halfway, but before I set it down, untie Mayla and Tom."

Laughing, Marianna showed her sparkling white teeth. "Deal."

Mayla groped for Tom's hand as Madeleine slowly put one foot in front of the other. When she reached the middle, she crouched down and placed the stone on the rocky ground. However, she didn't let go of it as she looked at them. "Now you!"

Marianna couldn't help but grin as she raised her wand and Mayla and Tom's bindings fell to the ground. Mayla slowly circled her shoulders and raised her hands in front of her body.

"Careful," Marianna warned, keeping an eye on her and Tom as well as Madeleine. "One wrong move and I'll kill you, fire witch." Turning to Madeleine, she shouted, "On the count of three, let go and jump together. I don't want to see you here for another minute. One..."

Madeleine pulled herself up a little. "Two..."

"THREE!"

Instead of Madeleine releasing the stone, countless witches popped up around her and surrounded Marianna and her men. Mayla quickly spotted the high priestesses, who had jumped next to Madeleine, along with her grandmother, Georg, and Violett, who appeared beside the sisters.

Melinda fearlessly ran toward Marianna and sent the huntress crashing to the stone floor with a spell. Georg and the others also attacked, sending their opponents to their knees, but they quickly stood up again. Their magic was stronger. And they laughed as if they had expected it. More hunters burst out from behind the temples, hurling curses at them.

"Quickly, Mayla and Tom, come!" Behind them stood Gabrielle, who immediately grabbed Mayla's hand. Next to her, she spotted Phylis and Andrew.

"We must unite the ancient magic."

"But Marianna can use ancient magic with the help of a potion, as can the rest of the hunters."

Tom held Mayla and Andrew's hands. "Remember what I told you. United, we stand a chance."

Before she knew it, they were standing in a circle, hand in hand, eyes closed. In her mind, she saw the fight against Bertha and Vincent and she immediately remembered the necessary incantation.

"Aer et terra,
ignis et aqua,
nostro iussu,
foedus facite!"

Their voices rose in chorus across the ancient temple landscape and a purple glow formed between them. Slowly, Tom and Andrew released their hands so that they stood in a line, keeping an eye on their enemies.

Marianna clutched her amulet key, intending to escape with the four magic stones. Melinda tried her best, but her strength wasn't enough to stop her.

Mayla and her allies imagined the purple glow encompassing the entire area, stopping the Perduce spell. The high priestesses seemed to cast an additional spell so that no one could escape. It was their territory, which meant their power exceeded that of the hunters. When Marianna's spell failed, Mayla cheered.

"Very good," Melinda cried out, "now imagine thick walls around them." She rushed to them and took Tom's hand, strengthening the combined magic. The five high priestesses also stood next to her and held hands.

Anna hurried over to Madeleine with Georg and Violett next to her, and standing alongside them were Angelika, Artus, John, Matthew, Pierre, Susana, and Nora, who took Andrew's hand. They had all come. The bond fueled their magic as they focused on their task as one. They formed a semicircle around their enemies and extended the purple shield over the entire area, preventing the hunters from performing magic.

"Now charm them unconscious!" Melinda's command rang out and they all shouted together, "Animo linquatur!"

The hunters fell motionless to the ground, including Marianna. Her hand was outstretched, the four magical stones lying in her palm.

"Keep the spell going!" Georg shouted, slowly breaking away from the protective circle. Violett immediately grabbed Anna's hand so that the human chain was once more intact. From Georg's wand there appeared shackles that immediately wrapped around the hunters. Teresa leaped forward and grabbed the four magical stones, and then Marianna was bound up just as tightly.

"Vola!" Georg shouted, and the hunters and Marianna floated into the air before lining up neatly next to each other on the rocky ground. "Now repeat after me, Aperi, carcer!"

"Aperi, carcer!" they shouted in unison, and purple bars appeared around the hunters like a prison cell.

"Wonderful. We did it!" Melinda clapped, and the allies hesitantly released one another's hands. Mayla waited anxiously, her hands still raised defensively, but the shimmering purple prison remained.

She glanced around happily. The high priestesses rushed to one another. Their faces were beaming with joy, and even Madeleine had taken off her hood and was laughing. The Metal Circle

Stone was still in her hands and Aura was holding the other four fragments tightly. Luckily, without knowing it, Marianna had chosen one of their holy sites for the exchange. The high priestesses' magic was stronger in this ancient mystical place, which was why they had been able to stop the hunters.

Angelika and Artus examined the prison with Melinda, and Georg explained how it was constructed. Violett said something as she stood with the others from Donnersberg Castle. John and Andrew stayed close to Mayla and winked at her, grinning. Was everything okay again between them?

Violett came bounding toward her and threw her arms around her neck. "Mayla, I'm so glad you're okay!"

"What happened? Were you the one who brought everyone here?"

"No, that was Madeleine, the high priestess. Georg felt so well this morning that he didn't want to stay in the hospital a second longer. When we came out of the room, we heard Melinda making a ruckus as she discharged herself. Then, the three of us jumped out of the hospital to Donnersberg Castle. Madeleine arrived there with her sisters. They explained who they were and what had happened to you. We immediately realized that the only way to stop Marianna and her stupid companions was to work together."

Mayla laughed. "And then you came?"

Violett nodded, her long red hair bouncing around her shoulders. "Marianna negotiated the handover with Madeleine and suggested this ancient place of the high priestesses. What a lucky coincidence, right? Magic is definitely on our side."

"I'm so happy." Mayla looked up at Tom with a smile. "Is it truly over?"

"Yes, we did it, together with our friends." Tom took her face in both hands and even though they were standing in the middle of their allies, he kissed her in front of them all.

26

"What happens to the stones now?" Angelika von Donnersberg asked, bringing Mayla and Tom back to the present.

Teresa stepped forward, her four sisters behind her. Madeleine had naturally fallen in line with them as if there had never been any differences. Mayla was pleased to see that not only was this coming from her, but that the other high priestesses were accepting her into their midst. "Our sister Madeleine has already told you who we are."

All eyes looked reverently at the high priestesses, but only Melinda stepped forward confidently. "I'm honored to meet you. We circle heads will once again keep the stones safe."

Mayla stepped next to Melinda. "No, Grandma, I think it would be wiser if the high priestesses returned to their duties. They help protect the source of magic and maintain the balance of power."

Melinda's white eyebrows drew together and a deep crease appeared between them. "What are you talking about? It is our job as circle heads to protect the source."

Teresa placed her hand assertively on the five magical stones. "The balance has been threatened by the division of magic. We must reunite the fragments and we will protect the source."

"But..."

Mayla held her grandmother's arm. "I think it's a good idea."

Gabrielle stepped next to Mayla and smiled at her. "I vote for it too. For too long, the sisterhood has been robbed of its mission. It's time the stones were returned to their care."

"I'm also for it," stated Tom, and all eyes turned to Andrew.

Breathing in deeply, he approached the women. "It will not affect the magic of my coven if you keep the stones, correct?"

Smiling, Aura stepped forward. Her yellow-brown eyes sparkled. "My magic is yours too. I vow to take care of the stone and never use its power to hurt other witches."

Agatha came to stand next to her. "My magic is that of water, and I also promise to carry out my task diligently and not to harm anyone."

Ignatia tossed her fiery red curls over her shoulders and joined her sisters. "I cast fire magic and vow to use my role as guardian of the stone to keep harm away from all witches and wizards."

Teresa looked around with a smile. "Earth magic rests in my soul. I will give my life to protect the united magic stone."

Spellbound, everyone watched as Madeleine hesitantly pulled the hood off her head. A collective gasp rose as the resemblance to Tom immediately caught everyone's eye. "I vow to use my metal powers to protect the united magic stone, just as I will from now on protect my family and my sisters." She looked at Tom, who was staring back at her. His face remained expressionless, but Mayla took the eye contact as a good sign. She peered excitedly at the other witches and her grandmother, who were looking at each other, perplexed. Finally, Melinda spoke up.

"If the new generation of head witches is unanimously in favor of it, I will not stand in the way. Nevertheless, I wonder how you plan to reunite the fragments. You need someone who can perform the ancient magic and the spell would kill Tom."

"We already have a suitable candidate in mind." Teresa turned to one of the temples and called out, "You may come, little guardian."

When Mayla saw the little girl emerge from the shadows of the temple wrapped in a cloak like the ones the guardians wore, she clutched her heart. "Emma!" She ran toward her little one and pulled her into her arms, lifting her and hugging her tightly. "My little darling, we can finally be together again. Everything will be okay now." Tears glistened in her eyelashes as Emma's short arms wrapped around her neck.

"Mommy!"

Tom wrapped his arms around both and buried his nose in his daughter's dark curls. Mayla heard him take a deep breath and smiled.

All too quickly, Emma grew restless, whereupon Mayla let her down. "I have to go to my sisters."

"Your sisters?" Mayla looked at the high priestesses skeptically.

"Yes, I liked being with them and they said that soon, I'd be accepted into their sisterhood."

"Is that so?" Mayla looked searchingly at one high priestess after the next.

"Emma is the next generation. The old magic is united within her and she is a direct descendant. She will be a wonderful guardian."

At Teresa's words, everyone exchanged surprised glances. Except for Georg and Violett, no one knew Emma possessed the ancient magic within her. Had Teresa intentionally mentioned it? Angry, Mayla put her hands on her hips.

"You can't force her! She is a good child. Just because she has the old magic within her, no one needs to be afraid of her." She addressed her last words to her friends, who were staring at Emma. Was there distrust in their eyes? Were they going to ostracize Emma like they had done with Tom?

Georg suddenly spoke up. "Just because this dear child has the ancient magic within her doesn't mean she's dangerous. As a guardian, she will use this magic for the good of us all."

The others murmured and Georg spoke up again. "Still, I think it's important we keep Emma's powers to ourselves. It is important for the child to develop freely and that others do not view her with suspicion."

Angelika and Artus exchanged a meaningful look as did John and Matthew, but then it was Andrew who surprised them all. "No one can help what magic flows within them. Nobody should be judged for that. No one will find out from me what magic lies within your daughter."

The murmur grew and everyone gradually agreed. Mayla and Tom exchanged glances. Hopefully they could count on that.

"In order to put magic on the right track," Teresa spoke up, "we must unite the fragments."

"Let me," Emma squealed happily.

"No!" Tom and Mayla shouted at the same time, and Mayla restrained her little one before she could run to Teresa. "It's too dangerous. If the spell was too powerful for Tom, it will be even more powerful for Emma!"

Madeleine shook her head. "For her, it isn't. The old magic has been resting within her, even before she was born. She's the only one who can safely cast the spell."

Mayla's pulse pounded in her ears. Did the high priestesses truly want to risk their daughter's life?

Tom stiffened beside her. "And if not?"

"She can do it," Ignatia said, joining the conversation. "And we will support her."

"How are you going to do that?" Tom demanded. "How can you guarantee our daughter's safety?"

"We will draw a protective circle around her and the stones as she casts the spell. In this way, we'll support her with our power."

Tom stepped in front of Emma. "Then cast a protective spell around me. I will cast the spell. If what you say is true, nothing will happen to me."

Madeleine shook her head. "You would die despite our assistance. I would never allow that."

"Do you believe I'll allow my child to die?"

Madeleine smiled wistfully. "Do you think I'd let my granddaughter die?"

"Granddaughter?" Mayla heard Susana whisper.

"She's Tom's mother," Anna whispered to her. At this, the Spanish woman let out a soft, "Really?" Mayla barely even noticed the conversation. She was standing next to Tom in front of Emma, who quickly squeezed between their legs.

"Please, Mommy and Daddy, I want to do it. It will help us all."

"The little one is right," Melinda said, putting a hand on her arm. "Mayla, she has the power to do this. You can't always be afraid that she'll overextend herself. It's her magic. You have to allow her to use it."

Everything inside Mayla was crying out, but she took a deep breath and looked at Tom, who seemed to be fighting the same battle. When their eyes met, she knew he would agree if she did. She closed her eyes for a moment. Darn, her grandma was right. She couldn't deny Emma her path or insist she hide her true power. Regardless of the consequences if more and more people inevitably found out, it would be far more terrible for Emma if she suppressed her true powers forever.

She slowly bent down and took Emma's hands. "Do you honestly want to do this, my star?"

Emma grinned. The little girl immediately sensed that Mayla was about to cave. "Yes, Mommy, absolutely. I can do it."

Worry clutched at her heart, and its rhythm faltered. She glanced uncertainly at Tom, who nodded. "All right, then do it."

The little girl wriggled out of Mayla's hands and ran to Madeleine. With a beaming smile, she took her grandmother's hand as if she had known her all her life. Tom's expression softened before he put his arm around Mayla.

"We are on consecrated ground," Teresa pointed out. "That is why we will perform the magic in this world fold. Up ahead, there is an open-air temple. Columns support the ceiling, but there are no brick walls. It is the Temple of Power. That's where Emma will perform the ritual, and you can watch without setting foot on the sacred ground."

Mayla and Tom nodded hesitantly. They held each other's hands tightly, still filled with worry, but united. As if in a procession, they followed Emma and the high priestesses as they marched to the designated temple with the others joining them. Directly behind Mayla and Tom were Georg, Violett, and Melinda. It felt good to have them nearby for emotional support.

The Temple of Power was huge. The thick pillars that supported the massive stone ceiling rested on three steps that Mayla and the others were not allowed to climb. Emma entered the sacred area with the high priestesses as if she had been doing it her whole life. They remained in the middle of the holy place. The high priestesses drew something on the floor that Mayla couldn't see. Presumably, it was the protective circle in which Emma had to stand. They placed the fragments in the little one's hands and stood in a circle around her.

"Wait until we cast the protection spell, Emma. Then cast the spell as we explained, okay?"

"Yes, sister." Mayla heard Emma's high-pitched voice respond and her heart clenched. She squeezed Tom's hand so tightly that he stroked the back of her hand with his thumb.

They didn't hear the spell the high priestesses cast, but one by one, glowing orbs appeared over their heads: red over Ignatia, white over Aura, blue over Agatha, brown over Teresa, and a red-grey one over Madeleine, with protruding tails that met in the middle above Emma. White magic enveloped her daughter, surrounding her like a protective cocoon, and at that moment, Mayla knew nothing would happen to Emma. She was doing what she was born to do.

Emma focused on the five fragments in her small hands before closing her eyes. She murmured a spell, speaking it so softly that Mayla couldn't understand a word. Maybe it was intentional. The magic of the high priestesses should remain secret. In her daughter's hands there appeared a blinding light that turned purple. The fragments shone so brightly that Mayla raised a hand to shield her eyes, but she didn't want to miss anything, and neither did Tom, who didn't take his eyes off his daughter for a second.

The brightness slowly diminished, with only the purple light still glowing in Emma's hands. She slowly opened her eyes and cheered.

"I did it!" Like a victor, she held up a large stone that glowed purple in her grasp. It was so big she needed both hands.

The high priestesses gradually lifted the protective spell. Their cloaks were no longer dark, but pure white like Emma's. Smiling, they approached her. Mayla was about to rush up the temple steps to her daughter when Tom held her back.

"We are not allowed to enter the sacred site."

Shoot. She desperately wanted to join Emma, wanted to celebrate the moment with her, not just the joining of the stones, but also that she had survived, that she was obviously fine, and that her magic was extraordinary.

Teresa took the stone into her care and unhurriedly carried it outside to Mayla and the others. She held it before her like the greatest gift in the world — and maybe it was. The fragments had been seamlessly reassembled without a visible crack, shimmering in purple hues. It seemed as if its energy radiated beyond the stone itself.

Emma skipped happily next to Teresa and leaped into Tom's arms. He immediately placed her on his shoulders.

"You did great, my darling."

"It was so much fun, Daddy. I felt white magic inside me. It was really beautiful and tickled, and at the same time, I felt really warm. Here, look." She pointed to her chest, and Mayla smiled sweetly and squeezed her tiny hand firmly.

Melinda leaned forward, but Teresa kept the magical stone on holy ground.

"We will never break our vow. We protect the source of the magic and it will never be to your detriment." Teresa held the stone so that everyone could see it but no one could reach it. Everyone paused in awe and marveled at the magic stone.

"We will reactivate our offering houses and spread the word that we still exist and are carrying on the task of our ancestors. The High Priestess Society has been reawakened." With those words, the sisters took each other's hands and Madeleine waved to Emma, who waved back enthusiastically before everything began to spin and the complex, the temples, and with them, the five venerable women in their bright robes disappeared, as if it had all just been a dream.

27

T he big day had arrived. Mayla heard church bells ringing in her mind as she peered at herself in the mirror in her white dress. It was not customary for witches to wear white at their weddings, but Mayla liked the tradition of normal people and it had always been her dream to marry her true love in a white dress. The fact that a cute little whirlwind swept through the dressing room and excitedly stood next to her was more than she could have ever imagined.

"Mommy, you look so beautiful."

Moved, she leaned toward Emma, who looked even more beautiful in her white dress. "Thank you, my star. Oh, look at you."

They gazed at each other in the mirror, both wearing daisy wreaths around their heads. Mayla's was white, Emma's pink. They happily smoothed out their dresses.

But Emma wasn't captivated by her reflection

for long. She spun excitedly in a circle and ran to the window. "When will it start?"

"Violett and Georg will pick us up at any moment."

"Why doesn't Daddy pick us up? And why didn't he get pretty with us?"

Mayla smiled. This was also an unusual custom for witches, but Mayla wanted to do it anyway. "Because it is bad luck for the groom to see the bride on the wedding day before the ceremony has been performed."

"Great-grandma said that is human nonsense."

"I wouldn't call it nonsense, my darling. Everyone has their traditions and customs. I've spent many years of my life living among normal people, so I've picked up some of their habits."

"Great-grandma said that you'll soon believe it's bad luck if Karl or Kitty crosses your path from left to right."

"That is nonsense."

"Are you ready?" Georg's voice rang out from the hallway of the inn.

"Yeah!" Emma immediately dashed out of the room. Mayla grabbed the bouquet of white and purple hydrangeas and followed her, smiling. The big day was here.

Mayla hadn't known until a few days ago, but there were world folds specifically designed for weddings where the marriage ceremony could be performed. They were created in such a way so that all witches could access it since it was not uncommon for marriages between different covens to take place. You could just as easily get married in any other part of the world, but since the house on the Rhine was no longer an option for Mayla and the secrecy was finally over, they had decided to get married in one.

They had chosen a world fold in Tuscany to commemorate the mini-trip through Italy when they had been on the run from the hunters, which Mayla remembered fondly despite how anxious she had been. She was looking forward to taking many trips with Tom and Emma from now on and her wedding was merely the beginning.

The sun was shining as she stepped out of the inn where countless brides had prepared for their big day before her. There were one or two clouds in the otherwise blue sky, but fortunately, they didn't appear to be rain clouds. The scent of lavender filled her nostrils as she walked toward the central square in the middle of the fields where a fire burned. Standing in front of the fire was the priestess who would carry out the ceremony and next to her was Melinda who, as head witch, would then ritually welcome Tom to the Fire Circle.

Tom waited for them beside the magical fire. He had swapped his dark leather jacket for a dark blue suit with a white shirt and had styled his hair to the side. He had left the stubble and Mayla looked forward to feeling the short hairs tickle her lips and cheeks during the wedding kiss.

Mayla was incredibly happy that Madeleine was standing next to Tom. Who would have thought that one day their wedding would include not only her family but also Tom's?

The situation wasn't easy for Tom. After many years, he and his mother would have to become reacquainted and learn to trust each other. But, with Mayla and Emma by his side, he hadn't hesitate for a moment to invite her to the wedding.

The little girl was hopping toward her grandma, scattering rose petals along the path that Mayla walked with Georg and Violett on her arms. Unfortunately, Heike couldn't attend the ceremony, but they were planning a big party to make up for it.

As Mayla walked the petal-strewn path, her long train swishing behind her, she only had eyes for the man standing up front, who smiled at her, who was there for her, and who finally realized they were stronger together than apart.

When she reached him, Violett hugged her and Georg kissed her hand. Then her friends joined Madeleine on the chairs arranged in a row where her other friends from Donnersberg Castle had already taken their seats. Apart from Madeleine, none of the other high priestesses were present, but that wasn't necessary.

Tom took her hands and kissed the fingertips, then smiled down at her. She would have liked to kiss him straight away, but even this she would handle like regular humans.

As they turned to the priestess and her grandmother, Melinda looked at them tenderly.

"My darling, the day is finally here. I am so incredibly happy that we have come this far, that we have overcome all the obstacles, and that you two have not let anything or anyone separate you. Your love is true and everyone present can attest to that."

Emma put her hand over her mouth and giggled, prompting all the guests to laugh, even Melinda. "And your child, my great-granddaughter, is living proof of that." Melinda stroked Emma's curls, and the little girl chuckled happily and placed herself between Melinda and her parents. She watched the priestess's every move with curiosity.

Beaming, the priestess clapped her hands together. She was an old, gray-haired woman whose face was lined with countless wrinkles. She wore a white robe similar to that of the high priestesses — and who knew if she too was part of that ancient mystery. "Welcome, Mayla and Tom, to this special day. Come closer and join hands." She reached into a wicker basket on the ground next to the fire and took out herbs and flowers, scattering them one by one over the fire.

"Roses for the love that will bind you forever,

Cornflowers, so your feelings will never fade,

Juniper berries, so you may always ward off evil,

Leaves of an apple tree for fertility,

And pine needles, so you may be forever happy."

A flame erupted from the fire, shooting green, red, yellow, and blue smoke into the air before the flames turned dark red.

"Mayla and Tom, we hereby approve this

sacred bond of marriage. May the blessings of the ancient magic rest upon you forever." The priestess held her hands over Mayla and Tom's entwined hands and wrapped a red ribbon around their wrists. Then, she smiled at them. "From now on, you are bound to each other. Your magic is one, as are your hearts. I wish you all the happiness on earth." With those words, she withdrew and Melinda clasped her hands in front of her body.

"It is with great pleasure that I welcome you, dear Tom, son of the von Eisenfels family, into our fire circle. May the dispute between the founding families be history forever and may you feel as at home with us as if we were your native circle." She took Mayla and Tom's hands, which were still bound by the red ribbon, between hers. Heat radiated from her until that warmth materialized into a shimmering flame. It remained transparent, burning neither Mayla nor Tom. Their hands lit up with this reddish glow until Melinda gently blew out the magical flame.

"Welcome to the Fire Circle, Tom. And now, as Mayla requested, the groom may kiss the bride."

Mayla's knees weakened as Tom placed a hand on her cheek. Goosebumps spread across her body as she lifted her chin and stood on her tiptoes. Tom slowly leaned down and placed his lips against hers. She heard Emma and the other guests cheering. Georg whistled and Angelika clapped and shouted, "Let's hear it for the couple!" Tom and Mayla, however, didn't break away from each other. They lost themselves in the kiss that was both a beginning and an end.

The time of uncertainty was over. They belonged together and no one would come between them. With the marriage and the kiss, Tom was no longer affiliated with the Metal Circle. Time would tell what would happen to the members of the circle, but Mayla had not forgotten her promise. She would do everything within her power to integrate those witches into the community.

And at the same time, the kiss was the beginning of their marriage, a new time. No matter if other children followed, where they lived, or what jobs they performed, from now on, they promised each other they would do things together. United. Married. Together forever.

Mayla stroked his cheek and felt his stubble tickle her lips. This wonderful man was finally hers.

THAT'S IT! The Charms & Chocolate saga has come to an end. But wait, there's more... Want to read an exclusive, unpublished chapter of Mayla, Tom, and Emma visiting the Iron Coven? Don't miss out! Subscribe to my Magic Mailing List now and instantly download this exciting bonus scene!

http://jennyswan.com

I'm so excited to have you join!

THE NEXT ADVENTURE IS
ALREADY WAITING ...

Enchanted in Time – Fairy Tale for Women

How would you react if you received an invitation to a ball from a king you'd never heard of?

As a single mother, Hannah has hardly any time for herself. She has to do everything on her own to keep herself and her children financially afloat. One morning, an invitation to a royal ball makes its way to her door and lands in her hands. She's never heard of this royal family. And the place where the ball is to be held is nothing more than a crumbling ruin.

When a coach with six white horses appears in front of her building that same evening, she has to decide: should she break with her daily routine and find out what this mysterious invitation is all about? Will she dance with the prince? And what if he's harboring some incredible secret?

This is a fairy tale for women that is full of wonder, love, magic, and excitement. Don't you also dream of having a fantastic adventure and dancing with a fairy-tale prince?

Find out more on Amazon

Every magical tale in The Enchanted Over 30 Series stands on its own, weaving a complete story from 'once upon a time' to 'happily ever after.' Feel free to dance through these enchanted pages in any order your heart desires – each book is a self-contained adventure waiting to sweep you off your feet!

NOT A FAN OF FAIRY TALES?

No problem. I've got something even more exciting for you. Coming soon, my SECRET WHISPER SAGA will hit the shelves. If you love witches, vampires, Italy, and wine mixed with sparkling dialogues and lovable characters, you'll fall head over heels for this series.

Unlock the enchanted scroll! Join my Magical Mailing List and never miss a new spellbinding release!

http://jennyswan.com

WOULD YOU DO ME A FAVOR?

It would be enchanting if you could sprinkle a little magic by writing a review. Even a short one — just a sentence or two would be wonderful. Your words mean the world to me.

Thank you so much for your support.

I can't wait to whisk you away on our next magical adventure!

Yours, Jenny Swan